— *The* —
Truth About
HILLARY

ALSO BY EDWARD KLEIN

NONFICTION
All Too Human: The Love Story of Jack and Jackie Kennedy
Just Jackie: Her Private Years
The Kennedy Curse
Farewell, Jackie

NOVELS
If Israel Lost the War
(with Robert Littell and Richard Z. Chesnoff)
The Parachutists

ANTHOLOGIES
About Men
(with Don Erikson)

The
Truth About
HILLARY

*What She Knew,
When She Knew It,
And How Far She'll Go
To Become President*

Edward Klein

SENTINEL

SENTINEL
Published by the Penguin Group
Penguin Group (USA) Inc., 375 Hudson Street,
New York, New York 10014, U.S.A.
Penguin Group (Canada), 90 Eglinton Avenue East, Suite 700,
Toronto, Ontario, Canada M4P 2Y3 (a division of Pearson Penguin Canada Inc.)
Penguin Books Ltd, 80 Strand, London WC2R 0RL, England
Penguin Ireland, 25 St. Stephen's Green, Dublin 2, Ireland
(a division of Penguin Books Ltd)
Penguin Books Australia Ltd, 250 Camberwell Road, Camberwell, Victoria 3124, Australia
(a division of Pearson Australia Group Pty Ltd)
Penguin Books India Pvt Ltd, 11 Community Centre, Panchsheel Park,
New Delhi – 110 017, India
Penguin Group (NZ), Cnr Airborne and Rosedale Roads, Albany,
Auckland 1310, New Zealand (a division of Pearson New Zealand Ltd)
Penguin Books (South Africa) (Pty) Ltd, 24 Sturdee Avenue,
Rosebank, Johannesburg 2196, South Africa

Penguin Books Ltd., Registered Offices:
80 Strand, London WC2R 0RL, England

First published in 2005 by Sentinel,
a member of Penguin Group (USA) Inc.

1 3 5 7 9 10 8 6 4 2

Copyright © Edward Klein, 2005
All rights reserved

LIBRARY OF CONGRESS CATALOGING-IN-PUBLICATION DATA

Klein, Edward.
The truth about Hillary: what she knew, when she knew it, and how far she'll go
to become president / Edward Klein.
p. cm.
Includes bibliographical references and index.
ISBN 1-59523-006-8
1. Clinton, Hillary Rodham. 2. Presidents' spouses—United States—Biography.
3. Women legislators—United States—Biography. 4. Legislators—United States—
Biography. 5. United States. Congress. Senate—Biography. 6. Clinton, Bill.
7. Presidents—United States—Election—2008. 8. United States—Politics and
government—1993–2001. 9. United States—Politics and government—2001– I. Title

E887.C55K57 2005
328.73'092—dc22
[B]   2005044072

Printed in the United States of America
Set in Janson Text
Designed by Jaime Putorti

Without limiting the rights under copyright reserved above, no part of this publication may be reproduced, stored in or introduced into a retrieval system, or transmitted, in any form or by any means (electronic, mechanical, photocopying, recording or otherwise), without the prior written permission of both the copyright owner and the above publisher of this book.

The scanning, uploading, and distribution of this book via the Internet or via any other means without the permission of the publisher is illegal and punishable by law. Please purchase only authorized electronic editions and do not participate in or encourage electronic piracy of copyrightable materials. Your support of the author's rights is appreciated.

For
Karen and Steven, Alec and Julie-Ann,
Rob and Ruth, and Melissa and James

CONTENTS

Prologue   1

PART I: THE BIG GIRL

Chapter 1: The Impossible Dream   11
Chapter 2: Hillary's Bubble   15
Chapter 3: Tacky Kaki   19
Chapter 4: First Lovebirds   26
Chapter 5: Celestial Ambitions   37

PART II: THE BOOK OF LIFE

Chapter 6: Toughening Up   47
Chapter 7: The Great Debate   53
Chapter 8: The Radical   56
Chapter 9: The Intern   66
Chapter 10: Grooving at Cozy Beach   68
Chapter 11: The Other "Smoking Gun"   74
Chapter 12: The Misfit   83

Chapter 13: A Night to Remember　　　　　　　　90
Chapter 14: All the Governor's Women　　　　　　93

PART III: THE WHITE HOUSE YEARS

Chapter 15: Her Husband's Keeper　　　　　　　103
Chapter 16: "Bill Owes Me"　　　　　　　　　　110
Chapter 17: Payback Time　　　　　　　　　　　114
Chapter 18: Hibernation　　　　　　　　　　　　121
Chapter 19: Hillary's Brain　　　　　　　　　　　125
Chapter 20: "This Is War"　　　　　　　　　　　129
Chapter 21: "Screw 'Em"　　　　　　　　　　　132
Chapter 22: The Human Bridge　　　　　　　　　135
Chapter 23: The Wronged Woman　　　　　　　141

PART IV: THE CANDIDATE

Chapter 24: Run, Hillary, Run!　　　　　　　　　149
Chapter 25: The Education of Hillary Clinton　　　153
Chapter 26: Blowing Them Away　　　　　　　　158
Chapter 27: "Boob Bait for the Bubbas"　　　　　163
Chapter 28: Distortion　　　　　　　　　　　　　167
Chapter 29: "The Martians Have Landed"　　　　170
Chapter 30: The Juice　　　　　　　　　　　　　173
Chapter 31: Hillary's Problem　　　　　　　　　　180
Chapter 32: "A Legend Imploding"　　　　　　　186
Chapter 33: The Turnaround　　　　　　　　　　190
Chapter 34: "Pure Hollywood"　　　　　　　　　194

PART V: THE ROAD BACK TO THE WHITE HOUSE

Chapter 35: The "Phenom"　　　　　　　　　　201
Chapter 36: "The Perfect Student"　　　　　　　206
Chapter 37: Where's Waldo?　　　　　　　　　　211

Chapter 38: The 800-Pound Gorilla — *214*
Chapter 39: "So Hillary" — *219*
Chapter 40: Hillary from Chappaqua — *224*
Chapter 41: Shut Out? — *232*
Chapter 42: Hedging Her Bets — *235*
Chapter 43: Gearing Up — *240*
Chapter 44: Nixon's Disciple — *249*

Epilogue — *253*

Acknowledgments — *257*
Selected Bibliography — *259*
Note on Sources — *263*
Notes — *265*
Index — *297*

— *The* —
Truth About
HILLARY

PROLOGUE

Monica Lewinsky hadn't seen the Big Creep since she was banished from the White House. And now, on this sultry August evening in 1996, she found herself close to him again—so close she could reach out and touch him.

"He had this big fiftieth birthday party at Radio City Music Hall," Monica recalled, "and [beforehand] there was a cocktail reception [at the Sheraton Hotel], and when he and [Hillary] came to do the rope line . . . I had my back to him, and I just kind of put . . . my hand behind me and touched him [in the crotch area]. And it . . . was . . . maybe sort of grazing of that area, but . . . it wasn't how you might imagine it if someone described this, from a scene from a movie, it wasn't like that, but it was, you know. . . ."[1]

For a moment, Monica faltered, and her eyes welled with tears. Then she managed to pull herself together and say in a voice choked with emotion:

"... I don't even know if he *remembers*."[2]

And that thought tormented her.

She had flown to New York City at her own expense, and fondled the President's penis in the presence of his wife, who was a few feet away on the rope line and probably saw her do it, and yet Monica couldn't be sure that Bill Clinton even remembered the incident.

Was that *all* she meant to him?

And not only that...

When Monica reached behind her to touch the President, she glanced over her shoulder and flashed him one of her big toothy smiles—and all at once she noticed that the Big Creep wasn't wearing the Ermenegildo Zegna necktie she had sent him for his birthday.

"I like it when you wear my ties," Monica had told him shortly before his birthday, "because then I know I'm close to your heart."[3]

So how close *were* they?

She was feeling more than her usual edgy, insecure self as she left the Sheraton New York Hotel after the cocktail reception and hailed a taxi to take her to Radio City Music Hall for the President's birthday bash.

Manhattan was a ghost town on this Friday evening in August. But the ticket lobby of Radio City Music Hall was jammed with rich Democratic donors. Many of them had interrupted their summer vacations in the Hamptons or on Martha's Vineyard in order to help Bill Clinton celebrate the Big Five-O.

Tonight's extravaganza was being produced by Jeff Margolis, who had staged several Academy Awards ceremonies. It featured Whoopie Goldberg as emcee, and the usual lineup of liberal stars—Jon Bon Jovi, Aretha Franklin, Kenny Rogers, Nathan Lane, and Rosie O'Donnell.[4]

Prologue

At twenty-three years of age, Monica was the youngest person in the ticket line. She had gained a lot of weight over the past few unhappy months, and she was bursting the seams on her thin, sleeveless summer dress. She felt conspicuous as she entered the Music Hall's Grand Foyer, a soaring Art Deco space whose proportions were magnified by mirrors of gold-backed glass. The entrance was dominated by a mural titled *Quest for the Fountain of Eternal Youth*—an appropriate theme for a fifty-year-old president who acted as though he was still a horny teenager.

Entering the vast six-thousand-seat auditorium, Monica checked her ticket stub. For the first time, she noticed that she had been relegated to the cheap seats in the back of the orchestra.

Suddenly, she lost it.

Blinded by all the rage and resentment that had accumulated since she was exiled from the White House the previous spring, Monica turned on her heels and raced back up the crowded aisle, pushing and shoving people out of her way.

"I need to be near him!" she shouted.

People stared at her as she dashed into the lobby.

"*I need to be near him!*"

She disappeared into the ladies' room.

Nearby, the telephone rang in the office of the Democratic National Committee official who was in charge of the night's fund-raiser.

"I had an emergency phone call from my deputy that Monica was having a meltdown in the ladies' room," the DNC official recalled in an interview for this book. "Monica came unglued. I could hear her over the phone, saying the President's name over and over—'Bill! *Bill! Bill!*' "[5]

The official made her way to the ladies' room and found Monica crying hysterically.

"Monica had been hired by the DNC to be an unpaid intern in the White House," the official said, "and I was shocked when I heard that she had been promoted to a *paid* job. She had had bad grades in college. She had no skills. A paid job in the White House is one of the most coveted jobs in Washington. Somebody obviously gave her special treatment. I always wondered who.

"I handed her a tissue, and she told me, 'I need to be near him! I need to be near him on his birthday! *I need to be up closer!*'

"Suddenly, I put two and two together. *Monica had a relationship with the President!* That was the only possible explanation. I had heard that several women in the White House were sleeping with the President, but I was fearful that Monica might be different in one respect: she might be a dangerous stalker.

"So I alerted a few people to what was going on. I told the Secret Service agent in charge that I was concerned that Monica would go running up on the stage.

"And I discovered that nobody was surprised about Monica. The Secret Service knew all about her. Everyone I talked to knew she was obsessed with the President. And when I say everyone, I mean everyone—including *Hillary*."

HILLARY CLINTON HAD EYES AND EARS EVERYWHERE IN THE White House.

Her main watchdog was Deputy Chief of Staff Evelyn Lieberman, a short, overweight, gray-haired woman, who had befriended Hillary back in the 1980s when they served together at the left-leaning Children's Defense Fund. In the White House, Hillary assigned her loyal friend the task of monitoring the sexual activity of Bill Clinton—a role that helped earn Evelyn the nickname "Mother Superior."

Acting on Hillary's behalf, Evelyn tracked Monica Lewinsky from the first day the buxom young woman appeared in the West Wing wearing a low-cut blouse and bright red lipstick and nail polish. She repeatedly shooed Monica away from the Oval Office, and when the staff began to catch on to the fact that something was up between the President and the intern, Evelyn transferred Monica to the Pentagon.

If Monica had any doubt about who was behind her transfer, her confusion was cleared up during a twenty-minute telephone conversation with the President on April 12, 1996. During that call, Bill Clinton revealed that Evelyn Lieberman, a.k.a. Mother Superior, had "spearheaded" Monica's removal from the White House, because he had been paying too much attention to her. Monica didn't have to be told that Evelyn was Hillary's chief spear-carrier.[6]

After Monica's banishment, it became harder and harder for her to arrange a tryst with the President. By the fall of 1996, Bill Clinton was totally consumed by his reelection campaign, and the President's private secretary, Betty Currie, had to be extra careful to schedule Monica's visits when Mother Superior wasn't around to see the young woman slip into the Oval Office.

However, in early November, Monica managed to gain entry to a fund-raiser for Senate Democrats that was attended by Bill Clinton. She sidled up to the President and had her picture taken with him. This time, he was wearing one of her neckties.

"Hey, Handsome," she told him, "I like your tie."[7]

That same night, Bill Clinton telephoned Monica for some phone sex, and she mentioned that she planned to be at the White House on Pentagon business the next day.[8]

"Stop by the Oval Office," the President said.

But when Monica showed up at the White House the following day, she spotted Mother Superior standing near the Oval

Office, keeping an eye on the President for the First Lady. Not daring to defy Hillary Clinton, Monica left without seeing the President.

ONCE BILL CLINTON'S AFFAIR WITH MONICA BECAME PUBLIC knowledge in January 1998, Hillary acted as though she was just as scandalized by the news as the rest of the country.

Many people found that hard to believe. And so Hillary set out to convince people that the *first* First Lady ever to occupy serious real estate in the West Wing of the White House; a woman who interviewed potential White House appointees, oversaw the President's daily schedule, and ran many important White House meetings; a woman who deployed a legion of loyalists (not just Evelyn Lieberman) to keep an eye on her sex-addicted husband; a woman who once said, "[Bill] and I talk about everything. Anyone who knows us knows that we worked together on everything"[9]—that such an all-seeing, all-knowing, all-powerful woman had been unaware of the existence of Monica Lewinsky.

Hillary worked hard at making the country believe *she could kill Bill.*

"The estrangement was vital," wrote political consultant Dick Morris, "for it helped substantiate the idea that they had a real marriage [to begin with]. And a rapprochement was essential, allowing [Hillary] to attract the money and political support she would need to run [for public office in the future]."[10]

Hillary had been interested in power all her life, but without Monica Lewinsky, she would have remained a scandal-scarred, unpopular First Lady without a promising political future. It was Monica who transformed Hillary overnight into a sympathetic figure and national martyr. And it was Monica who paved the way for Hillary to become a U.S. Senator.

"The great irony of [Hillary's] life," remarked Michael

Tomasky, a seasoned political observer, "[was] that she achieved her highest stature, reached her apogee as a public person, not because of widespread admiration for something she had done, but because of public sympathy over something that was done to her."[11]

PART I

The Big Girl

CHAPTER ONE

The Impossible Dream

January 21, 1998

Bzzzzzzzzz!
  The Big Girl was buzzing for breakfast.
  BzzzzzzzZZZBBBBBBBBBZZZZZZZ!
In the pantry on the second floor of the White House, the harsh metallic noise caught the staff off guard. One of the butlers glanced at his watch: it was several minutes shy of six o'clock in the morning.[1]

Something was out of kilter.

As a rule, the President went to bed late and got up early, while the Big Girl—as members of her inner circle called Hillary Rodham Clinton—went to bed early and slept in late. Come to think of it, none of the personal staff could recall a single occasion when she had gotten out of bed before her husband.[2]

The senior servants in the White House were intimately acquainted with the daily habits of the First Couple. Bill and Hillary Clinton could not have been more different. While the President was erratic and unpredictable, you could set your watch by the Big Girl. She was a *perfectionist*—a woman who had a compelling need to exert iron control over the lives of others as well as her own.

What could possibly have made her alter her routine?
BzzzzzzzZZZBBBBBBBBBZZZZZZZ!

The butler picked up a tray with a glass of orange juice, a carafe of coffee, and several morning newspapers, and set off down the long, wide center hallway of the family residence, which was adorned with a Cézanne, a de Kooning, a Cassatt—and a bronze sculpture of President Calvin Coolidge's pet chow, Tiny Tim. The Big Girl had found Tiny Tim while rummaging through the White House storerooms and had put this piece of kitsch on display (to the dismay of White House historians) as an example of her taste in art.[3]

The butler made his way across the West Sitting Room to the eat-in kitchen. The Big Girl and the President took breakfast in the kitchen, rather than in their second-floor bedroom suite. Few of the downstairs staff in the West Wing knew what went on inside that bedroom, and as a result, there was always a great deal of water-cooler gossip regarding the Big Girl's sleeping arrangements with her husband.

Was it true they slept in separate beds?

Were there any telltale signs on the presidential sheets that they ever had sex with each other?

For that matter, did the Big Girl have any interest in sex with a man?

Or, as was widely rumored, was she a lesbian?

Some people were offended by such impertinent questions about the First Lady. But Hillary Clinton only had herself to blame for the talk about her sex life. Most women, faced with a chronically unfaithful husband like Bill Clinton, would have divorced him long ago. Hillary, on the other hand, not only stayed married to her husband; she displayed a curiously detached attitude toward his infidelities.

"It's hurting so bad," Hillary once told a friend during the Gennifer Flowers bimbo eruption in 1992.[4]

But you had to wonder *why* she felt pain.

Was it because of her husband's breach of faith? Or was it because his breach of faith had become public?

Over the years, a roster of distinguished journalists, biographers, and historians had struggled to answer those questions. Many of them had come to the conclusion that Hillary was more interested in power than she was in sex.

"[Hillary] kept her eye on the real ball," wrote the historian Paul Johnson. "Each presidential peccadillo led her to demand and get more political say, with her own future political career in mind. . . ."[5]

That was true, of course. But it still did not explain what made Hillary tick. After all this time, and all the effort that had been devoted to understanding her, the essential Hillary remained one of the great mysteries of our time.

What made her so difficult to understand was the fact that she was motivated not by one, but by many different feelings, ideas, and impulses—some conscious, others repressed—and that these feelings, ideas, and impulses were frequently at odds with each other.

She was a mother, but she wasn't maternal.

She was a wife, but she had no wifely instincts.

She said she was passionately in love with her husband, but many of her closest friends and aides were lesbians.

She inspired fierce loyalty among her followers, but she frequently stabbed them in the back.

She professed to be a devout Christian, but she cheated and lied at the drop of a hat.

She was a liberal who promised to use her power to help the weak and disenfranchised, but she acted more like a misanthrope who distrusted people and avoided their company.

For years, she denied she had any plans to run for president, yet she had always harbored the grandiose dream of succeeding her husband in the White House, and creating an empire of her own.*

In short, everything about Hillary was ambiguous; everything she stood for, she stood for the opposite. She seemed to lack the innate knowledge of good and evil, right and wrong, and the obligation to tell the truth.

---

*Commenting on Hillary's decision not to run for president in 2004, Bill Clinton told ABC's *Good Morning America*: "She doesn't want to be president *this time*" [italics added].[6]

CHAPTER TWO

Hillary's Bubble

THE BUTLER FOUND THE SECOND-FLOOR HALLWAY COMpletely deserted. Not a single Secret Service agent was in sight.

Early in the Clinton administration, the Big Girl had a fit when stories began appearing in the press saying that she had thrown a lamp at Bill and called him a "stupid motherfucker."[1] Another time, it was reported, she had burst into a room looking for her husband, and shouted at a Secret Service officer, "Where's the miserable cocksucker?"[2]

She blamed these press leaks on the plainclothes Secret Service officers who were stationed in the private residence, and she had them banished from the family quarters, where they had stood vigil since Ronald Reagan's presidency. The officers were moved down one level, where they could no longer witness the Clintons' *Jerry Springer*–style free-for-alls.

Hillary didn't trust the White House ushers, either.

Until her ill-conceived decision to fire the entire Travel Office blew up in her face, she was planning to fire all the ushers as well, and replace them with people she knew and trusted.³ When she realized she would have to live with the current crop of ushers whether she liked it or not, she placed restrictions on their access to the family quarters.

During the day, they were allowed to bring important papers—such as résumés of Supreme Court nominees and other applicants for high office—directly to the Big Girl, who signed off on all White House appointments. But once the President and First Lady retired for the night, the ushers had orders to leave messages on a table outside the elevator, where the doors to the residence were firmly shut.⁴

Some of the staff felt that the Big Girl's extreme suspicion of people and their motives bordered on paranoia. When she first arrived in Washington and realized she could not control the White House press corps, she tried to move the reporters out of their quarters in the West Wing and into the Old Executive Office Building. The reporters howled in protest, and Hillary was forced to abandon her plan.⁵

However, her defeat only made her more determined than ever to rein in the obstreperous press. She had the White House pressroom sealed off from the rest of the West Wing so that the reporters could not have easy access to the President's press secretary.⁶ What's more, when she traveled domestically, she did not allow reporters to fly on her plane, because, as she explained, she did not like to be scrutinized by journalists during her downtime.

This obsession with privacy extended to the White House switchboard, whose operators were famous for being able to reach anybody anywhere in the world at a moment's notice. Hillary ordered the installation of bedside telephones that did not go through the switchboard, so that she and her husband could talk on the encrypted phone lines and not worry about someone listening in. Every Sunday, the Army Signal Corps came to the White House to check the phones for taps and to make sure they were secure.[7]

And so, by January 1998—the start of the sixth year of the Clinton presidency—Bill and Hillary Clinton governed America as co-chief executives from inside a giant protective bubble. All presidents live inside a bubble, but Hillary's bubble was unique, because it was designed to conceal her moral imperfections. She always had to look perfect in her own eyes and everyone else's.

"Bill learns from his mistakes," noted Dick Morris. "Hillary doesn't make any."[8]

Hillary's bubble was an effective political tool. It camouflaged the moral decay in the Clinton White House, and misled many people into believing that the Clintons were the victims of their political adversaries, rather than the other way around. It helped deflect Kenneth Starr's quest for the truth about Whitewater, and left him sputtering in frustration. And it helped Bill Clinton win reelection—the first time in more than a half century that a Democratic president had won a second term in office.

THESE TRIUMPHS SHOULD HAVE THRILLED HILLARY, AND GIVEN her a sense of self-satisfaction. But that was not the case. Instead, as this morning's frantic summons for the butler demonstrated, she was in an anxious state of mind.

The reason for this was not hard to find. All of Washington was abuzz with talk that Bill Clinton had gotten himself into woman trouble again, and that this time he might not be able to wriggle out of it. Members of Hillary's staff had alerted her several days before that *Newsweek* magazine and the *Washington Post*, the paper whose Watergate investigation had led to the resignation of Richard Nixon, were hot on the trail of an equally sensational story—this one involving sex in the Oval Office between Bill Clinton and a young White House intern.

While Hillary brooded over what to do about the brewing

scandal, she had stopped speaking to her husband. Everyone in the White House could feel the tension that existed between the Big Girl and the President, and a sense of panic began to engulf the place. Staffers sniped at each other in the corridors of the West Wing. Senior aides spoke in hushed tones into their cell phones. And a few battle-scarred veterans of past Clinton wars—such as press spokesman Mike McCurry and damage control chief Lanny Davis—tried to put some distance between themselves and what they saw as the coming apocalypse.

"The mood inside the West Wing . . . had never been grimmer," *Newsweek* noted. "Staunch defenders who had lived through all the various -gates were disconsolate. There were tears and anger and a sense that maybe this time Clinton the great survivor was pushing his luck."[9]

Suddenly, Hillary's bubble had burst.

CHAPTER THREE

Tacky Kaki

When the butler entered the First Family's eat-in kitchen, he found the Big Girl, dressed in pajamas and a robe, seated at a table before a small mirror. She was being fussed over by Isabelle Goetz, a slender young Frenchwoman who worked at Salon Cristophe, Washington's trendiest and most expensive hair salon. (Cristophe, the legendary Belgian stylist, cut Bill Clinton's hair. The President once held up air traffic at Los Angeles Airport while he got a $200 haircut from Cristophe aboard Air Force One.) When summoned by the White House, Isabelle came roaring over on her motorcycle.

The tip of the Big Girl's nose was crimson, and the dusky bags under her eyes were puffier than usual. A wastepaper basket by her side was brimming with used tissues. She was nursing a bad head cold.

This room had once served as Margaret Truman's bedroom. It had been done over, along with the rest of the White House, by Hillary's Little Rock decorator, Katherine "Kaki" Hockersmith, who was known by some of her colleagues in the world of interior design as Tacky Kaki.

Kaki had a weakness for the Victorian period, and she had heaped yards of heavy velvet upholstery and gold Napoleonic laurel leaves on the public rooms of the White House.[1] When she was through with the Lincoln Sitting Room, critics said it looked like Belle Watling's whorehouse parlor in *Gone With the Wind*.[2]

On the other hand, Kaki had shown uncharacteristic restraint when it came to the family quarters. She had replaced the eighteenth century–style hand-painted wallpaper that Nancy Reagan had chosen for the master bedroom because its pattern of birds in flight spooked Bill Clinton, who said it reminded him of Alfred Hitchcock's movie *The Birds*.[3]

The kitchen resembled the Clintons' eat-in kitchen in the Arkansas governor's mansion; it was decorated in florals, chintzes, and linens to create an English country feeling. Comfortable white faux-wicker chairs flanked the table, which always had a fresh arrangement of flowers. The walls were covered in a fruit-patterned wallpaper by Country Life.

Hillary liked to say that she was involved in every detail of Kaki's White House redecoration. But those who knew Hillary's lack of interest in the domestic arts were more than a little skeptical.

"When Barbara Bush took [Hillary] on a tour of the White House after the election," Richard L. Berke reported in the *New York Times*, "Mrs. Clinton expressed no interest in decorating chores and was far more preoccupied with building bookshelves for her huge collection...."[4]

Nonetheless, Hillary wanted to make a political statement by erasing the Republican ambiance created by Nancy Reagan and Barbara Bush and putting her own Boomer stamp on the White

House. No one knew exactly how much money Kaki and Hillary had lavished on their White House project. Some estimates ran as high as $400,000, about a quarter of a million dollars more than had been budgeted. The Clintons claimed that all the money came from private donations.

Christopher Emery, a White House usher who was fired by Hillary for chatting on the phone with former First Lady Barbara Bush,* told the author of this book that Hillary had not only exceeded her budget allotment, but had secretly tapped into Historical Association funds.[5]

Whatever the final figure, one thing was clear: there was more to the redecoration project than met the eye. It was one of the factors leading up to the apparent suicide in July 1993 of Deputy Counsel Vincent W. Foster Jr., Hillary's colleague from her Rose Law Firm days in Little Rock, who handled all of her private affairs in the White House, and who guarded her secrets.

Vince Foster and Hillary had met years before while working with the Legal Services Corporation. In Little Rock, they spent countless hours together, established an intimate bond, and consoled each other about their unhappy marriages. Several Arkansas state troopers charged that Vince and Hillary had been lovers, and that when Bill Clinton was out of town, Vince would spend the night with Hillary at the governor's mansion. There were also reports that Hillary and Vince stayed together overnight in a remote cabin in the woods.[6]

"Within the small circle of politically clued-in people in Little Rock, it was accepted as a fact that Hillary and Vince were sleeping with each other," said Michael Galster, a medical

---

*Hillary feared that Christopher Emery was passing on information to Barbara Bush about the Clintons' private life, and that Mrs. Bush was behind the embarrassing anti-Clinton rumors that appeared to be originating in Houston, where the Bushes lived.

worker whose wife, Vali, was a good friend of Hillary's and worked closely with her on children's educational issues. "Hillary and Vince's love affair was an open secret."[7]

As the person she trusted most in the world, Hillary often assigned Vince the sensitive task of cleaning up the political messes created by her careless and corrupt husband. One of the worst messes involved the notorious Arkansas penal system, which had awarded a lucrative contract to Health Management Associates (HMA), a company run by Leonard Dunn, a Clinton crony.

When Michael Galster, who held an orthopedic clinic in the Cummins state prison once every two weeks, discovered that HMA was harvesting tainted blood from prison inmates by paying them $7 a pint, he threatened to blow the whistle. He was prepared to testify that the blood, some of which was infected with hepatitis C and the HIV virus, was being sold with the knowledge of prison authorities and Governor Clinton to brokers, who in turn shipped it to several foreign countries, including Canada.[8]

"Vince Foster was then–Governor Clinton's liaison on prison issues," Galster told the author of this book. "One day, Foster came to visit me at my office in Pine Bluff. One of the prisoners was threatening to sue HMA over a non-blood issue, and Vince wanted me to get involved and convince the prisoner not to sue. But those HMA doctors were hacks, and I refused to get involved."

"Vince started bullying me," Galster went on. "He said, 'You know what your noncooperation means as far as the state's renewing your orthopedic conract, don't you, Mike?'

"And I said, 'Yes, I know what you're talking about.' And he said, 'It's going to be hard for you to maintain your contract with the prison system.' And I said, 'I know.' And he said, 'I just want to make sure you know how things work.' And, sure enough, they fired me. And knowing how close Hillary was to Vince, I never had any doubt that she knew all about it."

After he came to Washington, Vince fell into a suicidal depression once he realized that Hillary, as First Lady, could no longer be his intimate friend—and that he, in turn, could no longer protect her from scandal and her flagrant disregard for the law. He was right. The night of his death, Hillary launched one of the most shameful—and illegal—cover-ups of her entire career.

She sent two of her most trusted White House loyalists—Maggie Williams, the First Lady's chief of staff, and Patsy Thomasson, who was in charge of White House administration—into Foster's office to retrieve embarrassing and incriminating documents related to Whitewater and Hillary's other personal affairs. While White House Counsel Bernard Nussbaum barred investigators from entering Foster's office, Maggie Williams, Patsy Thomasson, and Craig Livingston, Hillary's director of White House security, removed armloads of files and loose-leaf binders.[9]

In addition, a White House staffer allegedly tampered with the titles of several memos and removed the First Lady's initials in an effort to erase her role in improper behavior. For instance, the staffer changed "HRC's Travel Office Chronology" to "Chronological Analysis of Travel Office Events."[10]

In a note found in Vince's briefcase several days after his suicide, he alluded to the huge cost overruns in the White House redecoration project, and wrote cryptically: "The Usher's Office plotted to have excessive costs incurred, taking advantage of Kaki and HRC [Hillary Rodham Clinton]."[11]

"GOOD MORNING, MRS. CLINTON," THE BUTLER SAID. "I HOPE YOU enjoyed a good night's sleep. It's twenty-nine degrees outside, with a wind-chill factor that makes it feel thirteen. The weather report calls for the low forties, with no rain or snow."

The Big Girl blew her nose.

"I have to go to Baltimore this morning to deliver a speech," she said, staring at her reflection in the mirror. "Make sure everything's ready."

The butler recognized the steely tone that crept into her voice whenever she was out of sorts. As he bent to place his serving tray on the table, he stole a sidelong glance at her (the staff had strict orders never to look the Big Girl directly in the eye).

Hillary Clinton was the kind of homely woman whose features seemed to improve with age. She was better looking at fifty than she had been at forty-five, when she first arrived at the White House.

There was an explanation for this remarkable physical transformation. As First Lady, Hillary received the kind of personal care that was available only to A-list stars in Hollywood. Thanks to her pals Harry Thomason and Linda Bloodworth-Thomason, the husband-and-wife television producers of *Designing Women*, *Evening Shade*, and *Hearts Afire*, some of Hollywood's top makeup artists came to the White House on a regular basis to improve Hillary's appearance. In addition, Cliff Chally, the *Designing Women*'s costume designer, helped pull her wardrobe together.[12]

According to her friends, however, none of this dolling up altered a basic fact: Hillary still saw herself as an ugly duckling.[13] In particular, she hated her body. A small-boned woman from the waist up, she was squat and lumpy from the waist down, with wide hips and thick calves and ankles.

She had not always been that way. Though Hillary was never a standout beauty, she had had a nice figure in high school and college. Indeed, several of her Wellesley College classmates, who played sports with Hillary, described how she looked in a

T-shirt and shorts. They said she had a tiny waist, slim legs and ankles, and small buttocks.[14]

However, after giving birth to Chelsea on February 27, 1980, Hillary's silhouette changed dramatically. Though she never released her medical records, a physician who had observed her at close quarters told the author of this book that he suspected Hillary had contracted an obstetrical infection, which was serious enough to damage the lymphatic vessels carrying excess fluid from her legs back into central circulation. He said that she was left with a condition called chronic lymphedema, an incurable (though not fatal) disorder that causes gross swelling in the legs and feet, which Hillary covered up with wide-legged pants.[15]

In private, some of her friends suggested that Hillary's discontent with her body type predated her lymphedema, and might have explained her onetime neglect of personal grooming.[16] When she looked in the mirror, these friends said, the perfectionist in her saw only faults. As a young woman at Yale Law School and later in Arkansas, Hillary had felt so hopelessly unattractive that she did not bother to shave her legs and underarms, and deliberately dressed badly so that she would not have to compete with more attractive women in a contest she could not possibly win.

The one thing she *could* control about her looks was her hair, and she had experimented endlessly with different hairdos. But when Isabelle Goetz started coming to the White House on her motorcycle, Hillary's hair ceased being a problem—and a source of late-night jokes by David Letterman and Jay Leno.

Now, as Isabelle Goetz set to work with a straightening iron, Hillary reached for the stack of newspapers that had been placed at her side by the butler. She went straight for the *Washington Post*. And there, in big black letters, splashed across the top four columns of the front page, was the reason Hillary Clinton had not been able to sleep in late this morning.

CHAPTER FOUR

First Lovebirds

**CLINTON ACCUSED OF
URGING AIDE TO LIE**
*Starr Probes Whether President Told Woman to Deny
Alleged Affair to Jones Lawyers*
Independent counsel Kenneth W. Starr has expanded his investigation of President Clinton to examine whether Clinton and his close friend Vernon E. Jordan Jr. encouraged a 24-year-old former White House intern to lie to lawyers for Paula Jones about whether the intern had an affair with the president, sources close to the investigation said yesterday. . . .[1]

FOR HILLARY, IT WAS THE WORST POSSIBLE NEWS IN A WEEK OF BAD news.

Four days earlier, on Saturday, January 17, Bill Clinton had submitted to a secret deposition conducted by the attorneys for

Paula Corbin Jones.* Though Hillary and the President had tried every legal trick in the book to delay his appearance, the U.S. Supreme Court had voted unanimously that the Paula Jones case could proceed to trial while Bill Clinton was still in office.[2]

The federal judge presiding over the Paula Jones case, Susan Webber Wright, compounded the Clintons' legal problems by ruling that Paula Jones's lawyers could put *other* women on the stand in an effort to prove a pattern of sexual harassment by Bill Clinton.[3]

These two findings threw open the political floodgates, and as the date for the President's deposition drew near, Hillary went into full battle mode. The person she turned to for help was her political guru, Harold Ickes, who had managed the Clinton-Gore reelection campaign and had served as the President's deputy chief of staff.

Harold Ickes (pronounced *ICK-eez*) was a tall, skinny, seedy-looking man with thinning reddish hair. Until he came to Washington, he was best known as a combative left-wing activist on Manhattan's Upper West Side, and as a lawyer who represented labor unions, some of which reportedly had ties to organized crime.† In political circles, Ickes was known as "the dark prince," because of his abrasive, foul-mouthed manner and his instinct for the jugular.

---

*In her suit, Paula Jones alleged that Bill Clinton asked her for sex in a Little Rock hotel suite in 1991 while she was a state worker and he was governor.
†Among the unions represented by Ickes's law firm was the New York City District Council of Carpenters, charged in a 1990 civil racketeering suit with being controlled by the Genovese crime family. The union later agreed to install a federal judge to monitor its operations.[4]

An old-style New Deal Democrat (his father served as secretary of the interior under Franklin Roosevelt), Ickes had frequently backed losing left-wing presidential candidates like Eugene McCarthy, George McGovern, and Jesse Jackson. Then in 1992, he signed up with the Clinton-Gore campaign, ran the Democratic National Convention that summer, and found himself for the first time in his life on the winning side of a national election.

To advance her left-wing agenda, Hillary had planned to appoint Ickes as White House chief of staff in her husband's second term. But Ickes's reputation was so badly tarnished by his involvement in the administration's campaign-finance scandal that the President had no choice but to fire him.*

"From the unions to Whitewater and campaign-finance practices," wrote Micah Morrison, a senior editorial page writer for the *Wall Street Journal*, "Mr. Ickes' true role, performed brilliantly, has been as consigliore to the dark side of the Clinton presidency."[5]

Even after his banishment, Ickes continued to serve as Hillary's secret consigliore. Several months before, Hillary told Ickes that her main concern about the Paula Jones deposition was not Paula Jones's lawyers, but her own lawyer—David Kendall, the attorney from the white-shoe Washington law firm of Williams and Connolly, who had been defending Hillary and her husband in all their Whitewater legal problems. Kendall might be a skilled attorney, Hillary said, but he didn't like soiling his hands by dealing with the press—and when he did, he wasn't very good at it.[6]

---

*Charles La Bella, the head of the Justice Department's campaign-finance task force, identified Ickes as the "Svengali" behind every aspect of the fund-raising scandal.

Should she stick with Kendall, whom she personally liked, or should she get somebody else? Hillary asked Ickes.

Dump Kendall and get Bob Bennett, Ickes replied without a moment's hesitation.

Hillary asked Ickes to arrange a meeting for her with Bob Bennett, and to prep him in advance.

HAROLD ICKES AND ROBERT BENNETT HAD A LOT IN COMMON. The short, heavyset Bennett was as pugnacious as the tall, skinny Ickes. (Bennett liked to boast that he was a former amateur boxer from the streets of Brooklyn.) And as lawyers, both Bennett and Ickes had made their names representing criminals.

A senior partner in the Washington office of Skadden, Arps, Slate, Meagher & Flom, Bennett was known as one of the best criminal defense lawyers in America. He charged his clients $475 an hour for his services, and had already represented Ickes and TV producer Harry Thomason in their own tussles with the Whitewater special prosecutor. Like his younger brother, William Bennett, the former secretary of education and drug czar, who was among Bill Clinton's most vocal *Republican* critics, the *Democrat* Bob Bennett was expert at spinning the media.*

"This is an election year," Ickes told Bennett when they met. "And this case is political. But Kendall is not giving us the kind of political help we need."[8]

---

*"Shortly after Jones filed her lawsuit," wrote Jeffrey Toobin, "Bennett even invited a [writer for] *The New York Times Magazine*, Ruth Shalit, to his vacation home in Montana, took a business call there in private, then informed the journalist of the (unspecified) coup he had just engineered for a client. 'That's called getting intelligence. That's knowing people. That's getting the inside track,' Bennett told Shalit. 'That's having inside your head a kind of wiring diagram of how Washington works.' "[7]

Several days later, Bennett was ushered into a room in the West Wing, where he met Hillary for the first time.

They spent fifty-five minutes together. Bennett was taken aback by how charming and attractive Hillary was. During their conversation, Hillary asked many questions.

"What would you do? . . . How should we handle this? . . ."

Bennett told her, "You have to treat this as ninety percent political and ten percent legal. It's not enough to wait to the end of the day, because you could lose the [off-year 1998] election and then everything would be all over."

Shortly after his meeting with Hillary, Bennett got a call from Lloyd Cutler, the President's in-house legal counsel. The two men had breakfast at the Four Seasons Hotel in the Georgetown section of the capital.

"We'd like you to come aboard and have a seat at the table, not merely for Paula Jones, but everything—Whitewater and all the other issues," Cutler told Bennett.

"The next thing I know," said Bennett, "I'm being escorted into a room with the President. And that's how it went—from Ickes to Hillary to Cutler to the President—and I was hired."

Based on his discussions with Paula Jones's lawyers, Bennett was confident that Paula Jones would agree to a reasonable cash settlement and a watered-down apology from the President. His advice to the Clintons was simple and straightforward: *Pay Paula Jones to go away.*[9]

But Hillary vetoed the idea.

Her attitude puzzled Bennett. After all, she had to know that the names of many of her husband's lovers, including that of Monica Lewinsky, would surface during his deposition. If Hillary had once harbored any illusions about her husband, surely she had wised up by now.

However, Bennett was only slightly acquainted with Hillary Clinton. He did not yet understand that, after years of covering up for her husband, Hillary was convinced that candor, honesty, and truthfulness only invited disaster.

MANY OF HILLARY'S DEFENDERS HAD A DIFFERENT EXPLANATION for her behavior. They claimed that Hillary lived in a state of denial when it came to her husband's affairs. They subscribed to what might be called the *she-didn't-know-what-she-didn't-want-to-know* theory of Hillary's relationship with Bill Clinton.

"We know things at many different levels," said a psychotherapist who supported this theory of Hillary's behavior. "If our marriage partner is unfaithful to us, we may find it so painful that we choose not to recognize it *consciously*, even though we know it *intuitively*. That seems to be how Hillary's mind works. When she needs to blind herself to her husband's infidelities, she creates a fantasy."[10]

Yet, a dispassionate examination of the Clintons' marriage failed to support that theory. The fact was, Hillary had been *consciously* aware of Bill Clinton's character flaws—and especially his sexual addiction—practically from the day she met him nearly thirty years before.

Prior to their marriage, Hillary dispatched her father and her younger brother Tony to Arkansas to keep an eye on her future husband, who, as she had heard, was fooling around with other women.

In his biography of Bill Clinton, *First in His Class*, author David Maraniss quotes Paul Fray, a ranking Clinton campaign aide in Arkansas, as saying, "Hillary had put the hammer on her daddy to go down there and make sure everything was hunky-dory. It was her little spying mission."[11]

Hillary didn't rely solely on her daddy; she did some sleuthing on her own. After she and Bill were married, she "went through Bill Clinton's desk on a search-and-destroy mission to tear up phone numbers she knew he collected during the day's campaigning," wrote Barbara Olson. "Most self-respecting women would have left. Hillary chose to stay."[12]

Later, in the early 1980s, Hillary hired private detectives to identify the women her husband was sleeping with, and to intimidate these women so they would not go public with their stories.[13]

"Hillary learned about private investigators in her work [while at Yale Law School] on behalf of the Black Panthers and the Communist apologists Robert Treuhaft and Jessica Mitford," wrote Barbara Olson. "Now Hillary was constantly checking up on Bill, not just to learn the extent of his betrayals, but to assess the danger he posed to their joint political career."[14]

As first lady of Arkansas, Hillary used the governor's chief of staff, Betsey Wright, to fish him out of countless bedrooms all over the state. In 1988, when Clinton planned to run for his party's presidential nomination, Hillary thought his woman problem could be "handled." But Betsey Wright knew better, and made him withdraw from the race.

According to David Maraniss, Betsey Wright "said that he was having a serious affair with another woman, and was not even being discreet about it. Everyone knew, she said. She knew, the troopers knew, *Hillary knew.*"[15]

In 1992, on the eve of the critical New Hampshire presidential primary, it was Hillary who forced her husband's handlers to face topic A: the issue of Bill Clinton's philandering.

"The hired hands still felt queasy discussing the subject in his or her presence in any terms more specific than 'character,' " reported *Newsweek* in its exhaustive postcampaign ticktock, *Quest for the Presidency 1992.* "They needn't have worried; [Hillary's] tone, when she raised [the topic], was clinical—the attitude not of a woman scorned but of an adviser addressing a matter of practical politics. . . ."[16]

Upon her arrival in the White House in January 1993,

Hillary put together a team of aides whose primary job was to keep an eye on her faithless husband. They reported back to the First Lady on any suspicious sexual activity by the President.

Given this well-documented history, it seemed absurd to argue that Hillary didn't know about Bill's affairs—or (what amounted to the same thing for a woman in her position) that she didn't *want* to know.

"The wife who deludes herself about her husband is a cliché," wrote political commentator Michael Kelly. "But Mrs. Clinton was not only a wife. She was a central figure in her husband's campaigns and his gubernatorial administrations. She was in a position to know the truth about her husband, and she did know it; and she joined the likes of George Stephanopoulos, Paul Begala and James Carville in a cynical and immoral effort to hide the truth from voters and to savage those who told the truth."[17]

Of course, it was in Hillary's interest to preserve the fiction that she didn't know the truth about Bill's philandering. She found many creative ways to circulate the idea that she and Bill were a normal, happily married couple. For instance, she would occasionally drop a tantalizing remark that all was sweetness and light in the presidential bedroom.

"Buddy," she would say, referring to their dog, "jumped in bed with us this morning."[18]

Two weeks before the Paula Jones deposition, Hillary and the President flew to St. Thomas in the Virgin Islands for a brief Christmas vacation. There, despite her negative feelings about her body, the First Lady donned a one-piece bathing suit and led the President onto the beach, where they began slow-dancing. Though they were guarded by the Secret Service, a lone French photographer was allowed to breach the security perimeter. The subsequent photograph of the half-naked First Lovebirds was printed in practically every newspaper in America.

But such transparent efforts at manipulating public opinion didn't work. Instead, Hillary's stubborn refusal to settle the Jones case had disastrous consequences.

"When Bill Clinton went into the deposition," said David Schippers, chief counsel to the House Managers for the Impeachment Trial of President Clinton, "he thought he could take care of questions about Kathleen Willey and all the other women. And he also felt that Monica was in the bag. He was smug, cocky, arrogant."[19]

The President wasn't prepared to be put through the third degree.

"Have you ever given any gifts to Monica Lewinsky?" one of Paula Jones's attorneys asked him.

"I don't recall," the President replied in a tentative tone of voice, sensing that his opponents might possess some physical evidence that could be used against him. "Do you know what they were?"

"A hat pin?" the attorney said.

"I don't . . . I don't remember," the President stuttered. "But I certainly . . . I could have."

"A book about Walt Whitman?"

"I give . . . let me just say, I give people a lot of gifts," the President said, "and when people are around I give a lot of things I have at the White House away, so I could have given her a gift, but I don't remember a specific gift."

"Did you have an extramarital sexual affair with Monica Lewinsky?" the attorney asked.

"No," the President lied. ". . . I have never had sexual relations with Monica Lewinsky. I've never had an affair with her."

The deposition dragged on for several hours, during which time the President denied having even met Paula Corbin Jones, or having had sexual relations with her or the other "Jane Does."

But he did drop one unexpected bombshell.

"Did you ever have sexual relations with Gennifer Flowers?" the attorneys asked him.

"Yes," Bill Clinton replied.

"On how many occasions?"

"Once," he said.

"After the deposition was over," wrote Michael Isikoff of *Newsweek*, "the Jones lawyers were ebullient. They felt they had scored some significant points and laid the groundwork for some useful trial testimony. David Pyke [one of the lawyers] actually thought Clinton's concession on Flowers was the biggest coup. Contrasted with his 1992 denials of a sexual relationship between him and Flowers, he thought it conclusively established Clinton as a liar on matters relating to his relations with women."[20]

As soon as the President emerged from the deposition, his media-savvy attorney Bob Bennett began putting a positive spin on the event. Everything had gone just as they had planned, Bennett told the waiting reporters.

Privately, however, Bennett was puzzled by the flurry of questions about Monica Lewinsky. He began to wonder if his client had told him the whole truth about his relationship with the White House intern.

Matt Drudge, for one, wasn't buying Bill Clinton's story.

At 2:32 A.M. Sunday morning, January 18, Drudge posted a "World Exclusive" item on his Web site. He revealed that the editors at *Newsweek* magazine, after considerable internal debate, had decided to withhold a story from their upcoming issue about the President's affair with a twenty-one-year-old intern. Drudge correctly described the story as "destined to shake official Washington to its foundation."[21]

Then came the *Washington Post* exposé, which was quickly followed by reports on ABC radio and in the *Los Angeles Times*.

The same morning, George Stephanopoulos, who had once been Bill Clinton's closest aide and was now a commentator for ABC News, appeared on *Good Morning America*, where he made a shocking prediction.

"I talked to the White House this morning," Stephanopoulos said, ". . . and obviously these are very serious allegations. And they're taking them very seriously. But right now, we know two things about this investigation. One, these are probably the most serious allegations yet leveled against the President. There's no question that . . . if they're true, they're not only politically damaging, but it could lead to impeachment proceedings."[22]

CHAPTER FIVE

Celestial Ambitions

THE "I WORD"—IMPEACHMENT—ROCKED HILLARY TO her foundation.
As a young attorney fresh out of Yale Law School, she had worked on the House Judiciary Committee's impeachment inquiry staff, drawing up articles of impeachment against Richard Nixon. She still remembered the day when a delegation of congressional Republicans trooped over to the White House and convinced President Nixon that he had no alternative but to resign from office. Now, she feared that a similar delegation of congressional Democrats would come to visit her husband, carrying the same grim message.

Her fears were not unfounded. She and Bill Clinton had barely managed to survive an endless series of blunders and transgressions. The sorry record included:

- THE $100,000 CATTLE-FUTURES WINDFALL: At the outset of Bill Clinton's first term as governor of

Arkansas, Hillary invested $1,000 with a disreputable commodities broker named Robert L. "Red" Bone and managed to walk away with $100,000. She claimed she made the $99,000 profit by studying the *Wall Street Journal*. But she lied. At the behest of Arkansas power brokers who wanted to curry favor with the new governor, Hillary was allowed to profit while others would have certainly lost their shirts.

- THE GENNIFER FLOWERS BIMBO ERUPTION: In 1992, in the midst of the New Hampshire presidential primary campaign, the lounge singer Gennifer Flowers revealed that she had had a seventeen-year affair with Clinton. At first, Clinton denied her story. But after she released tapes of their intimate phone conversations, the candidate went on *60 Minutes* to save his campaign. Seated next to him was Hillary, who said: "You know, I'm not sitting here, some little woman standing by my man like Tammy Wynette." But that was exactly what she was doing.
- THE HEALTH-CARE DEBACLE: In 1993, President Bill Clinton launched his new administration's major domestic program—health-care reform—and appointed his wife to head the task force. With typical arrogance, Hillary proceeded to hold secret meetings, keep powerful figures in Congress in the dark, and create a comically complex and hugely expensive plan that came to be known as Hillarycare. As a result, the program was killed, the Republicans won both houses of Congress in the next midterm election, and Hillary was politically discredited for the next four years.

- THE TRAVEL OFFICE PURGE: In 1993, Hillary ordered the entire staff of the White House Travel Office to be fired because, she claimed, the office was grossly mismanaged. In fact, she had an ulterior motive: she wanted to funnel the travel business to her Arkansas friends Harry Thomason and Linda Bloodworth-Thomason, who had an interest in their own travel agency. Hillary denied she had anything to do with the firings—a claim that was contradicted by David Watkins, an assistant to the president for management and administration, who wrote in a memo that there would be "hell to pay" if Hillary's Travel Office orders were ignored.
- THE PURLOINED FBI FILES: In 1993, Craig Livingstone, a former bar bouncer, dirty trickster, and official in the White House office of personnel security, collected several hundred FBI background files on Republican opponents. Some assumed that Hillary had directed Livingstone to collect the files. Hillary denied knowing Livingstone—a claim that was discredited by a White House intern who testified to having seen the First Lady greet Livingstone warmly in a White House hallway.
- THE FOR RENT SIGN ON THE LINCOLN BEDROOM: Throughout their eight years in the White House, the Clintons turned the place into the most expensive bed-and-breakfast in the world. Rich backers—Steven Spielberg, Steve Jobs, David Geffen, and others—who were treated to overnight stays in the Lincoln Bedroom and Queen's Bedroom donated $4.4 million to Bill Clinton's 1996 reelection campaign and other Democratic causes.

- THE MISSING ROSE LAW FIRM FILES: While a lawyer back in Arkansas, Hillary did legal work for a savings and loan institution that backed the Clintons' investment in a land deal that came to be known as Whitewater. She later denied representing the S&L, and the billing records of her legal work mysteriously disappeared. They surfaced conveniently in the White House in 1995—two days beyond the statute of limitations.

All of these crimes and misdemeanors paled by comparison with the latest charge leveled against the President. Nothing short of the Clintons' political survival hung in the balance. Which meant only one thing to Hillary, whose whole life had been built on grandiose dreams of acquiring fame and power.

As a teenager in the early 1960s, Hillary had set her heart on becoming the first woman astronaut.[1] Early space voyagers like Alan Shepard (who became the first American in space in 1961) and John Glenn (the first American to orbit Earth in 1962) were routinely offered the chance to serve in the president's cabinet or run for the Senate. A career as an astronaut greased the path to national power faster than any other possible approach, and Hillary was more than willing to risk life and limb for the prize.

But Hillary's celestial ambitions were thwarted by a catch-22. In order to qualify as an astronaut, you first had to be a fighter pilot, but women couldn't become fighter pilots because they were banned from combat. Then, of course, there was the minor problem of Hillary's famously poor eyesight, which ruled her out as a candidate for space travel regardless of her gender.

Barred from applying to the space program, Hillary was despondent. To cheer her up, her mother encouraged her to set her sights on the Supreme Court; she could become the first female justice on the Court. But eventually, Hillary became fixated on an even bigger prize. Whoever occupied the White House, she decided, had the power to affect vast numbers of people through legislation and executive action.

"From an early age, she dreamed of living in the White House," said Hillary's first mentor, the Reverend Don Jones, her youth group minister.[2]

At Wellesley College, Hillary's classmates frequently talked about her becoming the first woman president of the United States. At Yale Law School, Bill Clinton joined the chorus of those who believed that Hillary had the right stuff to make it all the way to the White House.

"If she comes to Arkansas," he said, "it's going to be my state, my future. *She could be president someday.* She could go to any state and be elected to the Senate. If she comes to Arkansas, she'll be on my turf."[3]

Nonetheless, Hillary hitched her star to the charismatic Bill Clinton. She followed him back to Arkansas because, as she told several friends, she believed that he was going to be president one day.[4] According to the Reverend Don Jones, Hillary and Bill started plotting his run for the White House as early as 1982—almost ten years before he actually declared his candidacy.[5]

During those years, the country's attitude toward women shifted dramatically under the compelling force of the women's movement. And this revolutionary change in the status of women allowed Hillary to dream an even bigger dream: succeeding her husband in the White House.

That audacious dream was never far from Hillary's mind. At times, she found it hard to accommodate her fantasies of power and glory with her carefully cultivated public image as a selfless, holier-than-thou person. But over time, she managed to convince herself that she wasn't a hypocrite, that her dream was pure and untainted, a virtuous obligation, not an exercise in selfishness. Indeed, she came to believe that the world would be a far better place with Hillary Rodham Clinton as president.

"What Mrs. Clinton seems in all apparent sincerity to have in mind," wrote Michael Kelly, "is leading the way to something on the order of a reformation: the remaking of the American way of politics, government, indeed life. A lot of people, contemplating such a task, might fall prey to self-doubts. Mrs. Clinton does not."[6]

Shortly after Hillary and Bill moved into the White House, her aides in the East Wing put up signs proclaiming: HILLARY FOR PRESIDENT!*

West Wing staffers thought it was a joke.

But it was no joke.

The cadre of feminists who surrounded Hillary in the White House thought that she had made a big mistake marrying Bill Clinton. Being First Lady was beneath her, they said. *She* should be president, not *Bill*.[7]

"Hillary never wanted to be a wife," said a White House official who worked closely with her. "She wanted to be president."[8]

Now, AS THE BUTLER PREPARED TO LEAVE THE KITCHEN, HILLARY read the *Washington Post*'s story about her husband's reckless affair with Monica Lewinsky. Although the butler could not tell what she was thinking, he noticed that her hands holding the newspaper visibly trembled.

Hillary understood her husband well enough to know that this latest dalliance meant nothing to him; he never had any empathy or compassion for the women he slept with. Yet this affair

---

*The signs started coming down after the Travelgate and health-care fiascos.

was different from all the others, for it had the potential to derail the Clintons' copresidency.

She had to save Bill in order to save herself.

Otherwise, everything she had dreamed about since childhood would come to naught.

PART II

The Book of Life

CHAPTER SIX

Toughening Up

1958 (Forty years earlier)

It was three o'clock in the afternoon, and the fifth-graders in Park Ridge, Illinois, had just been dismissed from class. The schoolyard was a scene of frolicking, screeching children. However, one of the kids, a somber-looking eleven-year-old boy by the name of Jim Yrigoyen, was not in the mood to play.

He gathered up his courage and approached a girl who was wearing thick round eyeglasses.

"Hi," he said.

"Hi," Hillary Rodham replied.

Jim handed Hillary a set of dog tags embossed with his name and address.

"Will you wear these?" he asked in a rather timid voice.

"Okay," she replied nonchalantly, and immediately tied a knot in the chain as a symbol that she and Jim were going steady.

"Hillary and I were both standouts in our class," Jim Yrigoyen recalled many years later. "She was on every committee and involved in all the activist groups, as well as being a straight-A student and an outstanding athlete.

"While the other girls were jumping rope," he continued, "Hillary insisted on playing softball or dodgeball with the boys. And she was always picked in the first rounds to be on a team, because she was good and a tough competitor. She was an intimidating figure to many of our classmates, but not to me, despite the chance she could haul off at any time."[1]

Hillary's reputation as one of the toughest kids in Park Ridge—then, as now, a predominately Republican suburb of Chicago—went back to the time when she was four years old and came home in tears complaining to her mother of the treatment she had received at the hands of Suzy O'Callaghan, the neighborhood bully.

Hillary's mom, Dorothy Howell Rodham, was the product of a grim childhood. At the age of eight, she was abandoned by her teenage mother and sent on a cross-country train ride with her three-year-old sister to Alhambra, California, where her grandparents lived. Her grandparents abused Dorothy until she finally ran away from home. Years later, after she married Hugh Rodham Sr. and moved to the suburbs, she retained the attitude of a tough tomboy.

"If Suzy hits you," Dorothy told little Hillary, "you have my permission to hit her back. You have to stand up for yourself. There's no room in this house for cowards."[2]

This story, which was legendary among the children in Park Ridge, and would eventually become part of Hillary's hagiography, ended with Suzy on the business end of Hillary's fist, and the two girls becoming fast friends.

But Hillary's career as a pugilist was just getting started.

Her first steady boyfriend, Jim Yrigoyen, now a high school guidance counselor in Lake Zurich, Illinois, remembered being ordered by Hillary to guard a warren of baby rabbits, and not give any of them away to neighborhood boys, no matter how much they begged. Jim readily agreed, but when Hillary's next-door neighbor asked for just one rabbit, Jim couldn't refuse.

"Hillary immediately counted the rabbits," Jim recalled. "She knew exactly how many she had. She looked at me with disdain and said, 'Did you do this?' When I admitted I did, she became pretty enraged. She yelled, 'Jim, I trusted you! You big jerk!' Then, she hauled off and punched me in the nose. I was stunned. I reached up and found my nose was bleeding a lot. She had really hurt me.

"Not only was it extraordinary for a girl to punch a boy," Jim went on, "but fighting even among boys was very much frowned upon in Park Ridge. I had transferred from an inner-city Chicago school, where you practically had to fight your way through the school day. When I came to Park Ridge I had one dustup and was promptly told that fighting would not be tolerated. So it was pretty much of a shock that Hillary, the teacher's pet and best all-around student, so quickly let her temper flare into violence like that."[3]*

Despite Hillary's combative nature, she and Jim Yrigoyen continued to go steady. After school, they tramped over to Hillary's yellow-brick, Federal-style house at the corner of Wisner and Elm streets, where they did their homework together.

As the eldest of three siblings, Hillary occupied a choice bedroom with a large veranda overlooking the yard. Her parents

---

*The quick and easy violence Hillary practiced as a child would come to characterize her relationship with Bill Clinton. There is at least one account of Hillary beating Bill with her fists in the face, and clawing him in the jaw, leaving a prominent mark. Close Clinton friend Linda Bloodworth-Thomason told author Gail Sheehy that it was great that Hillary had "smacked [Bill] upside the head."[4]

had a similar bedroom on the other end of the house. Hillary's younger siblings, Hugh Jr. and Tony, shared a room.

Hillary's father ran the household like a boot camp, which was to be expected from a one-time Penn State football scholarship student who majored in physical education and served in World War II as a navy drill instructor. He idolized Gene Tunney, the former world heavyweight boxing champion, who had been in charge of the U.S. Navy's wartime physical fitness program, and he lost no opportunity to apply the "Tunney Method" to toughen up Hillary for the hard knocks of life that lay ahead.[5]

Like his idol Gene Tunney, Hugh Rodham Sr. made a religion of physical fitness. He believed that body-contact sports such as boxing and wrestling did more than build muscle; they built self-confidence, self-reliance, self-discipline, and poise. He encouraged Hillary to be mentally tough and physically aggressive, and to fear no one.

Some visitors to the Rodham home recalled Hugh Sr. as a scary figure—a barrel-chested man with a booming voice, who was always criticizing Hillary's posture and telling her: "Head up, chin in, chest out, stomach in!" An acquaintance once described him as "rougher than a corn cob, as gruff as could be."[6]

Hillary received no special consideration from her father because she was a girl. He expected her to compete with boys in sports, feats of physical strength, and academics. When Hillary came home with straight A's on her report card, her perfectionist father's only comment was: "That must be an easy school you go to."[7]

Some biographers believed that the hyper-macho Hugh Sr. was responsible for Hillary's mistrust of men—an attitude so noticeable later in high school that she was compared by her classmates to a sexually frigid nun, and nicknamed "Sister Frigidaire."[8]

"Among both relatives and friends," wrote Roger Morris in *Partners in Power*, "many thought Hugh Rodham's treatment of his daughter and sons amounted to the kind of psychological abuse that might have crushed some children."9

But that was a misreading of Hillary's relationship with her father.

"For all his grouchiness," wrote Joyce Milton in her biography of Hillary, *The First Partner*, "Hugh was devoted to his family.... He taught Hillary to read the stock tables; and when she fretted about her low batting average in school softball games, he took her out to the park and threw her one pitch after another until she learned to connect with a curveball.

"Hillary and her father often seemed to be involved in a contest of wills," Milton continued. "She did everything he asked, and he would respond by raising the bar a few inches higher. Hillary's brothers had no doubt that she was their father's favorite, a daddy's girl who could do no wrong in his eyes.... In later years ... Hillary would insist that her father's behavior was 'empowering.' "10

In short, Hillary did not feel abused by her father. She did not construe his demands as criticism of her. On the contrary, those demands, which were supported by her mother, only reinforced Hillary's feeling that she was special—and that she was slated to become a champion.

When her father told her, "You can do better," Hillary interpreted that to mean, "He wants the best for me, because he believes I should be better than others." She experienced her father's demands as a loving challenge, and incorporated his perfectionism as her own.

Hillary learned several life lessons from her father and mother.

Lesson No. 1: Never allow yourself to be a victim.
Lesson No. 2: If somebody hits you, hit him or her back harder.
Lesson No. 3: Stay in control of your own destiny.

As the daughter of two perfectionist parents, Hillary seemed to come unglued whenever anyone dared to criticize or cross her. One of her closest friends was a boy named Rick Ricketts. Like Hillary, he was also a superachiever and a class leader. But when he infuriated Hillary by carelessly bumping his bike into hers, she gave him a good punch in the face.[11]

And Jim Yrigoyen's little romance with the future First Lady also ended on a note of violence.

"We were in a snowball fight with a bunch of other kids and I hit her a few good ones," he recalled. "She got pretty angry, and came after me, punching and hitting me in the chest and face. I couldn't punch her back, because she was a girl, so I tackled her. Then I guess I got carried away and rubbed her face in the snow, way too hard. By punching me she had gotten me all wound up and things got out of control.

"That was the end of the relationship," he continued. "The next day, when I got to school, my dog tags were on my desk, the knot undone. Hillary couldn't have made it plainer."[12]

CHAPTER SEVEN

The Great Debate

WHEN SHE WAS SIXTEEN YEARS OLD, HILLARY RODHAM composed a bitter letter to her church's youth minister, the Reverend Don Jones.

She had just been defeated for president of the senior class at Maine South High School. As she described it in the letter, she had lost as a result of "dirty campaigning" by chauvinist opponents who were "slinging mud" at her.

"We did not retaliate," she wrote the Reverend Jones, using the royal "we." "We took the high road and talked about motherhood and apple pie."[1]

Four decades later, in her memoir *Living History*, Hillary recalled that moment. Still as bitter as ever, she accused one of her Maine South High School opponents of saying that "I was really stupid if I thought a girl could be elected president."[2]

Timothy Sheldon, the boy who defeated Hillary, and who was now an Illinois circuit court judge, had a far different memory of events.

"It's incredible that it still rankles her after all these years," he said in an interview for this book. "There was nothing to sling mud about, because there were no issues, no debate.

"The so-called race was just a popularity contest," he went on. "Normally, boys ran for president and girls for secretary. Rightly or wrongly, that was just the way it was done in those days. I remember it vividly: it was the first time a girl had run for student council president. The reason I won was I was the star running back on the football team. It was as simple as that."[3]

But it wasn't that simple for Hillary.

"The reason Hillary still makes excuses for her loss, suggesting dirty tricks were somehow played, is that she had then—and apparently continues to have—a sense of infallibility," said a former member of the Maine South student council. "It is not possible that she could have lost even a high school election simply because she was not the most popular candidate. She was bitter and furious at the loss back then, and even in her own mind probably has convinced herself there was chicanery."[4]

THAT SAME YEAR, HILLARY TOOK PART IN A MOCK PRESIDENTIAL debate. It was well known that her father was a conservative, and that Hillary was actively campaigning for the Republican candidate, Barry Goldwater. However, she recalled that her government teacher, Jerry Baker, "in an act of counter-intuitive brilliance—or perversity—assigned me to play President [Lyndon] Johnson" in the debate.[5] She said that Ellen Press, the only Democrat she knew in her class, was assigned to take the role of Barry Goldwater.

As she told the story, Hillary at first resented having to research Lyndon Johnson's Great Society policies. Gradually, however, she came to find herself arguing the president's liberal positions with "more than dramatic fervor."[6] She went on to suggest that it was a political turning point for her and Ellen Press.

However, the October 30, 1964, edition of *Southwards*, the Maine South student newspaper, directly contradicted Hillary's story about the debate. The paper mentioned no such switch of political affiliation on the part of Hillary and Ellen. Rather, it identified Hillary as a Goldwater Republican, not a Johnson Democrat as she later claimed.

In an interview with the author of this book, Jerry Baker, Hillary's government teacher, who later went on to become the legislative counsel for the Airline Pilots Association, said that his recollection about the forty-year-old high school debate was a bit fuzzy.

"Hillary's version of the debate makes a good story," Baker said. "However, it may not have been the way she portrayed it."[7]

CHAPTER EIGHT

The Radical

Big Hugh Rodham swung his Cadillac out of the driveway and aimed its flying-wings hood ornament east, toward his daughter's future.

During the thousand-mile journey—from Park Ridge, Illinois, through the rust belt of the upper Midwest, over the Appalachian cordillera, eastward across the rolling farms of Pennsylvania, north through the New Jersey wetlands, and east again across the abandoned mill towns of Massachusetts—Hugh worked on a wad of chewing tobacco, while his wife, Dorothy, kept up a constant patter to help him stay alert.

Hillary, their demure, well-scrubbed, neatly coifed seventeen-year-old daughter, seemed lost in the enormous backseat of the car. She kept the driver's side back window shut to avoid getting splattered by her father's flying tobacco spit.

"When Hillary left Park Ridge for Wellesley College, she was still a conservative Park Ridge girl," said Penny Pullen, a high school classmate. "She chose an all-girls college that catered to the upper crust, but the seeds of a radical left-wing political philosophy had been planted by her Methodist youth group minister, Don Jones. And those seeds would be watered and fertilized at Wellesley College.

"The next time I saw her," Penny continued, "was on television as a guest on *The Irv Kupcinet Show*. She looked like a hippy with big glasses, shapeless clothes, and hair that looked like it hadn't been washed in a month. Kupcinet patted her on the head in praise. My recollection is that she was yelling about a university strike over a rent increase on student housing."[1]

The transformation of Hillary Rodham—from a neatly groomed Goldwater Girl to a scruffy left-wing radical—began in earnest in the backseat of her father's Cadillac. Throughout the long journey across America, Hillary rarely took her nose out of the books and magazines she had brought along. One of her favorite publications was *motive*, whose logo was spelled with a lowercase *m*. The magazine was destined to have a profound influence on her way of thinking.

The Reverend Don Jones, Hillary's youth minister at the Park Ridge United Methodist Church, had given her a subscription to *motive* as a high school graduation present. It was easy to see why Jones—who would soon be fired by his congregation for advocating "socialist" views—thought so highly of *motive*. The Division of Higher Education of the United Methodist Church had published the magazine since 1941, and its original editorial mission was to help Methodist college students keep in touch with their church's principles of "piety and service." But by 1965, the year of Hillary's high school graduation, the magazine was trumpeting a very different tune.

It would come to resemble such New Left underground publications as the *East Village Other* and the *Berkeley Barb*. Indeed, *motive* was gleefully vulgar; it editorialized that words like *fuck, bitch,* and *shit* should be printed "in tact." Photo features included a birthday card for Ho Chi Minh and a picture of a pretty coed with an LSD tablet on her tongue.

Marxist writers were featured in the pages of *motive*. Renegade priest Daniel Berrigan contributed anti–Vietnam War poems. Nat Hentoff defended student militancy. Convicted cop killer Huey Newton was lauded as a victim and a visionary. Advice was dispensed on draft dodging, desertion, and flight to Canada and Sweden.

According to the Methodist Church's archives, during the 1960s and early 1970s *motive* espoused "highly politicized, left-wing ideology, which favored Cuba, socialism, the Black Panthers, SDS [Students for a Democratic Society] . . . obscene and vulgar language, and anti-American ideology." As the archives pointed out, *motive*'s stance "did not win it popularity among the Methodist faithful."[2]

In 1972, the last year of its publication, *motive* devoted an entire issue to a radical lesbian/feminist theme, which emphasized the need to destroy "our sexist, racist, capitalist, imperialist system."[3] Two of the editors of the issue were Rita Mae Brown, author of the lesbian novel *Ruby Fruit Jungle*, and Charlotte Bunch, a lesbian militant.

"At this time," the editors wrote, "we are separatists who do not work with men, straight or gay, because men are not working to end male supremacy. Only a complete destruction of the whole male supremacist system can free women."[4]

Brown and Bunch defined lesbianism as a political faith, and they made it clear that even a woman who did not choose to participate in sex with another woman could still live philosophically under the rubric of political lesbianism.

"Male society," they wrote, "defines lesbianism as a sexual act, which reflects men's limited view of women: they think of us only in terms of sex."[5]

In a 1994 interview with *Newsweek*—more than two decades after *motive* folded—Hillary proudly stated: "I still have every issue they sent me."[6]

HILLARY HAD READ HER COPIES OF *MOTIVE* COVER TO COVER BY THE time Hugh Rodham got off at exit 14 of the Massachusetts Turnpike and headed toward the Wellesley College campus—five hundred acres of woodlands, hills, meadows, and ponds, and miles of footpaths and trails that bordered Lake Waban. The beautiful campus was virtually unchanged from the day it opened to its first female students almost one hundred years before.

Hillary soon discovered that the college's rules and regulations hadn't changed much, either. She was assigned to a suite of rooms with four other girls in Stone-Davis Hall. The imposing neogothic dormitory had recently undergone a renovation. The first thing Hillary noticed when she entered the building was a bell desk, whose distinctive chimes announced whether a visitor was male or female. An upperclassman, who offered to give Hillary and her parents a tour of Stone-Davis, pointed out two glass-walled "fishbowl" date rooms, where girls met boys under the wary eye of housemothers—middle-aged, nonfaculty college employees, who lived in the dorm and enforced 10:00 P.M. weekday and 1:00 A.M. weekend curfews.

It did not take Hillary long to decide that Wellesley was stuck in a Victorian time warp. Out of an incoming class of 420 women, only five were African Americans. Jewish students were housed with other Jews, Catholics with Catholics. Bible classes were mandatory.

In one of the college's most degrading traditions, freshmen were required to strip to their underwear, have reflective stickers attached to their spines, and then be photographed to determine what areas of their posture—such as overly prominent buttocks—needed improvement.[7] The girls were told: "The buttocks [should be] neither unduly prominent nor having that 'about to be spanked' look."[8]

The freshmen were warned they must adhere to Wellesley's long-established parietal regulations, which forbade boys from entering the living quarters of the dorms except on Sunday afternoon, and then only when doors remained wide open. The rules also prohibited the girls from having a car on campus, and from wearing pants.[9]

Much of the Wellesley curriculum was finishing-school material that was designed to educate a woman to be a skilled wife and homemaker. There was mandatory instruction on serving tea, how to walk in high heels, and the proper way of getting out of a car in a skirt. The marriage lectures taught the young women how to talk to their husband's boss, and how to maintain a slender figure so that their husband did not lose his interest in them. The few married students who lived on campus were officially put on notice that they were not to share the "secrets of married life" with single girls.[10]

IN THE HIGHLY CHARGED ATMOSPHERE OF THE 1960S, WELLESLEY was ripe for change. Toward the end of her freshman year, Hillary was elected sophomore senate representative on a platform that promised to reform Wellesley's course requirements. Her inflammatory rhetoric brought her some unexpected notoriety. The conservative *Boston Herald* wrote that Hillary and her Wellesley College allies resembled "the Bolshevik women's auxiliary, in their fur caps and high boots. . . ."[11]

"Theirs was a generation that imagined it would reinvent the world," wrote Miriam Horn in *Rebels in White Gloves*, an exhaustive study of Hillary's 1969 graduating class at Wellesley. "Self-conscious iconoclasts and pioneers, the women of '69 would experiment boldly with sex and work and family and religion and politics.... The feminist insight that 'the personal is political' meant that ... all sorts of seemingly intimate choices—what kind of underwear one wore, whether and how and with whom one had sex—were political as well as personal, a way of confronting social rules as to how a lady behaved and of interrogating the complicated relationship between power and sexual consent...."[12]

Hillary's chief lieutenant at Wellesley College was Eleanor Acheson, the granddaughter of former Secretary of State Dean Acheson. "Eldie" had the easy nonchalance that went with inherited wealth, and at first she was contemptuous of Hillary's desire to achieve power, influence, and access. Yet eventually, a strong bond developed between the two young women.

While Hillary was still in the early stages of exploring her sexual nature, Eldie was already sexually reckless and bawdy. When she and Alison "Snowy" Campbell, another girl with a patrician background, designed the Class of 1969 yearbook, they decided to make a brazen reference to the sexual position 69. They illustrated the cover of the book with a sexy shot of Mae West, right side up; on the back cover, Mae West was shown upside down. The title page of the yearbook was illustrated with a picture of the bare behinds of Eldie, Snowy, and two other girls.[13]

Penny McPhee, who was editor-in-chief of the *Wellesley News*, recalled: "I wasn't surprised that they did it, by any means. Around the same time, I posed in a bikini made out of newspaper, which we ran in the *News*. So that kind of thing was definitely in the air. But I would have been shocked if they had gotten it in the yearbook."[14]

They didn't. The president of the college, Ruth Adams, put her sensible heels down, and the offending yearbook pages were left blank.

* * *

HILLARY'S YEARS AT WELLESLEY LEFT AN INDELIBLE IMPRINT ON her personality and character. Her role models were the strong-willed, ideologically passionate, sexually adventurous feminists who rejected dependence on men and despised the old-fashioned feminine wiles typically used by women to attract the opposite sex. Her feminist classmates refused to wear pretty dresses, style their hair, use coy remarks, or deploy any of the trappings that might make them appear subordinate to men. As a result, they sometimes appeared mannish.

There was a long tradition of lesbianism at Wellesley, though it had not always been called by that name. In the late nineteenth and early twentieth centuries, Wellesley girls who had lesbian relationships called them "smashes," "mashes," "crushes," and "spoons." Men were not permitted to attend college dances; instead, upper-class women donned tuxedos and black ties, and brought gowned freshmen and sophomores as their "dates."[15]

In those early days of the college, Wellesley women who loved other Wellesley women did not consider themselves strange, since the relationships they formed were the norm rather than the exception. So many of the college's female professors lived together in lesbian relationships that a union between two women came to be known as a "Wellesley marriage" or "Boston marriage." By the turn of the century, when 90 percent of the adult women in America were married, more than half of Wellesley graduates remained single, and only one female faculty member out of fifty-three was married.[16]

In Hillary's day, the young women at Wellesley were just as determined as their predecessors to change the college, society, and themselves. At least two women who were close to Hillary—Eldie Acheson and Nancy Wanderer—would become out-of-the-closet lesbians who felt that it was important to break their bonds of "imprisonment" to male sexuality.

"The notion of a woman being a lesbian was fascinating to

Hillary," said one of her Wellesley classmates. "But she was much more interested in lesbianism as a political statement than a sexual practice. . . .

"A lesbian was suddenly not the eccentric old maid of Victorian literature, but a dynamic young woman who had thrown off the shackles of male dominance," this person continued. "Hillary talked about it a lot, read lesbian literature, and embraced it as a revolutionary concept."[17]

To be a lesbian, it was not necessary for a woman to have a physical relationship with other women. Such a relationship could be romantic *and* asexual. Forty years before Bill Clinton tried to redefine the meaning of sex by saying, "That all depends on what your definition of *is* is,"[18] Hillary and her Wellesley classmates confronted the same question: what is sex?

"This question has the potential to be tremendously important in defining a lesbian relationship," Esther D. Rothblum and Kathleen A. Brehony wrote in *Boston Marriages*.[19]

And the feminist Naomi McCormick added: "Female bisexuality and lesbianism may be more a matter of loving other women than of achieving orgasm through genital contact. . . . The absence of genital juxtaposition hardly drains a relationship of passion or importance."[20]

At Wellesley, while many of her classmates were falling in and out of love with men—or other women—Hillary did not seem to be interested in either gender for the purpose of having "genital juxtaposition."

During her last three years at Wellesley, Hillary dated a boy by the name of David Rupert, who, as Hillary would eventually discover, was a classmate of Bill Clinton's at Georgetown University in Washington. Hillary's attraction to David Rupert seemed more political than sexual: they marched against the Vietnam War, talked endlessly about changing society, smoked pot, and eventually—in her senior year—briefly slept together.[21]

But their relationship began to sputter when Rupert insisted that Hillary spend weekends at his shack in Bennington, Vermont, where he loved to ski both cross-country and downhill. Hillary refused to ski, and Rupert, finding a chink in her armor, teased her about her fear of appearing vulnerable and out of control.

Their testy discussions about skiing—which might have been a substitute for an honest discussion about Hillary's sexual frigidity—often ended with Hillary retreating into an icy silence. She refused to let Rupert—or any man, for that matter—get the upper hand. Their relationship abruptly ended the week Hillary met Bill Clinton at Yale Law School.

"I never stated a burning desire to be president of the United States," said Rupert. "I believe that was a need for her in a partner."[22]

FROM HER DAYS IN WELLESLEY ONWARD, HILLARY WAS OFTEN MIStaken as asexual.

"People who claim that they were born asexual are operating under a false assumption," said Dr. Claudia Six, a clinical sexologist. "There is always a psychological reason for their behavior. Chief among these reasons is a fear of losing control, a feeling of vulnerability when one is sexually active with a partner, a deep underlying anxiety about having sex. That fear can be so strong that it leads a woman to shut down all her sexual feelings."[23]

Unlike most college-age girls, Hillary did not come of age sexually in Wellesley. Nonetheless, she retained a feeling of solidarity with the members of the Wellesley College Class of 1969. In addition to appointing several of her classmates to high government posts during her husband's administration, Hillary invited many others for sleepovers at the White House.

Most of the members of her Wellesley class attended a twenty-fifth reunion that was held in 1994 at the White House.

One of these women was Nancy Wanderer. Nancy married in her junior year, but after decades of marriage, she began a sexual relationship with another woman. For a short time, she played musical beds with her husband and girlfriend under the same roof. But she finally divorced, went back to school and became a law professor, and moved into a full-time lesbian relationship with her lover.[24]

At the class's twenty-fifth reunion dinner, Hillary made a point of sitting next to Nancy Wanderer. The two old friends chatted for an hour or so—not about their mutually tumultuous marriages, but about menopause and other middle-age health concerns.

At one point, Hillary leaned toward Nancy and asked if she could touch her closely cropped hair.

After Nancy recovered from her surprise, she gave Hillary permission to go ahead.

Hillary reached out and ran the palm of her hand over Nancy's butch cut.

"Maybe," said Hillary, "I'll get a haircut like this and really shock everyone."[25]

CHAPTER NINE

The Intern

AS THE SUMMER OF 1968 APPROACHED, HILLARY WAS LOOKing forward to an internship in Washington, D.C. Some of her best friends at Wellesley College had already lined up choice assignments. Kris Olson was going to work at the Office of Economic Opportunity on the social, psychological, and vocational rehabilitation of indigent defendants caught up in the Washington criminal justice system. Likewise, Nancy Gist would be working for Representative John Conyers, an African American who was active in the Southern Christian Leadership Conference and the upcoming Poor People's March on Washington. Cynthia Harrison was assigned to Senator Albert Gore of Tennessee. Jan Krigbaum would spend the summer at the Agency for International Development, working on Latin American antipoverty programs.[1]

But when Hillary's assignment was announced, she was crushed. She was being sent to Washington to work on the Republican House Conference, the legislative research and planning group that was laboring to help the GOP in the upcoming fall election.

"By this time," said her old friend Sarah Calvedt, "Hillary had come full circle. She started off at Wellesley as a Goldwater Republican, and had become a fully converted liberal Democrat."[2]

But things worked out better for Hillary in Washington than she had expected. She wound up interning for Representative Charles Goodell, a liberal Rockefeller Republican. And, even more exciting, she was invited by Goodell to attend the Republican National Convention in Miami.

"We all stayed at the Fontainebleau Hotel in a room with a bunch of girls, and we took turns trying to grab some sleep," one of Hillary's classmates recalled in an interview for this book. "One night, a couple of the girls brought some guys back to the room. They had been drinking, and things got a little rowdy.

"Hillary, who was in bed and apparently asleep, jumped up and stormed out of the room," her classmate continued. "The surprising thing was that she had been in bed fully clothed—I guess to ward off any unwanted sexual advances by randy politicians.

"She was completely indignant, and refused to come back until the guys were gone. She made it clear she was going to go to Congressman Goodell if it happened again. She was still far too straight for that sort of thing.

"We all got hit on by some of the delegates and congressmen. A couple of times Hillary looked like she was about to haul off and smack some of these guys. They were really grabby and obnoxious. I have to think that she would have come away from that experience feeling that young interns should really be protected from lecherous older guys."[3]

CHAPTER TEN

Grooving at Cozy Beach

THE YOUNG WOMAN STROLLING ACROSS THE CAMPUS OF Yale Law School in the fall of 1971 was a sight to behold.

She was wearing a sleeveless blouse, black silk pajama bottoms, sandals, and a pair of thick glasses in red plastic frames. Her hair looked as though it hadn't been shampooed in weeks. As she bounced along on the balls of her feet, she was shouting at the young man by her side, gesticulating wildly, and revealing that she did not shave under her arms.

The young man towered over her by more than a head. He was a beefy fellow, well over two hundred pounds, and he sported an orange-colored beard, hair down to his shoulders, and a shabby army surplus jacket. Somebody had once told him he sounded like Gomer Pyle.

Hillary Rodham and William Jefferson Clinton were always arguing about something. Today, it was over a speech they had just heard at Trinity Church Parish House in nearby New Haven. It was delivered by a spellbinding orator and one of Hillary's heroines—Marian Wright Edelman, a civil rights lawyer and the first black woman trustee of the Yale Corporation.

In her remarks, Marian Wright Edelman criticized liberals who suffered from "issue nymphomania." And she predicted that the recent orgy of violence at Attica State Prison, where prisoners bludgeoned and slashed each other to death, would happen "all over the country if changes are not made."[1]

These apocalyptic predictions came from a woman who was known by her left-wing followers as "Saint Marian." She and her husband, a white man who once served as an aide to Robert Kennedy in the Justice Department, believed in big government programs, and were skilled at playing upon white liberal guilt to pass legislation on behalf of poor, mostly black children.

At Yale, the Edelmans were mentors to promising young radical law students like Hillary Rodham. Shortly after Hillary graduated, Marian Wright Edelman founded the Children's Defense Fund. Despite its modest-sounding name, the organization had grandiose ambitions. As Marian once confessed:

"The country was tired of the concerns of the 1960s. I got the idea that children might be a very effective way to broaden the base for change."[2]

According to an article in *The New Republic* by Mickey Kaus, Marian's strategy "requires that [the Children's Defense Fund] reduce every issue of anti-poverty to a question of 'protecting children who can't speak for themselves.' Not only are Head Start, WIC [the Special Supplemental Food Program for Women, Infants, and Children] and immunization cast as children's issues, so are welfare, day care, housing and employment."[3]

The issue of children's rights was custom-made for Hillary. After all, who could be against children? Better yet, children were hardly in a position to write Op-Ed articles in the *New York Times* pointing out that Marian Wright Edelman and Hillary Rodham didn't speak for them.

* * *

HILLARY'S PASSION ABOUT SUCH CAUSES FASCINATED BILL CLINton. He had never met a female firebrand quite like her. And that was saying a lot, since he had slept with dozens of women. In fact, women were never far from Bill's mind; he was addicted to them as surely as his alcoholic stepfather had been addicted to fermented spirits. Normally, Bill was able to juggle several women at the same time.

"Bill's pattern," said a fellow Yale Law student, "was seduction and betrayal. The latter seemed to come as naturally to him as the former. He would do anything as long as he got what he wanted from people."[4]

Bill Clinton's seductions were conducted in his off-campus bedroom, which was located on the second floor of a Victorian house along a wind-swept stretch of Long Island Sound. Between love bouts with women, he took long solitary walks on the beach. Dressed in his heavy army surplus jacket and a ski mask to protect his face from the stinging cold, he contemplated his future.

After he graduated from law school, he planned to return to Arkansas and run for public office. He had already picked out what he thought was a safe congressional district, and had secured a $10,000 loan from his uncle Raymond—far more than was customarily spent on such Arkansas contests. Since the age of seven, Bill's goal had been to become president of the United States. His mother, his teachers, and his friends all told him he was going to make it. The only missing ingredient in his calculus was a wife.

And that was where Hillary Rodham fit in. Years later, Hillary would tell a story about how she and Bill met at Yale. According to this tale, Hillary caught Bill staring at her across the room in the law library, and marched over to the moonstruck

Arkansan and introduced herself. The anecdote had a nice feminist ring to it: a woman took the initiative and forced the issue.

The only trouble was, Hillary's story was blatantly untrue.

In fact, Bill first became aware of Hillary through her work as coeditor of a far-left journal called *The Yale Review of Law and Social Action*.[5] In its debut issue in the spring of 1970, there was an article titled "Jamestown 70."[6] It proposed the migration of like-minded leftists to one of the fifty states for "the purpose of gaining political control and establishing a living laboratory for experiment." The article rejected working within the established social order. "Experimentation with drugs, sex, individual lifestyles or radical rhetoric and action within the larger society," it stated, "is an insufficient alternative. Total experimentation is necessary."[7]

In a later special double issue of the *Review*, Hillary and one of her former Wellesley classmates, Kris Olson, coedited articles that focused on the violence-prone Black Panthers and the ongoing trial of several Panthers for the torture-murder of their colleague Alex Rackley. Hillary and Kris believed that the accused murderers had been denied their full legal rights. In that same special issue, an unsigned article criticizing a New Haven police raid on the Panthers' headquarters caught Bill Clinton's eye. It was illustrated by a cartoon depicting the police as oinking, hairy, snot-nosed pigs.[8]

While Bill Clinton was an admirer of the *Yale Journal of Law and Social Action*, he had serious reservations about lending his name to the magazine, for fear that such a move might come back to haunt him in politically conservative Arkansas. Nonetheless, he asked Jeff Rogers (the son of William Rogers, President Nixon's secretary of state) to introduce him to Hillary Rodham. Bill had seen Hillary around the campus, and though she was hardly his physical type, he was interested in meeting her.

Jeff Rogers was the ideal person to make the introduction. He and Kris Olson, Hillary's coeditor, lived together in a commune called Cozy Beach, which was affiliated with Ken Kesey's Oregon Hog Farm commune. The Magic Bus riders, immortalized in Tom Wolfe's *Electric Kool-Aid Acid Test*, were regular visitors.

"Jeff Rogers and Kris Olson had [Bill and Hillary] over to their commune for dinner," a friend recalled. "That meant sitting on the floor or on their broken furniture and eating take-out pizza or something. But the introduction was made and they hit it off right away.

"Hillary was soon a regular at Bill's group house in Milford, and the relationship took off," this friend continued. "Hillary was clearly smitten. She seemed to hang on him. But Bill was not nearly as enamored. In fact, he continued to see other women, even after they moved into an apartment just off campus."[9]

DURING THEIR REMAINING TIME AT YALE, BILL AND HILLARY often grooved the night away at Cozy Beach, spinning the latest Jefferson Airplane platters and eating Kris Olson's hashish brownies. When Kris's long-suffering Republican parents finally became fed up with her counterculture ways and cut off the flow from her trust funds, she donned a jumpsuit with her name stenciled on the back and produced drug-inspired psychedelic light shows to make ends meet.[10]

It was clear to friends that Bill and Hillary had a relationship in which the normal rules of courtship did not apply. Their romance (if it could be called that) was not based on mutual physical attraction. Bill frequently found sexual release elsewhere.[11] And Hillary, who had never placed much store in sex, did not seem to mind.

Bill treated Hillary as one of the boys, and never talked down to her because she was a woman. He reinforced the idea in

Hillary's mind, which had been planted there by her parents, that she was a special person, and that there was nothing beyond her reach—including becoming the first woman president of the United States.

What's more, Hillary believed that Bill had the makings of a Great Man. He offered Hillary something that her father could never give her: the chance for Hillary to transcend her gender. As a woman coming of age in 1971—still the infancy of the feminist movement—Hillary knew she could not achieve power on her own. She needed Bill Clinton to take her to the mountaintop.

CHAPTER ELEVEN

The Other "Smoking Gun"

At the first faint light of dawn, Hillary Rodham emerged from her basement apartment on Dupont Circle. She was twenty-six years old, less than a year out of Yale Law School, and she was dressed in her customary spinster-lady fashion—opaque black stockings and large brown-tinted eyeglasses.[1] Off in the distance, she could see the Capitol dome brightening as the sun came up on another steamy summer day.

Hillary made her way to the Congressional Hotel, a down-at-the-heel establishment on Capitol Hill. There, she showed a photo I.D. to the guards and passed through two separate security checks. Inside, the doors had thick steel locks, and the windows were covered with iron bars. Each office was furnished with two wastebaskets—one for normal trash, the other for sensitive papers relating to the impeachment inquiry of President Richard Milhous Nixon.

Hillary was one of three women on a staff of more than forty lawyers who were looking into President Nixon's Watergate abuses of power in the late fall of 1974. Her tiny office, which looked out on a back alley, was located near the coffee machine, on which someone had posted a notice:

> *The women in this office were not hired to make coffee. Make it yourself or call on one of these liberated men to do so.*[2]

Hillary unlocked a safe and gathered some papers. Then she headed for the office of her boss, John Doar, the special counsel of the impeachment inquiry. As always, the door was closed, and Hillary knocked before she entered.

John Doar kept the window shades drawn in his second-floor office to prevent people from looking in and lip-reading his conversations.[3] It took Hillary a few moments to adjust to the gloom. First, she saw the immaculate desk. ("A clean desk," Doar lectured his staff, "represents a methodical mind.") Then, she saw Doar himself, a tall, thin, ascetic-looking man, who was said by his admirers to resemble Gary Cooper in *High Noon*.

Doar first made his mark on the national stage in the early 1960s while working for Deputy Attorney General Burke Marshall in the civil rights division of the Justice Department. During the racial violence in Montgomery, Alabama, he faced down white mobs and impressed Burke Marshall and President John Kennedy with his physical courage. Later, when Doar became chief of the civil rights division under President Lyndon Johnson, he prosecuted the murderers of three civil rights workers—Andrew Goodman, Michael Schwerner, and James Chaney—in Neshoba County, Mississippi.

Despite his impressive résumé, however, John Doar was hardly the incorruptible *High Noon* hero portrayed by his friends. During the Johnson administration, Doar engaged in many of the activities that he now described as "abuses of power" by Richard Nixon. Among other things, Doar had recommended the creation of a secret computerized intelligence file on American citizens who were considered to be dangerous dissidents.[4]*

Doar insisted that he was nonpartisan in his role as special counsel to the Nixon impeachment inquiry. But, according to writer Renata Adler, who was one of Doar's closest confidants, that was not the case. As Adler would later write:

"The fact that underlay the [impeachment] ordeal was that most of the work, almost all of the time by almost all of the staff, was a charade. . . . Doar himself was working mainly with a small group of about seven people, five of whom were old friends who had worked with him before and who were not on the regular staff [Adler herself was a member of this group].

"There was never any doubt among Doar and this small group that . . . the object of this process was that the President must be impeached. Doar had, in fact, been the second non-radical person I knew, and the first [nominal] Republican, to advocate impeachment—months before he became special counsel, long before the inquiry began. Doar customarily spoke . . . in terms of 'war' and 'the Cause.' "[6]

AMONG HIS IMPEACHMENT STAFF, JOHN DOAR WAS NOTORIOUS FOR being stingy with praise. His rare pats on the back were known as "Doar fixes."[7] But he treated Hillary Rodham differently from all the others. She was his favorite. Though junior in rank, she

---

*In 1975, a commission headed by Vice President Nelson Rockefeller was created by President Gerald Ford to investigate the CIA. The Rockefeller Commission revealed that John Doar recommended the establishment of "a single intelligence unit to analyze the FBI information we receive about persons who make the urban ghetto their base of operations." Other sources of dissident information suggested by Doar included the Intelligence Unit of the Internal Revenue Service and the Post Office Department.[5]

was given choice assignments and invited by Doar to accompany him to confidential executive sessions of the full Judiciary Committee.

Hillary had come to Doar's office this morning to deliver a draft report written by a committee of eminent scholars chaired by the Yale historian C. Vann Woodward. Doar had assigned Hillary to supervise the historians' work as they investigated the record of past presidential abuses of power.

There was no need for Doar to explain the critical importance of the project to Hillary. As part of Richard Nixon's defense, White House lawyers were prepared to argue that Nixon's abuses of presidential power were no worse than those committed by other presidents, including John F. Kennedy, who made illegal political assassinations a secret instrument of his foreign policy.[8]

"When Nixon entered office, he was very serious about foreign affairs," recalled Geoffrey Shepard, a lawyer who worked in the Nixon White House during the impeachment inquiry. "President Nixon immediately began pushing the hell out of [CIA director] Richard Helms, demanding to know who screwed up the Bay of Pigs, who stood by while [South Vietnamese president] Ngo Dinh Diem was assassinated. Those were exactly the kinds of things that Teddy Kennedy did not want explored about his dead brother's administration."[9]

Indeed, Nixon's doomsday threat to expose the "crimes of Camelot" posed a serious problem for Senator Edward M. Kennedy, the front-runner for his party's presidential nomination in 1976. If Nixon was impeached, he was prepared to reveal what he knew about JFK's programs to assassinate foreign leaders and illegally wiretap the telephone conversations of American citizens.

Such bombshell revelations would not only irrevocably

tarnish the reputation of John Kennedy, they would likely derail Teddy Kennedy's plans to restore Camelot in the White House.

The question was: Did Nixon have enough ammunition to carry out his threat against Teddy Kennedy?

The answer was contained in the C. Vann Woodward report that Hillary now placed on Doar's desk, with its title page facing up:

> *Responses of the President to Charges of Misconduct Including Accusations of High Crimes and Misdemeanors from George Washington to Lyndon Johnson: An Authoritative History Requested by Counsel John Doar for the Impeachment Inquiry Staff Investigating Charges Against Richard M. Nixon.*[10]

Less than a year out of Yale Law School, Hillary Rodham seemed an unlikely choice to supervise such a sensitive project. But then, Hillary was no ordinary rookie lawyer.

While Hillary was at Yale Law School, her fiery radicalism had brought her to the attention of Marian and Peter Edelman. They, in turn, had sung Hillary's praises to Professor Burke Marshall, the former Kennedy Justice Department official who had been one of the first people Teddy Kennedy turned to for help after Chappaquiddick.[11]

Now, as the attorney-general-in-waiting of the Camelot government-in-exile,[12] Marshall was the secret éminence grise behind the impeachment inquiry. From his professor's perch at Yale Law School, he had personally recommended or vetted most of the lawyers who were hired by his protégé, John Doar. Hillary was hired on the basis of Marshall's glowing reference.[13]

Shortly after she arrived in Washington, Hillary received a crash course in the kind of bare-knuckles politics that would come in handy later in Arkansas and Washington, D.C. Among other things, she learned that Teddy Kennedy had used his considerable clout to shield his assassinated brother from embarrassing exposure.

First, Teddy successfully lobbied for the appointment of an old friend, Harvard professor Archibald Cox, as the Watergate special prosecutor. Cox was a fierce Kennedy partisan; he had been an adviser and speechwriter for John F. Kennedy and served as solicitor general in the Kennedy Justice Department. In addition, Teddy sponsored an amendment to the bill establishing the Senate Watergate Committee. His amendment, which was passed by the Senate, barred the Watergate Committee from investigating past misconduct by the executive branch, the FBI, or the CIA.

In addition, Hillary learned that the lineup of pro- and anti-impeachment forces in Washington was not at all what she expected. Many Republicans, including Senator Barry Goldwater, believed that it would be better if Nixon were impeached sooner rather than later, so that his successor in the Oval Office would have time to reunify and strengthen the Republican Party. The Democrats, on the other hand, had a different agenda: they wanted to keep the fatally wounded Nixon in office as long as possible.

"Don Edwards of California, Robert Kastenmeier of Wisconsin, and other liberals . . . savored the prospect of Nixon remaining in office twisting in the wind until the end of his term," wrote Jerry Zeifman, chief counsel to the House Judiciary Committee, and John Doar's nominal boss. "As they saw it, that would pave the way for a staunch liberal such as Ted Kennedy to win the presidency easily."[14]*

Among those who agreed with Zeifman's analysis was Vice President Gerald Ford. He criticized Democrats who were

---

*Democrats also relished the prospect of running against a badly wounded Nixon in the 1974 off-year election.

"bent on stretching out the ordeal of Watergate for their own purpose," and accused a "relatively small group of political activists" of plotting to "cripple the President by dragging out the preliminaries to impeachment for as long as they can and to use the whole affair for maximum political advantage.... [T]heir aim is total victory for themselves and total defeat not only of President Nixon but of the Republican policies for which he stands."[15]

Doar and his ad hoc irregulars, including Hillary Rodham, conferred regularly on impeachment strategy with Burke Marshall at Yale. This group devised several ingenious legal strategies. They argued that a president was constitutionally shielded from impeachment for acts by his subordinates that he had not personally directed.[16] Under this legal umbrella, it would be difficult, for instance, to prove that President Kennedy was responsible for the use of Mafia hit men to assassinate Fidel Castro, because there was no direct evidence that he had ordered someone to do it.

The Doar irregulars further asserted that a president had neither the right to representation by counsel in an impeachment proceeding, nor the right to cross-examine witnesses.[17] This ruling would have prevented President Nixon's attorneys from examining witnesses who could testify that the Kennedy administration indulged in acts that had been blatantly unconstitutional.

These and other procedural rules, which were drawn up by Hillary Rodham and approved by Burke Marshall, had one principal object: to protect the reputations of John F. Kennedy (and, by extension, that of presidential hopeful Teddy Kennedy).

In the end, of course, Richard Nixon destroyed himself. In the famous "smoking gun" tape that led to his resignation, he could be heard ordering his aides to obstruct justice in the Watergate case.

But there was another, less famous "smoking gun." This was the report prepared under Hillary Rodham's supervision by C. Vann Woodward and a team of twelve scholars. Their report left little doubt that previous presidents, including John F. Kennedy, had engaged in immoral and unlawful abuses of power that were as bad as those perpetrated by Richard Nixon.

AFTER DOAR FINISHED READING THE REPORT, HE TURNED TO Hillary and warned her never to discuss it with anyone, not even with Doar's boss, Peter Rodino, the chairman of the House Judiciary Committee.[18] The report, he said, must remain "top secret."*

"When Congressman Charles Wiggins . . . insisted that the inquiry's failure to make such [a historic] study was unforgivable," wrote Renata Adler, "he was never told, nor were any other congressmen, that the project was *already under way* [italics added]."[20]

The decision to suppress the C. Vann Woodward report would have a long-lasting toxic effect on the impeachment process. Until Nixon, most constitutional lawyers had been of the opinion that a president who violated the spirit of the law and engaged in "immoral acts" was guilty of "high Crimes" as specified in the impeachment clause of the Constitution. However, after the badly flawed inquiry carried out by Burke Marshall, John Doar, Hillary Rodham, and the "irregulars," the immoral-acts standard for impeachment became so muddy that the ability to impeach a president was called into serious question.

"Now with our inquiry as a precedent," Michigan congressman John Conyers wrote in a separate opinion to the Judiciary

---

*In fact, all the internal memoranda and papers of the House Judiciary impeachment inquiry staff were later sealed for fifty years at Doar's recommendation.[19]

Committee Impeachment Report, "future Congresses may recoil from ever again exercising this power. They may read the history of our work and conclude that impeachment can never again succeed unless another president demonstrates the same, almost uncanny, ability to impeach himself. If this is our legacy, our future colleagues may well conclude that ours has been a pyrrhic victory, and that impeachment will never again justify the agony we have endured."[21]

Thus, a quarter of a century later, Hillary and Bill were able to argue successfully that President Clinton's depraved affair with Monica Lewinsky, his effort to suborn perjury, and his obstruction of justice were not sufficient reasons to throw him out of office.

CHAPTER TWELVE

The Misfit

WHILE HILLARY WAS STILL IN WASHINGTON WORKING ON the impeachment inquiry, two men in a late-model Cadillac with Illinois license plates pulled into the parking lot of the Clinton for Congress headquarters on College Avenue in Fayetteville, Arkansas.[1] Hugh Rodham Sr. and Tony Rodham, the younger of Hillary's two brothers, got out of the car.

"I'm Hillary's dad," Hugh Sr. announced.

"Well, how long are you going to be here to visit?" asked Ron Addington, Bill's campaign manager.

"Hell, I don't know," Hugh said. "Hillary told me I ought to come down here and help out."[2]

Though Hugh did not explain what he meant by "help out," it soon became clear.

"One of the worst-kept secrets at headquarters was that Clinton had become involved in an intense relationship with a young woman volunteer who was a student at the university [and who was known inside the campaign as the College Girl]," wrote David Maraniss in his well-regarded biography of Bill Clinton,

First in His Class. "According to Doug Wallace [the campaign press secretary], 'the staff tried to ignore it as long as it didn't interfere with the campaign.'

"Aside from the Fayetteville woman, the staff also knew that Clinton had girlfriends in several towns around the district and in Little Rock. Perhaps they could disregard his rambunctious private life, but could Hillary? There was some suspicion that one of the reasons she sent the men in her family to Arkansas was to put a check on her boyfriend's activities."[3]

It was clear from the way Hillary handled the College Girl problem that she knew about Bill's womanizing. She did not throw a fit. She did not confront the girl directly. She did not demand that Bill stop sleeping around. Instead, Hillary summoned her other brother, Hugh Jr., to Arkansas, and ordered *him* to give the College Girl the rush.

"That's exactly what he did," said Paul Fray. "Hughie stalked her every day, every way. She came to me and said, 'I want you to stop this son of a bitch bothering me.' I said, 'You're old enough to get rid of him yourself.' By the end of October, she was gone. She jumped up and married some other guy."[4]

"You should have seen her! No, you should have smelled her."[5]

The speaker was Dolly Kyle Browning, one of Bill Clinton's longtime girlfriends in Arkansas. She was describing her first impression of Hillary Rodham when she arrived from Washington, D.C., to work on Bill's race for Congress.

It would be easy to dismiss Dolly's remarks as the jealous reaction of a jilted lover, if it were not for the fact that a) Bill continued his affair with Dolly long after he married Hillary, and b) Dolly's portrayal of Hillary was echoed by virtually all of Bill's friends.

In 1974, appearances meant a lot in a small southern community like Little Rock, with its old families and old money, and Hillary's looks and behavior came as a shock to Bill's friends. True, Bill was a self-described redneck; he was from white trash. But southern girls were judged by stricter standards.

Southern girls were supposed to be cute and fun, but Hillary was neither of those things. She did not wear the right clothes. She spoke with a flat Midwestern twang, and preached about race relations, which southerners deeply resented. She had not gone to the right southern schools, attended the right debutante parties, or made the acquaintance of the right people. Even worse, the best families in Little Rock didn't know *her* people.

Hillary was a misfit.

Bill's mother, Virginia Kelley—a flashy woman who liked a good time—took an instant dislike to her son's plain-Jane girlfriend. Virginia had expected Bill to bring home someone more glamorous and sexy—someone, in fact, more like her—and she let Bill know of her disapproval in no uncertain terms.

"Virginia loathed Hillary then," recalled Mary Lee Fray. "Anything she could find to pick on about Hillary she would pick on. Hillary did not fit her mold for Bill."[6]

But Bill's mind was made up.

"Listen," he told Virginia, "I don't need to be married to a beauty queen or a sex goddess. I am going to be involved all my life in hard work in politics and public service, and I need somebody who is really ready to roll up her sleeves and work for me."[7]

What Virginia failed to appreciate was that she and Hillary were more alike than she imagined. Both women had boundless faith in Bill's potential for greatness. Both had pledged their lives to help him become president. And both stoked Bill's ambition, fed his political fantasies—and turned a blind eye to his promiscuous nature.

Bill Clinton chose Hillary Rodham for at least two reasons: first, because she was *like* his mother—an enabler; and second, because she was *unlike* his mother—a floozy. When he was a child, Virginia had brought strange men home in the middle of the night, traumatizing Bill and his younger brother, Roger.

"You have to remember," said a longtime Arkansas friend, "that Billy grew up where women who dressed flossy and used a lot of cosmetics were 'available,' and he wasn't ever going to *marry* that kind."[8]

IT WAS DURING THE 1974 CONGRESSIONAL CAMPAIGN THAT RUmors first began to fly through Arkansas that Hillary was a lesbian.

In large part, the rumors were founded on Hillary's tough, aggressive manner, her military barracks vocabulary, and her defiant refusal to do anything about her unkempt appearance. To Arkansans, she *walked* like a lesbian, *talked* like a lesbian, and *looked* like a lesbian. Ergo, she *was* a lesbian.

"If you looked at her in that day and age, the sack-o'-seeds dresses she wore, you'd understand that it wasn't that hard [to create a question about her sexuality]," said Paul Fray.[9]

Fray confronted Hillary, and told her that the lesbian rumors were hurting Bill's chances with the conservative voters of Arkansas.

"This rumor has to be faced," Fray said firmly.

"It's nobody's goddam business," Hillary shot back.

Fray stood his ground. He urged her to deny the rumors publicly, thereby putting them to rest.

"Fuck this shit!" Hillary replied.[10]

THOUGH BILL CLINTON OUTSPENT HIS RIVAL ALMOST TWO TO one, he went down to defeat in his race for Congress. Depressed, he returned to teaching law at the University of Arkansas at Fayetteville, while he and Hillary considered their next move.

Hillary recovered from the defeat a lot faster than Bill. He interpreted his loss at the polls as a personal repudiation. That seemed to take the stuffing out of him. The always-combat-ready Hillary began to wonder about the man for whom she had sacrificed her career. Did Bill Clinton have a glass political jaw?

Teaching bored Hillary. She yearned for the kind of action that could only be found in the public arena. In the summer of 1975, she visited friends back East, and explored her options outside Arkansas. She told her friends that she was considering leaving Bill because of his womanizing.

"I know he's ready to go after anything that walks by," she confessed. *"I know what he's doing."*[11]

But Hillary did not really care what Bill did with other women, as long as it did not hurt the Clintons' careers. The truth was, Hillary considered leaving Bill because she was worried that she had backed a loser.

During her absence, Bill discussed *his* options with Jim Guy Tucker, the attorney general of Arkansas. It just so happened that Tucker was planning to run for the House of Representatives in 1976, which would open the attorney general's slot for Bill. As Tucker later told a reporter, Bill would make a good attorney general, because he "was capable of understanding what you can and cannot do with the law."[12]

Hillary was delighted to hear that Bill was going to run again for public office. And when she returned to Arkansas, she accepted his proposal of marriage. Thus was sealed the Faustian bargain that would shape the rest of her life: Hillary accepted Bill's womanizing as the price of political power.

They set a wedding date for October 11, 1975. Dorothy Rodham flew down from Park Ridge, Illinois. Virginia Kelley drove up from Hot Springs, Arkansas. When Bill visited his mother on the morning of the wedding at the Holiday Inn where she was staying, he said he had something to tell her.

"Hillary's keeping her own name," he said.

"Pure shock," Virginia recalled. "I had never even conceived of such a thing. This had to be some new import from Chicago."[13]

At the time, no one saw the irony in Hillary's decision. She insisted on keeping her maiden name—and feminist credentials— because she wanted to be "a person in my own right" and not a " 'sacrificial' political spouse."[14] Yet, at the same time, she readily sacrificed her feminist principles and allowed herself to become a doormat to a man who was "ready to go after anything that walks by."

Hillary being Hillary, she believed she was *entitled* to have it both ways.

IN THE SPRING OF 1978, DURING ATTORNEY GENERAL BILL CLINton's campaign for governor, he and Hillary scheduled a joint appearance at a fund-raiser in Van Buren, a small town nestled in the foothills of the Ozark Mountains in Crawford County.

The chairman of the Crawford County Committee for the Election of Bill Clinton was an attractive thirty-five-year-old nursing home owner by the name of Juanita Broaddrick. She had volunteered to work for the young attorney general because, as she explained in an interview for this book, "all the women in this area were taken by his charisma, looks, and personality."[15]

But Juanita was no longer "taken" by Bill Clinton. In fact, she was dreading seeing him at this night's event, for the last time they were in the same room, he had raped her.

Just three weeks before, he had come up to her hotel room in Little Rock. "He turned me around and started kissing me," she said, "and that was a real shock. I first pushed him away and just told him 'no.' . . . The second time he tries to kiss me he starts biting on my lip. . . . And then he forces me down on the bed. I just was very frightened, and I tried to get away from him and I told him 'no.' . . . He wouldn't listen to me. . . . He was such a different person at that moment; he was just a vicious, awful person."[16]

Juanita did not tell her husband about the sexual assault.

"I felt responsible for what happened," she explained. "You go back to the nineteen seventies and allow a man to come to your hotel room, you feel you get what you deserved. I had accepted this guilt.

"When Hillary arrived with Bill at the fund-raiser, she made her entrance through the kitchen area," Juanita continued. "And I was going to leave immediately. But she made her way directly to me, making me very nervous. I was dumbfounded that she came straight to me.

" 'I'm happy to meet you,' Hillary said. 'Bill has talked a lot about you and what you have done for the campaign. And I want you to know how much I appreciate what you do for Bill.'

"I was falling apart emotionally. She would not let me go. She came close to my face.

" 'Everything you do for Bill,' she said, looking me stern in the eye. *'Everything.'*

"I extracted my hand from hers. And in that instant, I knew that *she* knew. I never thought for a moment there was any possibility that she didn't know that her husband had raped me."[17]

CHAPTER THIRTEEN

A Night to Remember

It was nearly one o'clock in the morning in June of 1979, and a group of boisterous vacationers were drinking and playing skittles, or nine pins, in the pub of the Horizons hotel in Bermuda. Among the collection of thirtysomethings was a couple from Arkansas—Hillary Rodham and her husband, Governor Bill Clinton.

As the hour grew late, the wives retired to their rooms, leaving their husbands, who had met for the first time this night, to demolish what was left of a case of beer.

After a few more beers, Bill Clinton—who normally was not a heavy drinker, and was clearly feeling no pain—made an announcement.

"I'm going back to my cottage to rape my wife," he said.[1]

His new friends laughed at his drunken boast, and bid him good night.

"The next morning, my phone rings at about eighty-thirty, and it is Bill inviting me and my wife for breakfast," recalled one of the men from the night before, an investment banker from

New York. "When we get there, the place looks like World War III. There are pillows and busted-up furniture all over the place. Obviously, Hillary's got pissed off at Bill, and threw a few things across the room. I guess that's the price he paid for going back to his room and taking the initiative and demanding sex.

"The irony of it is, about two months later the phone rings in my office in Wall Street. It's Clinton, calling from the governor's mansion in Little Rock. I've heard he's been hitting up Wall Street a lot. Investment bankers are always targets for governors looking for a contribution or two.

"Anyway, we talk for a while, and then he says, 'By the way, Hillary hasn't been feeling well recently. She went to the doctor, and the doctor called a press conference, and lo and behold, I'm holding the *Arkansas Gazette* reading that my wife is pregnant.'

"That's the way he learns that Hillary is pregnant with Chelsea—in the newspaper.

"But the fact that his wife didn't tell him that she was pregnant before she told a reporter doesn't seem to faze him one bit, because he says, 'Do you know what night that happened?'

" 'No,' I say. 'When?'

" 'It was in Bermuda,' he says. 'And you were there!' "[2]

AT THE TIME OF CHELSEA'S BIRTH, BILL CLINTON WAS CARRYING on a sexual relationship with Dolly Kyle Browning, a woman he had known since high school. Their affair, which started in the mid-1970s, would continue for more than twenty years, and as old friends as well as lovers, they indulged in a great deal of candid pillow talk.

"One time," Dolly recalled in an interview for this book,[3] "Billy told me he wanted to have a baby. I thought he meant with me, and I said, 'Do you think that's a good idea?'

" 'No, I don't mean with you,' he said.

"I said, 'What's the deal?'

"He said, 'It doesn't look good politically for me and Hillary not to have children, especially given the way Hillary is, and what people think about her.'

" 'Why are you telling me about this?' I asked.

" 'Because,' he said, 'I was hoping you might pray for me.'

"And I said, 'Is that what you really want?'

" 'Yes.'

" 'Okay, then,' I said, 'then I'll pray that you have a baby. But remember, you have to do your part.'

"I said that because I knew that he and Hillary never had much of a sexual relationship. Also, Billy had a low sperm count, and he and Hillary were going to a fertility specialist in California. They had been trying for quite a while without any success.

"But a month or so after our conversation [and after their trip to Bermuda], Hillary got pregnant. And the thing that shocked Billy was that he literally fell in love with his daughter. He was absolutely nuts about that child. But Hillary didn't have the mothering instincts, and she couldn't wait to dump this kid with a nanny and get back to work.

"And Billy was concerned about Chelsea, because he didn't think that Hillary was much of a mother. And he asked me, 'What can I do for my daughter?'

" 'Spend time with her and be a good dad,' I told him.

" 'What's the most important thing I can do?'

"And I said, 'Billy, unfortunately the most important thing you can do for your child is honor and respect her mother.' "

CHAPTER FOURTEEN

All the Governor's Women

AFTER CHELSEA'S BIRTH IN FEBRUARY 1980, HILLARY DEvoted less time to Bill and his political career.

Now, in addition to a baby girl at home, she had a demanding job as a partner at the Rose Law Firm, and commitments to various liberal do-gooder groups—such as the Children's Defense Fund and the Legal Services Corporation—which required that she travel outside the state every few weeks.

Bill—ever the needy narcissist—felt abandoned. He was overwhelmed by self-pity and resentment, and he compensated for these feelings by running after women—often in plain sight of his wife.

"At times," wrote Joyce Milton, "he flirted outrageously with women in front of Hillary, and even in front of the women's husbands. Moreover, now that he was Governor, Clinton had an escort of state troopers wherever he went, and he would regale them with lewd comments about the attributes of any attractive woman who happened to cross his path and occasionally ask the troopers to get the phone numbers of good-looking women he spotted at political rallies."[1]

"He had two levels of women: smart peers who he could tell were having trouble with their spouses, and of course the babes," said Nancy "Peach" Pietrefesa,[2] an ardent feminist who had been Hillary's best friend during her senior year at Wellesley, and who, after moving to Little Rock, was rumored to be Hillary's lesbian lover.[3]

"He knows human nature so well, he knows how to lay that little 'test' on a woman. Handfuls of women had their feelings hurt. Clinton would come on to them and then be distracted or interrupted. When he came back, he'd look at the same woman like he didn't know who she was.

"He was fucking a married woman in the bushes in the summer of 1980," Peach continued. "He'd go jogging and meet her. She was a former campaign volunteer who wasn't getting along with her husband. Bill would come home and talk about her to Hillary: 'Don't you think she's fabulous? She is such an incredible . . .' Hillary knew what he was doing and got pissed."[4]

Their marriage was on the rocks.

"One Saturday morning a friend stopped by the house and found [Bill] in the den, playing on the floor with Chelsea," wrote David Maraniss. "Rodham was in the kitchen. As he smiled and laughed with his one-year-old daughter, Clinton sang softly in the lilt of a gentle lullaby, but loud enough for the guest to hear: 'I want a div-or-or-or-or-orce. I want a div-or-or-orce.'"[5]

As governor, Bill was under constant media scrutiny, but he didn't allow that to put a crimp in his style.

"Bill was like a kid with a new toy that first term," a friend told Connie Bruck, a writer for *The New Yorker*. "The perks, the Mansion, having the most powerful people in the state paying court to you. And he always had a weakness for bleached blondes with big jewelry, in short skirts, their figures shown off to best advantage."6

He grew careless and sloppy and self-destructive. He wore his hair long, which did not go over well in his conservative state. He surrounded himself in the governor's mansion with bearded young aides, who looked as though they had stepped out of a Pink Floyd concert. And he was deaf to complaints about his northern-born, feminist wife.

People in small towns across Arkansas fumed that Hillary used her maiden name, dressed in "unfeminine" clothes, and was seen reading a book at an Arkansas Razorbacks football game. It all went to prove, said his political enemies, that Bill Clinton could "not even control his wife"—a grave sin in a macho southern state.7

The chickens came home to roost in the fall of 1980 during Bill Clinton's reelection campaign. Hillary was too busy flying back and forth to Washington, D.C., for board meetings to be of much help in the campaign. But Bill's Republican opponent, Frank White, made it a point to be seen everywhere on the campaign trail in the company of *his* wife, Gay. A traditional homemaker, Gay sat demurely on the speaker's platform, staring up at her man adoringly.

The contrast between Gay White and Hillary Rodham was not lost on the voters of Arkansas. And to drive the point home, White made Hillary a campaign issue, portraying her as a "bitch" who refused to take her husband's name.8

"I was her worst critic over that," said Richard Herget, Bill's campaign manager. "I think that issue cost us the election. And boy, if Hillary and I didn't tangle on that one. . . .

"I made a speech one time to a Democratic women's club during the campaign," he continued. "And the average age of the attendee was in the sixties. And I asked this group of ladies, afterward, before they opened up for questions, I said, 'Let me ask you a question.' I said, 'How do you feel about the issue of Hillary Rodham, you know, not being Hillary Clinton?' And, oh God, I wish I hadn't asked it. They unloaded on me. 'She's not good enough to take his name,' and that sort of thing. You've got to remember that this is the conservative South. Hillary just wasn't that in touch back then."[9]

The attacks on Hillary worked. When the ballots were counted, it was revealed that Frank White had upset Bill Clinton with more than 51 percent of the vote.

BILL'S DEFEAT WAS A TIPPING POINT IN THE CLINTON MARRIAGE.

"It shook both of them right down to their toes," said one friend.[10]

Bill felt guilty that he had failed Hillary. His greatest fear was that she might leave him, not because he had been unfaithful to her, but because he was a loser. *Her* greatest fear was that their mutual dream of living in the White House might now be unattainable.

"The experience of watching Bill screw up," said a Clinton adviser, "made Hillary realize she should jump into the breach.... She had to—he was so shaken, and was not a particularly good strategist anyway. There was no way he was going to win again unless she came in."[11]

Hillary made a calculated decision to reorder her priorities. From now on, her career would take second place to Bill's. Her feminist principles would be scuttled. Even her politics, which were far too liberal for Arkansas, would be toned down. Hillary consciously and deliberately set out to remake herself in the image of a conventional political wife.

On February 27, 1982—Chelsea's second birthday—Bill called a press conference and announced his candidacy for the upcoming gubernatorial election. Standing by his side was Hillary. She looked completely different. Gone were the thick Coke-bottle eyeglasses, replaced by tinted contact lenses that made her eyes look bluer. Gone, too, was the curly Little Orphan Annie hairdo, replaced by straightened and lightened hair. She wore makeup, a stylish dress, and sheer nylons rather than opaque black stockings.

"She conformed, eyes batting," said a Clinton aide. "She hated it, for a while resented it no end, but she became what Arkansas wanted her to be."[12]

One of the reporters at the press conference asked Bill Clinton if it was true that his wife had changed her name. Bill turned the microphone over to Hillary.

"I don't have to change my name," she said defensively. "I've been Mrs. Bill Clinton. I kept the professional name Hillary Rodham in my law practice, but now I'm going to take a leave of absence from the law firm to campaign full time for Bill, and I'll be Mrs. Bill Clinton."[13]

But that disingenuous answer did not satisfy the assembled journalists.

"Did you change your name legally?" one of them asked.[14]

Hillary tried to avoid giving a direct and honest answer.

"Did you change your name legally?" the reported pressed.

The next day's *Times-News* of McGehee, a small town in the eastern part of Arkansas, reported: " 'No,' came the ice cold answer from Arkansas' former first lady."[15]*

"The deal was," said Peach Pietrefesa, "she gave up her name and her integrity in exchange for his promise to take them where she wanted to go—to be president together."[16]

---

*It wasn't until the following May that she registered to vote as Hillary Clinton.

* * *

HILLARY'S MAKEOVER WENT BEYOND MERE WINDOW DRESSING.

She telephoned Dick Morris, the political consultant who had helped Bill win the governorship, and begged him to come back to work on her husband's next campaign. Morris was skeptical until Hillary convinced him that she was serious about using attack ads and attack campaigning—techniques that had been devised by communications consultant Roger Ailes to reposition Richard Nixon, and had since been made into a virtual art form by Morris.[17]

"Hillary was intrigued by the technique," said Morris. "Her reaction was not at all ideological, it was purely pragmatic: 'We need to learn how the bad boys do it.' "[18]

Hillary's next phone call was to Texas native Betsey Wright, a tough-as-nails political operative who had worked with Bill and Hill on the McGovern campaign and was now an activist in the women's movement. Hillary wanted Betsey to move to Little Rock, become Bill's campaign manager, and put together a whole new political machine—one that would move Bill away from the liberal positions carved out for him by his young, bearded staff and bring him toward the center of the political spectrum.

"Wright wasn't romantically interested in Bill, so Hillary could trust her around her husband without fear of a sexual relationship," wrote David Brock. ". . . Wright, a heavyset chain smoker with a famously foul mouth and a temper to match, built the political organization that Clinton lacked."[19]

Hillary's third phone call was to Ivan Duda, a well-known Little Rock private investigator.

"She asked to see me," Duda told the author of this book, "and when we met, she said, 'I want you to do damage control over Bill's philandering.' I asked her, 'What do you mean?' And she said, 'Bill's going to be President of the United States.' I laughed at that, but she said, 'No, I'm serious.'

"So," Duda continued, "I said, 'What do you want me for?' And she said, 'I want you to get rid of all these bitches he's seeing.' I said, 'Okay, I can do that.' And she said, 'I want you to give me the names and addresses and phone numbers, and we can get them under control.' "[20]

Hillary did not try to stop Bill from philandering; that would have been a fruitless exercise. All she asked of her husband was that he be more discriminating in his choice of women and not do anything to embarrass her in public. With Ivan Duda's reports in hand, Hillary was able to separate the "safe" women from the "trouble makers," and know who could be intimidated to keep their mouths shut.

On election night 1982, all of Hillary's efforts paid off: Bill won a resounding victory, garnering 54.7 percent of the vote. At the victory celebration, Hillary stood next to Bill on the stage, her hair blonder than ever, looking feminine in a form-fitting silk print dress. When she spoke, the crowd noticed that she had somehow acquired a southern accent.

"Hillary made her trade-offs early on," said her friend Jan Piercy, "and I think she steeled herself not to look back."[21]

PART III

The White House Years

CHAPTER FIFTEEN

Her Husband's Keeper

January 21, 1998

THE DAY THAT THE *WASHINGTON POST* BROKE THE STORY OF Bill Clinton's affair with Monica Lewinsky was the most painful day in Hillary's life. And because she felt so exposed and vulnerable, she was more determined than ever to fight back.

Late that morning, when she stepped out of a black chauffeured vehicle onto the pavement in front of Washington's Union Station, her hair was done in a glamorous shoulder-length pageboy. Her makeup was ladled on thickly for the cameras. And she was dressed in a long dark coat that reached to her ankles and made her look taller and thinner than usual. Despite the bitter cold January wind that swept down Massachusetts Avenue, Hillary made an effort to smile.

She did not want to look like a woman who was on the defensive. Which, of course, she was. Every twenty-four-hour cable news channel was carrying the story of how Monica Lewinsky had given Bill Clinton blow jobs in the Oval Office; radio talk show hosts were referring to the Oval Office as the Oral Orifice; people were e-mailing each other with Hillary jokes ("After Monica admitted to an affair with the president, Hillary phoned her up and asked her, 'What was it like?' ").[1]

"Whenever I go out and fight I get vilified, so I have just learned to smile and take it," Hillary said. "I go out there and say, 'Please, please, kick me again, insult me some more.' You have to be much craftier behind the scenes, but just smile."[2]

Her Secret Service detail escorted Hillary through the station's cavernous main hall, and under the barrel-vaulted ceiling. She was greeted by waiting Amtrak officials, who led her to a special car that would carry her to Baltimore. There she was scheduled to give a speech on race relations at Goucher College as a favor to an old friend, the Pulitzer Prize–winning author Taylor Branch.

No sooner had Hillary settled into her seat than her cell phone began ringing. The assistant in charge of the phone listened for a moment, then turned to Hillary.

"It's the President," the assistant said.

But when she tried to pass the phone to Hillary, the First Lady refused to take it.[3]

As the Amtrak train lumbered through the Maryland suburbs, the cell phone rang several more times. One call was from attorney David Kendall, who was now feuding openly with Robert Bennett over control of the President's legal representation. Kendall warned Hillary that Special Prosecutor Kenneth Starr planned to expand his Whitewater investigation into the Lewinsky matter, and nail the President for obstruction of justice.

Two other calls came from Bill Clinton, who was eager to apologize to his wife, and seek her forgiveness. He could have saved his breath. Hillary wasn't interested in apologies. She was searching for a way out of the Monica mess.

* * *

IRONICALLY ENOUGH, SHE HAD HELPED CREATE THAT MESS.

In the summer of 1995, Hillary's office received a phone call from Walter Kaye, a wealthy insurance mogul and Democratic donor who was especially close to the First Lady. Walter Kaye was calling to ask Hillary for a favor: a family friend named Marcia Lewis was trying to line up a summer job for her daughter, Monica Lewinsky, who, unlike her mother, had not changed her Jewish-sounding last name. Monica was graduating from Lewis and Clark, a small college in Oregon, and was looking for a job in Washington, D.C.

Walter Kaye carried a lot of weight; he had raised several hundred thousand dollars for the party, and had been an overnight guest at the White House. The First Lady's office sent a heads-up message to an official at the Democratic National Committee, who was in charge of hiring summer interns.

"I got a call from Walter Kaye asking me to interview Monica Lewinsky," the official recalled in an interview for this book. "Every summer, we would put five hundred kids in jobs as unpaid interns in the White House and other governmental agencies. At least fifty of them came through big donors. It wasn't a big deal."[4]

But it soon turned into one.

"Monica started working in the White House in November 1995, during the government shutdown," a high-ranking adviser in the Clinton White House told the author. "That shutdown, which was seen at the time as a brilliant political move by Bill Clinton against Newt Gingrich's Republican-dominated House of Representatives, turned out to be Bill's downfall.

"During the shutdown, we had to operate with only essential government personnel," the adviser continued. "Out of the normal White House staff, only about thirty people were allowed to come to work. Interns like Monica were allowed to work because they were not paid official staff.

"Everyone had the impression that the government worked better with fewer people. But during this time, Bill Clinton was wandering around the White House unchecked. And the incident in which Monica flashed her thong happened as he was wandering around the office. Normally, when Hillary's people were there, the President wasn't *allowed* to wander."[5]

HILLARY ALWAYS KEPT A SHARP EYE ON BILL. IN ORDER TO BE NEAR her husband, and exercise maximum control, she had refused to be exiled to the East Wing of the White House, the traditional realm of First Ladies, and fought for space in the West Wing. At first, she tried to grab the office earmarked for Vice President Al Gore, and when that didn't work, she settled for space on the second floor of the West Wing.

She ended up with two offices—a *social* office in the East Wing and a *political* office in the West Wing.

"We never saw her in the East Wing," said Kathleen Willey, who worked in the First Lady's social office for several months before she was groped by the President and left the White House in disgust. "All the event planning and state dinners were done in her office in the West Wing. Her social secretary, Ann Stock, would go to Hillary's office in the West Wing. Hillary was frankly not interested in any of the planning for the social events; she was only interested in being part of policy-making in the West Wing.

"Several months after the Clintons arrived in the White House," Kathleen Willey continued, "it was time to pick out the Christmas card design, and Hillary couldn't make up her mind. And I remember one day, I was walking by Ann Stock's office, and she had just come back from a meeting with Hillary, and she was frustrated by Hillary's lack of interest. And I remember Ann shouting, 'I just want to tell her, Hillary, get off your fucking ass and decide!' "[6]

Hillary's West Wing staff was so large that it had to be housed in the Old Executive Office Building next door to the White House. This staff, which soon became known as "Hillaryland," consisted of a group of strong, like-minded women who struck people, including several who were interviewed for this book, as masculine in appearance, dress, manner, and speech.

Hillary's old Wellesley College classmate, Jan Piercy, took charge of White House personnel and hired a large number of women whose first loyalty was to Hill, not to Bill.

"Hillary gave an ideological edge to Clinton's general fuzziness when he got to the White House," wrote the historian Paul Johnson. "She also stuck a feminist finger in the appointment pies, especially of women, sometimes with embarrassing, indeed hilarious, results. Thus Tara O'Toole, nominated assistant secretary of energy, turned out to be a member of a Marxist women's reading circle. Roberta Achtenberg, assistant secretary for fair housing, revealed herself as a militant lesbian who persecuted the Boy Scouts for not allowing homosexuals as scoutmasters. Joycelyn Elders, made surgeon general, after many public rows, had to go when she advocated masturbation."[7]

Another Wellesley classmate who worked for Hillary was Eleanor "Eldie" Acheson. Eldie—the granddaughter of former Secretary of State Dean Acheson—lived openly with her lesbian partner. She had served as cochair of the Clinton-Gore campaign in Massachusetts, where she minted "Vote for Hillary's Husband" buttons.[8] Hillary appointed Eldie assistant attorney general.*

Hillary scattered other friends through the Clinton administration. The First Lady was instrumental in appointing Donna E.

---

*In 2004, Eldie Acheson became John Kerry's liaison with the gay community, as well as a member of the Democrat GLBT (Gay, Lesbian, Bisexual, and Transgender) Caucus.

Shalala, the chancellor of the University of Wisconsin, who became secretary of health and human services, and Janet Reno, a prosecutor from Miami, who was made attorney general.

"In Clinton's cabinet," wrote gay conservative writer Andrew Sullivan, "almost everyone is married or divorced, but for two who aren't, Donna Shalala and Janet Reno, their orientations are shrouded in deep ambiguity."[9]

Another Hillary appointment was Susan Thomases, a tough and ruthless New York lawyer, who was known as the First Lady's "Red Queen." Susan Thomases whipped the staff into line through fear and intimidation.

Yet another appointment was the unfailingly loyal Evelyn Lieberman, who was given the title deputy chief of staff, and served as Hillary's eyes and ears in the White House.

"Evelyn was a force for order, and didn't believe in members of the White House staff doing their own thing," said a White House speechwriter. "She knew how she wanted the White House to look, and how people should behave. She exercised very tight control."[10]

Short, a little overweight, with grayish hair, Evelyn was precise, even prissy.

"She called one day, and asked if I could come over right away to the White House for a job interview," said a woman who ended up working for the administration. "I didn't have a chance to dress for the interview, but I had on a perfectly acceptable business suit. When Evelyn saw me, however, the first thing she said was: 'We wear stockings in the White House.' "[11]

Evelyn Lieberman was the head of an elaborate damage-control system that was set up by Hillary to keep dangerous women away from Bill Clinton—and Bill Clinton away from them.

"Bill couldn't have possibly seen Monica more than once or twice without Hillary knowing it," said the wife of a senator who dealt with the Clintons. "Hillary knew everything that happened in that White House. The only thing that surprised Hillary about Monica Lewinsky was how tacky the whole thing was. The thing that really embarrassed Hillary was that Bill was attracted to this trashy girl."[12]

"Sexual snobs from the Kennedy era always marveled at the 42nd President's terrible taste in women—big-haired Gennifer Flowers, skanky Paula Jones, pillowy Monica Lewinsky," wrote Tina Brown. "But terrible taste is the point. Has Clinton ever been linked to a woman who could remotely threaten Hillary?

"Washington was full of attractive, Harvard-educated, safely married policy babes who would have been far less embarrassing—but to Hillary far more dangerous—diversions," Tina Brown continued. "Blue dress or no blue dress, the irony is that if Bill had been arguing deep into the night with Monica about NAFTA, Hillary might have divorced him a long time ago."[13]

CHAPTER SIXTEEN

"Bill Owes Me"

Hillary's hall monitor in the White House, Evelyn Lieberman, a.k.a. Mother Superior, knew when to leave well enough alone.

She adopted a hands-off attitude when Bill Clinton indulged in affairs with women who were labeled "safe" by the First Lady. As a result, several of Bill Clinton's former girlfriends, who were known as the "graduates,"[1] were given cushy jobs in the White House. The most prominent of these was Marsha Scott, who described herself as "Bill's girlfriend from our hippie days."[2] Marsha was deputy director of White House personnel, but her power was far greater than her title suggested.

"The assumption among the women in the White House was that Bill took Marsha on political trips, and that she stayed with him in his hotel room," said a high-level White House staffer. "At one point, Leon Panetta [then the President's chief of staff] tried to fire Marsha, because, as he put it, 'Marsha's too close to the President.'

"Marsha came to me and asked me to help her save her job," this source continued. "My advice to the higher-ups was to keep Marsha Scott close. The biggest mistake with Monica was to send her to the Pentagon. They should have kept her close, in the White House, where they could have kept an eye on her. Maybe get her a boyfriend to keep her happy. Instead, they threw her out of the nest. That was Evelyn Lieberman's doing."[3]

The President had other rumored girlfriends stashed away in the White House. They allegedly included Catherine Cornelius, a blonde in her early twenties; Debra Schiff, a former flight attendant on Clinton's campaign plane and now a White House receptionist; and Robin Dickey, a former administrator of the governor's mansion in Little Rock and the mother of Helen Dickey, Chelsea's live-in nanny.[4]

Hillary's staff was perplexed by her casual attitude toward Bill Clinton's infidelities. Like everyone else in the White House, they spent endless hours gossiping about it. However, no one could come up with a satisfactory explanation for Hillary's behavior. The fact was, Hillary remained a mystery to her close associates for one simple reason: she never confided in anyone.

"She is so shrewd," Jan Piercy told the *New Yorker* writer Connie Bruck. "She has known all along that people around [the Clintons] would be placed in a position of being interviewed by the press—and, while she as a public figure has been very schooled in how you protect your privacy, she realized that her friends wouldn't have that sophistication. So she has kept her own counsel. She has not availed herself of what the rest of us do—crying on someone's shoulder. She has extraordinary self-possession and discipline."[5]

Others had a different explanation for Hillary's mystique.

"I'm not sure how many people are close to Hillary at all," said a major Clinton campaign donor. "My wife and I have spent hours and hours with her, but do I have a clue to what she's thinking? No. She's so closed, so guarded, so careful. I don't know what in her background led her to be that way."[6]

It appeared that Hillary operated on the bizarre theory that if she could handle her husband's betrayals without turning into his victim, then she, not Bill, would come out the winner. Bill Clinton might get a lot of "pussy"—to use one of his favorite words—but every time Hillary came to his defense, he fell deeper and deeper into her debt.

How many times had her aides heard Hillary say, "Bill owes me"?

"Watching [Bill Clinton] was very much like watching a golden retriever that has pooped on the rug and sort of just curls up and keeps his head down and is, like, 'I can't believe I did this,'" said David Gergen, who served as a senior adviser to Bill Clinton from 1993 to 1994. "And it put him in a situation where he was in the doghouse."[7]

Once in the doghouse, the guilty sex offender was at the mercy of his morally superior wife. Would she show tolerance and forbearance? Would she allow Bill to redeem himself? Would she forgive him? Each time Bill Clinton slipped up sexually and cheated on Hillary, the dynamics of their relationship tilted in Hillary's favor. In the never-ending struggle for dominance that characterized their marriage, control shifted from Bill to Hillary.

Hillary was selective about how she used the club of infidelity to beat her husband. For instance, she allowed him to keep a virtual harem under the roof of the White House. There were those who wondered whether Monica Lewinsky was included in this harem, since Evelyn Lieberman never said whether she informed Hillary about Bill's affair with the intern.

However, given Hillary's nearly thirty-year record of tracking Bill's relationships with other women—and the frequency of Monica's visits to the Oval Office—it seemed naïve to believe that the First Lady was kept in the dark about Monica by Evelyn Lieberman. After all, Evelyn's whole mission in life was to keep an eye on Bill for Hillary.

Furthermore, Hillary wasn't the only one who saw Monica as a danger.

"A Secret Service officer wanted to put Lewinsky on a watch list of people to be banned from the White House because he was concerned about Clinton's reputation," wrote the *Washington Post*, "but a commander overruled him, saying it was none of their business."[8]

Mother Superior repeatedly scolded Monica for her provocative way of dressing and for spending too much time hanging around the Oval Office. Ultimately, in April 1996, Evelyn—acting on behalf of the First Lady—banished Monica from the White House and transferred her to the Pentagon.

By that time, however, rumors about Monica and Bill Clinton had spread throughout the entire Democratic Party establishment. Marcia Lewis, Monica's mother, attended several Women's Leadership Forum events that were sponsored by the women's section of the Democratic National Committee. At these meetings, Marcia Lewis lost no opportunity to boast that her daughter was having an affair with the president of the United States.[9]

CHAPTER SEVENTEEN

Payback Time

"She was upset, but not visibly so—just chilly and withdrawn," said a White House aide who accompanied Hillary on the trip from Washington to Baltimore. "It was not an enjoyable train ride."[1]

As the train made its way south, Hillary stared at her reflection in the window. Though no one could tell what was going through her mind, it was a safe bet that she was thinking about her own reputation, which was inextricably linked to her husband's.

He had let her down again.

But then, in all fairness, hadn't she let him down as well?

Early in the 1992 presidential primaries, Democratic Party strategists began to realize that their candidate's biggest liability was not the "woman problem" as narrowly defined by the media. Gennifer Flowers, Paula Jones, and Juanita Broaddrick could be handled. The part of the "woman problem" that couldn't be so easily handled was Hillary Rodham Clinton.

"In the spring of 1992," said a senior adviser to the Clinton-Gore campaign, "I wrote [an analysis] saying that Hillary should take a page out of Barbara Bush's book. I said Hillary had misunderstood the role of the First Lady. What the public wanted to know was why she, his wife, loved this man."[2]

Hillary was a lightning rod for larger questions about the role of women in America. Many men said they didn't like her because she was a radical feminist. Many women said they couldn't stand her because she was willing to tolerate abuse from her husband in order to stay in power.

All this was well known to the people around Bill Clinton during the 1992 primary season. But no one on his campaign staff had the courage to confront Hillary. Instead, the staff came up with a roundabout way of getting that message across to their candidate. They conducted a focus group, and then showed the videotaped results to Bill Clinton.

"We were using these dial meters," recalled Paul Begala, one of Bill Clinton's chief political strategists. "So we would show videotape, talk about people, and the respondents in the group would dial up if they liked what they heard and saw, and [dial] down if they didn't."

"But we were sitting around the focus group, watching these dials," George Stephanopoulos added, "and until that point they'd been pretty steady. And then this picture of Mrs. Clinton comes on [the screen], and the dial groups go like [way down]—the footage that was used for Hillary was footage from [primary] election night, 1992, in New Hampshire, where she had this elaborate Nefertiti-style hairdo. And Clinton doesn't miss a beat. He just says, 'Oh, they don't like her hair.'"

Hair!

Everyone in the room knew it wasn't Hillary's *hair* that the focus group didn't like. It was *Hillary* who turned them off.

"I stuck my head under the table," James Carville said, "because I knew I could not look at anybody. And George was kicking me with his foot. And it was like I thought I was going to die because I couldn't come up for air, and I couldn't stop laughing."

"We were just holding it in," Stephanopoulos continued, "and [James] is grinding his fist into my thigh. And we finally—we're not breathing. We finally run out of the room, get into the hallway and just break up laughing."

"And it was like a sweet thing almost, you know?" Carville said.

"You know," Stephanopoulos agreed, "looking back, it was kind of sweet that Clinton said that. His instinct was to protect [Hillary]. Like, he's a smart politician and knew that . . . a lot of people had very strong feelings about Mrs. Clinton. And he was kind of just being protective of her at that moment. We didn't dwell on it for the rest of the day."[3]

"We found out from those focus groups that people actually thought the Clintons were rich and didn't have any children," said a party activist close to the campaign. "And after we got the results of those focus groups, Hillary had the first of her many makeovers."[4]

IN LATE APRIL 1992, BILL CLINTON'S TOP AIDES WROTE A CONFIdential memo laying out a strategy to rescue his foundering candidacy. The problem was clear: about 40 percent of the voters did not like Bill Clinton. And Hillary had even higher negatives. The memo set out an ambitious political plan to rehabilitate Hillary.[5]

DRAFT/CONFIDENTIAL

TO: Bill Clinton
Mickey Kantor and David Wilhelm*
FROM: Stan Greenberg, James Carville and Frank Greer†
RE: "THE GENERAL ELECTION PROJECT"

INTERIM REPORT

... The current presentation of Hillary Clinton and the Clinton marriage and family to the world is remarkably distorted. The absence of affection, children and family and the preoccupation with career and power only reinforces the political problem evident from the beginning. It also allows George Bush (and probably Perot) to build up extraordinary advantages on family values—32 points in the DNC survey.

We suggest the following steps to improve the situation, without endangering the family's privacy or trampling on reality:

o Hillary should have a lower profile in the immediate short-term, as we try to reintroduce Bill Clinton. It is important to do interviews with publications that have longer lead times, but, for the most part, Bill should appear alone on the popular culture shows. After the June primary, Bill and Hillary should do some joint appearances and Hillary should take up an aggressive schedule of interviews.

---

*Mickey Kantor was the campaign chairman and David Wilhelm the campaign manager.
†Stan Greenberg was the campaign's polling expert, James Carville its chief strategist, and Frank Greer its media consultant.

o Bill and Hillary need to talk much more of their own family, including Chelsea, and their affection for each other. If Chelsea cannot travel (which we understand) then we ought to figure out how protecting Chelsea from the press and protecting her childhood is an obsession of both parents. We need to make much more of Chelsea faxing her homework to Bill and/or something that Hillary does with Chelsea.

o The family needs to go on vacation together after the June primary, preferably in California (including Disneyland), though there is a minority for the Gulf Shores.

o After a short pullback period, Hillary needs to come forward in a way that is much more reflective of herself—both her humor and her advocacy work for children. Linda Bloodworth-Thomason has suggested some joint appearances with her friends where Hillary can laugh, do her mimicry. We need to be thinking about events where Bill and Hillary can "go on dates with the American public." There is a suggestion that Bill and Chelsea surprise Hillary on Mother's Day.

o Bill and Hillary need to clarify Hillary's role as First Lady. Ambiguity looks like a power game. It is very important that voters feel comfortable with Hillary's role and not see her as an empowered Nancy Reagan. . . .[6]

"What is most striking about the memo," wrote Michael Kelly, "is the degree to which its ideas were adopted, and were successful. In the months that followed, the Clintons did many of the things that their consultants advised. (But not all. They did not, as suggested, vacation in Disneyland, and no media-minded Mother's Day surprise was arranged for Mrs. Clinton.)"[7]

Hillary suddenly became a kinder and gentler woman. She had a new hairdo. She started palling around with Tipper Gore. And the Clintons and the Gores became two middle-class families that people would like to have in their homes.[8]

AFTER BILL CLINTON BECAME PRESIDENT, HILLARY REVERTED TO form, and swiftly became an even greater liability than before. In the first two years of the administration, she urged her husband to govern from the political left, even though he had been elected as a centrist. Her left-wing agenda was wildly unpopular among some influential figures inside the administration. Everyone from Treasury Secretary Lloyd Bentsen and Vice President Al Gore to Federal Reserve Chairman Alan Greenspan and political strategist Dick Morris knew that her approach was destined to fail.

During these early months of the new administration, Hillary competed openly with Al Gore for the President's time and attention. Things grew very tense. The President's top aides muttered that Hillary was a player who didn't know anything about Washington. She had spent most of her political life being the smartest person in Little Rock, Arkansas—which was a far cry from being the smartest person in Washington, D.C.*

"I told [the President] that he was terribly out of position, and that he had lurched to the left when he came in, and it sent

---

*Hillary's ambitions were such that she had originally wanted to be either attorney general or White House chief of staff. But the federal government's antinepotism law prevented her from assuming an official post.

signals to people like me, who thought he was going to be a centrist Democrat, you know, that he had lost his moorings," recalled senior adviser David Gergen.

Gergen continued: "I also had a private conversation with the First Lady saying, you know, 'It's widely perceived on the outside that you're the one who's pulled him left, and he can't govern from there.' They [the Clintons and their aides] didn't understand Washington very well. They didn't understand the dynamics of the press corps. They were having a hard time figuring out Capitol Hill."[9]

Of course, the President's costliest mistake was appointing his wife to head the administration's health-care reform initiative.

"Some in the White House saw [Hillary's appointment as health-care czar] as payback for Hillary Clinton's steadfast support of her husband during those difficult moments of the New Hampshire primary [when she defended him against charges by Gennifer Flowers]," said Chris Bury of ABC News.[10]

If it was payback, Bill Clinton paid dearly.

CHAPTER EIGHTEEN

Hibernation

As Hillary sat on the stage at Goucher College, waiting her turn to speak at the school's winter convocation, she played with the thick gold necklace around her throat.[1]

At one point during the ceremony, she was seized by a coughing jag, and had to cover her mouth with her hand. She had brought along cough drops to soothe her sore throat, and she popped one into her mouth just as her friend Taylor Branch, who was a visiting professor, finished his introduction of the First Lady.

Hillary rose from her seat in her black academic gown. It had a four-foot-long hood with a purple-colored velvet border signifying that she was receiving an honorary doctor of laws degree. She cleared her throat, smiled at the packed audience of students, their families, and faculty, and then turned to her prepared text.

"I am a product of my own experience," Hillary said in a voice whose raspy quality was amplified by the public-address system. "I [became] involved [in race relations] because of a youth minister. He arranged for us to go into the inner city of Chicago.... In 1961, I had the privilege of seeing Dr. Martin Luther King [and] when I heard Dr. King speak [it] simply changed my life...."

"We have a choice how to react," she went on. "We can be pulled down by these disappointments, or we can be made bitter and angry. But then, we are the losers...."[2]

She might have been talking about herself. The health-care fiasco had been the most humiliating defeat of her life, and most political analysts held her personally responsible for the 1994 conservative wave that swept Republicans into control of both houses of Congress for the first time in forty years.

That stunning defeat knocked Bill Clinton back to his senses, and with the help of Dick Morris, he started to govern from the center, rather than from the left. From all appearances, his leftist wife went into a kind of hibernation. Bill Clinton's aides put out word that Hillary no longer exercised significant influence over anything in the White House.

"After health care," noted a White House official, "Hillary did not show up at Cabinet meetings anymore, and she was not in the thick of things. You could watch Bill Clinton change. The longer he was in office, the more involved he became with foreign affairs. And as that evolution happened, Hillary had even less of a role. After all, what did she know about foreign affairs? After 1994, Clinton leaned on Al Gore, who was a centrist, and who was an expert on foreign affairs. So, after 1994, there are no more jokes in the White House about two vice presidents."[3]

It was during this difficult period that Hillary started channeling Eleanor Roosevelt, and making foreign trips with her daughter, Chelsea. In her public appearances, she stressed classical First Lady issues—children and women's empowerment. She even allowed the photographer Annie Leibovitz to capture her in a sultry pose for the cover of *Vogue*.

"And the public liked very much the Hillary Clinton that would go out in public and defend women and children, and fight for her agenda," said Dick Morris. "What they didn't like was the behind-the-scenes Hillary who would vet nominees for Attorney General, or who would make suggestions for the Cabinet, or who was the person who would formulate the inner working strategy on different issues, like health care reform. And they became very suspicious of that Hillary.

"But more importantly, Bill Clinton could not be seen as strong until Hillary Clinton was seen as weak," Morris continued. "Because the public assumed that the power belonged to one of them. It couldn't belong to both simultaneously, in their view.

"And therefore, it was very important for Hillary to kind of assume much more of a lower profile, and to focus much more on public advocacy than private machinations. I, in fact, felt that it was not a good idea for her to hide. I felt it was a good idea to talk about things like Agent Orange in Vietnam, or the Gulf War disease, or breast cancer, mammograms—issues where people would like her and identify with her on. But not to be seen as the power behind the throne."[4]

And so, for four long years—from the health-care debacle of 1994 to the Lewinsky scandal of 1998—Hillary kept up an outward show that she was no longer a major player in the White House. But as was frequently the case with the Clintons, appearances were deceptive.

"Although she was less visible now, devoting large blocks of time to handwriting revisions of her book *It Takes a Village*, the First Lady was still the most powerful liberal in the White House," wrote George Stephanopoulos. ". . . Although she was instrumental in bringing [Dick] Morris back, she also sensed the need for a liberal counterweight to him inside the White House. Several times a week, she'd call to check in and buck me up—often as she exercised. 'How're we doing today, George?' she'd ask, her measured breathing and the hum of the treadmill serving as a background for my morning updates."[5]

"I made my speech at Goucher's winter convocation," Hillary recalled, "then returned to the Baltimore train station, where a mob of reporters and camera crews was waiting for me. I hadn't been so swarmed in years."[6]

As she waited for a train to take her back to Washington, Hillary sat on a wooden bench, bathed in the flattering light that came through the stained-glass skylight overhead. The reporters were all yelling questions at the same time, and someone shouted above the rest, "Do you think the charges [against your husband] are false?"

"Certainly I believe they are false—*absolutely*," Hillary said. "It's difficult and painful any time someone you care about, you love, you admire, is attacked and is subjected to such relentless accusations as my husband has been. But I also have now lived with this for, gosh, more than six years. I have seen how these charges and accusations evaporate and disappear if they're ever given the light of day."

"Why is Bill Clinton being attacked?" another reporter asked.

"There has been a concerted effort to undermined his legitimacy as President," said Hillary, "to undo much of what he has been able to accomplish, to attack him personally when he could not be defeated politically."[7]

With those words—her first public comment on the Monica Lewinsky scandal—Hillary laid the foundation for all the lies that were yet to come.

CHAPTER NINETEEN

Hillary's Brain

I<small>N TIMES OF CRISIS, H</small>ILLARY <small>ALWAYS RETURNED TO THE SAME</small> playbook—the simple life lessons she had learned from her father and mother.

Lesson No. 1: Never allow yourself to be a victim.
Lesson No. 2: If somebody hits you, hit him or her back harder.
Lesson No. 3: Stay in control of your own destiny.

At some point on her way back from Baltimore, it seemed to have occurred to her that she did not have to be a victim of the Lewinsky scandal. On the contrary, she could turn the scandal to her own advantage. After four years of living in the political wilderness, she had the opportunity to get out there and fight "the neighborhood bully"—in this case, her political enemies on the right.

Upon her return to the White House, Hillary called Sidney Blumenthal. A former journalist, Blumenthal was an influential presidential policy adviser who understood the press better than anyone in the White House.

She needed to see him right away, Hillary told Blumenthal.

Sid Blumenthal went back a long way with Hillary. They had worked together on Gary Hart's doomed 1984 presidential campaign, where they discovered they had a lot in common. In college, Blumenthal had been a member of the radical Students for a Democratic Society; in law school, Hillary had worked on behalf of the violence-prone group known as the Black Panthers.

As members of the New Left, both Sid Blumenthal and Hillary Rodham manifested the qualities that historian Richard Hofstadter identified in his 1963 landmark study *The Paranoid Style in American Politics*—"heated exaggeration, suspiciousness, and conspiratorial fantasy."[1]

In fact, Hofstadter might have had Sid Blumenthal and Hillary Rodham in mind when he wrote: "Since what is at stake is always a conflict between absolute good and absolute evil, what is necessary is not compromise but the will to fight things out to a finish. Since the enemy is thought of as being totally evil and totally unappeasable, he must be eliminated. . . . It is hard to resist the conclusion that this enemy is on many counts the projection of the self; both the ideal and the unacceptable aspects of the self are attributed to him."[2]

Jeffrey Toobin, in his book *A Vast Conspiracy*, described Blumenthal as "perhaps the most partisan member of the Clintons' circle. . . . In a White House, and a capital, where people tried to slice issues into narrow, achievable objectives, Blumenthal saw the world in a broad sweep of ideological conflict between the Clintons and what he invariably called 'the right wing.' . . . Blumenthal's predilection for conspiracy theories prompted his colleague Rahm Emanuel to nickname him 'G.K.'—for Grassy Knoll."[3]

Blumenthal occupied a windowless basement office in a

room that used to serve as the White House barbershop. From these subterranean Phantom-of-the-Opera depths, he spun what the political writer Joe Klein described as "vast, obscure Manichean fantasies about the world outside the gates."[4]

Blumenthal plotted Hillary's defenses against the sinister forces of the media and the right. His enemies list included the *Washington Post*'s Susan Schmidt, who had broken many Whitewater stories and whom Hillary had tried to get fired.[5] Blumenthal was also behind a smear campaign against Special Prosecutor Kenneth Starr and his staff, some of whom he accused of being gay, or of having sex with members of the media.[6]

The West Wing reporters bestowed many nicknames on Blumenthal—"Sid Vicious," "Rasputin," "the dirt devil." But the one that seemed most appropriate was "Hillary's brain."

IT DIDN'T TAKE SID BLUMENTHAL LONG TO MAKE IT FROM HIS OFfice in the White House basement to the family residence.

Dressed in pinstripes and French cuffs, Blumenthal cut a dandyish figure. His hair, graying at the temples, fell in carefully arranged curls onto his forehead in the manner of the English actor Hugh Grant. In fact, Blumenthal was such an out-and-out Anglophile that some White House aides joked he spent more time on the phone with Prime Minister Tony Blair's aides in London than he did with anyone in the Clinton administration.

"[Hillary] explained that this [Lewinsky] story involved Clinton's concern for a person with personal problems, a common occurrence since she had known him," Blumenthal wrote in a typical example of the Big Lie. "His empathy, she went on, came from his relationship with his mother, an open, compassionate woman, and from Clinton's own difficult experiences growing up. I knew, of course, what she was referring to: being fatherless and poor, the often terrifying battles with his alcoholic, abusive stepfather.... In explaining what had happened, she relied upon her understanding of her husband. I assumed that she had spoken with him and that what she was saying reflected their conversation.

"For her," Blumenthal continued, "the stakes were greater than for anyone. They encompassed not only everything she had worked on politically for a lifetime, but her marriage. She had to defend both."[7]

Hillary could not admit that she had known about Bill's escapades with Monica Lewinsky. That would have only confirmed people's worst suspicions that her marriage was a political arrangement rather than a true love match.

CHAPTER TWENTY

"This Is War"

FRANKLIN ROOSEVELT CALLED IT THE "FISH ROOM," BEcause that was where he displayed his fishing trophies. John Kennedy carried on the nautical theme by mounting a sailfish on one of its walls. Richard Nixon took down JFK's fish and renamed the room in honor of his hero, Theodore Roosevelt. And in the minds of many people, Bill Clinton bestowed yet another name on the room:

The Liar's Corner.

At 10:35 A.M. on January 26, 1998—six years to the day after he had "absolutely leveled with the American people" on *60 Minutes* about Gennifer Flowers—Bill Clinton entered the small, windowless room. He was wearing a red and yellow necktie and a tense expression on his blotchy face. His wife was in the midst of presenting a new federally financed program for afterschool care, and the President took a place between her and Vice President Al Gore.

The assembled press, about fifty strong, had been tipped off in advance that the President would address the charges that he had had sex with Monica Lewinsky in the Oval Office, and had asked her to lie about it. Although he had denied under oath having done any such thing, there were reports that Kenneth Starr's investigators had already succeeded in getting Monica to make a tape-recorded confession.

What could the President say?

As one spectator described it, "The whole room seemed to hold its breath.... In six minutes of policy talk, Clinton folded his hands, stuffed them in his suit pockets, gripped the podium, and rifled the pages of his speech. Twice he paused and licked his lips. He glanced left, right and down, but not once did he make eye contact with the reporters or camera lenses watching intently from the back of the room.

"Then he spoke the words: 'But I want to say one thing to the American people. I want you to listen to me.'

"At that, he narrowed his eyes and trained a laser-like glare straight in the eye of the news cameras. Seven times he jabbed his finger. His forehead was shiny with sweat.

" 'I'm going to say this again. I did not have sexual relations with *that woman* . . . Miss Lewinsky. I never told anybody to lie. Not a single time. *Never*. These allegations are false.' "[1]

It took Bill Clinton just twenty seconds and fifty words to tell one of the most blatant lies in the annals of modern presidential history.

Behind him, dressed in a lemon-and-cream-colored suit that picked up the yellow in the President's tie, Hillary nodded in approval, even though she knew he was lying. The President's words echoed the advice that Hillary had received (and passed on to Bill) from her Arkansas friend Harry Thomason, who had moved into the White House and joined her war room team.

"We've had a slow-motion assassination in process for some time," Thomason had said. "Once everybody on our side falls in, this is war. Never give them a break. Never give them one inch.

Once you finally get that through your head, then you have to get out and fight this every way you can. My grandfather used to say that the Bible said when someone hits you, you turn the other cheek, but after that, you deck him."[2]

Dorothy Rodham, Hillary's mother, couldn't have said it better.

CHAPTER TWENTY-ONE

"Screw 'Em"

THE NEXT DAY, AN AIDE WOKE THE BIG GIRL AT FIVE o'clock in the morning in the presidential suite at New York's Waldorf-Astoria. Normally a late riser, it took her several minutes to become fully conscious.

After a light breakfast, she got the movie-star treatment from her hair stylist and makeup artist. As her dresser applied the finishing touches—a twisted choker of pearls and a large patriotic gold eagle pin with a pearl—her political aides stepped in and began to prep the Big Girl for a seven o'clock interview on the *Today* show.

The interview had been booked months before—back when Hillary was wandering in the political wilderness. At the time, the *Today* show's producers expected Hillary to address such traditional First Lady topics as historic preservation. But now, with her husband reeling from charges of sex in the Oval Office, Hillary saw an opportunity to return to the thick of battle.[1]

Dressed in a brown suit, every last strand of her blonde hair cemented into place, she told her staff that she was ready to rock 'n' roll. She was whisked into a private elevator and down to a waiting limousine for the short ride to Rockefeller Plaza.

"She was very relaxed on the ride over," said Melanie Verveer, her dark-haired mannish-looking chief of staff, who had worked with Hillary at the Children's Defense Fund. "Not uptight. Not apprehensive."[2]

Maybe so. But as she climbed out of the limousine in front of the NBC studios in Rockefeller Plaza, Hillary looked tense. The street was lined with a battalion of television satellite trucks, and Hillary flashed a smile for the cameras. However, she could not disguise her deep animosity toward the press. It was evident in the tight lines around her mouth.

Jeff Zucker, the executive producer of the *Today* show, poked his head into the makeup room while Hillary was getting a light powdering to hide the bags under her eyes. Hillary was a huge "get" for Zucker. But his star anchor, Katie Couric, was not present to exploit the moment; her husband had died of cancer the previous weekend, and she was on leave.

And so, the interview with the First Lady fell to Matt Lauer, who had been summoned back from vacation to handle the biggest political story since Watergate.

Ten minutes before Hillary was scheduled to go on air, she spoke on the phone one last time—to Sidney Blumenthal.

"I suggested that she say, 'There are professional forces at work whose only purpose is to sow division by creating a scandal,'" Blumenthal recalled.[3]

Once the cameras started rolling, Matt Lauer wasted no time getting to the point.

"There has been one question on the minds of people in this country, Mrs. Clinton, lately. And that is, what is the exact nature of the relationship between your husband and Monica Lewinsky? Has he described the relationship in detail to you?"

"Well, we've talked at great length," she answered. "And I

think as this matter unfolds, the entire country will have more information...."

"You have said, I understand, to some close friends, that this is the last great battle," Matt Lauer said. "And that one side or the other is going down here."

"Well, I don't know if I've been that dramatic," Hillary said. "That would sound like a good line from a movie. But I do believe that this is a battle. I mean, look at the very people who are involved in this, they have popped up in other settings. This is the great story here, for anybody who is willing to find it and write about it and explain it, is this vast right-wing conspiracy that has been conspiring against my husband since the day he announced for president."[4]

LATER, HILLARY'S ATTORNEY DAVID KENDALL CALLED TO congratulate her on her "vast right-wing conspiracy" remark, a phrase that would come back to haunt her.[5]

"I heard your words of wisdom ringing through my ear," Hillary told him.

"And which words of incredible wisdom were you hearing?" Kendall said, going along with the joke.

"Screw 'em!" Hillary said.

"It's an old Quaker expression," said Kendall, who was raised as a Quaker.

"Oh," said Hillary, "like 'Screw thee'?"[6]

CHAPTER TWENTY-TWO

The Human Bridge

THANKS IN LARGE PART TO HILLARY'S VIGOROUS DEFENSE of her husband, the President's poll numbers began to rise. By the spring of 1998, his favorable job rating was nearing an all-time high. The tide of public opinion appeared to have turned against Whitewater counsel Kenneth Starr, who was increasingly viewed as a puritanical, sex-obsessed prosecutor.

Even Hillary, who was normally the voice of doom and gloom in the White House, began to feel cautiously optimistic. Her standard strategy—lie, deny, parse, stonewall, go on the offense—seemed to have worked again.

Only it hadn't.

That summer, under mounting pressure, Hillary had to abandon her opposition to an appearance by the President before a federal grand jury. Then in July—less than a month before the President's scheduled grand jury appearance—Hillary learned that Ken Starr had offered Monica Lewinsky immunity in return for testimony revealing the lewd details of her sexual encounters with Bill Clinton. Monica was ready to testify that the President used a cigar to masturbate her, then put the cigar in his mouth.

These were devastating blows. But worse was yet to come. One of Starr's lieutenants sent a letter to David Kendall, the Clintons' lawyer, requiring that "President Clinton provide this Office as soon as possible with a blood sample to be taken under our supervision."[1]

Nobody had to tell Hillary what that meant. As part of Monica's immunity deal, she had given Starr's office a "GAP dress, size 12, dark blue," as the FBI report described it, and a test revealed the presence of semen. The Feds wanted to see if the DNA in the President's blood matched the DNA in the semen.

"I had some conversations with people in Ken Starr's office," said a source close to the Whitewater prosecutor. "When the stain proved to be Bill's semen, I said to one of the guys, 'Why the hell did you guys announce that match before Bill went into the grand jury? You could have leaked that it was cheese, and the DNA test had come out negative, and then the sonofabitch would have gone in there and lied like hell.

"The answer was, the test was done in the FBI lab, and the Clintons knew the results before we did. Someone in the Justice Department was leaking to them. The day the FBI got the test results, they trotted them right over to the White House. So, when the President went into that grand jury, he had to know the jig was up."[2]

And so did Hillary.

Yet Hillary decided to spin an implausible tale regarding what she knew, and when she knew it. In her memoir *Living History*, which was published two years later, she wrote that on the morning of August 15, her husband woke her up in their bedroom and "told me for the first time that there had been an inappropriate intimacy" with Monica Lewinsky.

"I could hardly breathe," she wrote. "Gulping for air, I started crying and yelling at him."[3]

But her version of events was not credible.

Months before, Hillary had taken charge of the White House's damage-control operation. She ran the meetings that prepped Bill Clinton for his grand jury testimony. She asked Robert Shrum, the highly regarded Democratic wordsmith, to write a mea culpa speech for the President to deliver on national television. She then vetoed Shrum's speech, because she found it too conciliatory, and instead urged her husband to "come out and hammer Ken Starr."[4]* She saw the headline in the *New York Times* of August 13—two days *before* her husband's alleged bedside confession to her about Monica—that said: PRESIDENT WEIGHS ADMITTING HE HAD SEXUAL CONTACTS.

The fact of the matter was, Hillary knew everything—and she knew it before anybody else. And yet, she never changed her tune. Even after the truth about Bill and Monica came out, Hillary continued to defend her husband. And while the lurid tale rocked the nation, Hillary recovered from the shock faster than everybody else.

In a gesture that was meant to rally the Clintons' African American base, Hillary invited the Reverend Jesse Jackson to the White House to "counsel" the First Family. After praying with the Clintons and watching the Superbowl with them, the

---

*Shrum has the draft of that speech, which the President never delivered, hanging outside his office to this day. In it, Shrum wrote: "I have fallen short of what you should expect from a President. I have failed my own religious faith and values. I have let too many people down. I take full responsibility for my actions—for hurting my wife and daughter, for hurting Monica Lewinsky, for hurting friends and staff, and for hurting the country I love. None of this ever should have happened."[5]

Reverend Jackson held a press conference, and—perhaps inadvertently, perhaps not—demolished Hillary's gulping-for-air story.

"Hillary's not naïve," Jesse Jackson said. "There was no great explosive shock and surprise moment. Hillary knows her husband well and has for twenty-five years. The best evidence of that is that Sunday as the drama was building, she was organizing his testimony, and so she knew what was going on."[6]

Nonetheless, Hillary stuck to her lie.

"She had no good options," said a White House official. "She could either abandon her husband and take herself completely out of power, or she could stick with him and make herself look like a cold, calculating woman.

"I would have advised her to leave her husband for three months," the official continued. "She should have stayed with her mother, then had a big reconciliation story with Bill. But Hillary didn't have the sense of a dramatic story line to do it that way. And nobody around her could or would advise her to do it that way.

"Al Gore and Tipper were furious at both Clintons. They felt betrayed that Bill had lied to Al. And Tipper was disgusted over Bill's affair with Monica, who was the same age as Tipper's own daughter. When the four of them went to New York for the premiere of the musical *The Lion King*, Tipper refused to leave her holding room to see the President. The relationship between the two couples was broken over this breach of faith."[7]

FOR A LONG TIME, HILLARY'S LIE WENT UNCHALLENGED BY THE news media. That was largely because it was overshadowed by the President's even bigger lie—that he didn't have sex with Monica—which he sustained for eight long months.

Indeed, if Bill Clinton's DNA sample had not matched the DNA on Monica's semen-stained dress, he might still be telling the same lie. But unhappily for him and Hillary, the DNA odds against him turned out to be 7.87 trillion to one.

"It was his digging in his heels and stonewalling for an incredible period of time, and overtly lying to the country, that really got him in trouble," Dick Morris said. "He could have dodged and weaved around this until the point more or less came out—leak it, get it out, get speculation out—and then have admitted it. In a situation like this, you need soft hands. You need to be able to be subtle about it and gradual, and not just do anything harsh like 'No.' "[8]

In August, Sidney Blumenthal watched the President's post–grand jury speech in Rome, where he was traveling with his wife. Ten minutes after the speech was over, the phone rang in his room.

"It was the President, asking what my reaction was," Blumenthal recalled. "I told him that it was all right. Hillary asked me what I thought. I told her the same. The President said he was pleased with it. Hillary also approved."

Then, as the White House phone was handed to James Carville and pollster Mark Penn, Blumenthal continued, "I could hear the President and Hillary bantering in the background. Whatever they would have to do between themselves to get over this episode, they were still working as a team."[9]

Their whole effort was now aimed at convincing people that Bill had lied to Hillary, and that the Clintons were an embattled couple. The cheated-on wife was not speaking to the cad of a husband. He had to suffer publicly before she would grant him remission for his sins.

BUT HOW WERE THE SPINMEISTERS IN THE CLINTON WHITE House to convey such a complex message to the American people? The answer came the following afternoon in a brilliantly staged scene on the South Lawn of the White House.

As they had so many times in the past, the First Couple emerged from the White House and walked across the South Lawn to a marine helicopter, which was waiting to take them to Martha's Vineyard for a long-planned summer vacation. But this time Hillary, who looked morose despite her TV-friendly turquoise jacket, ignored the television cameras and her husband's outstretched hand.

In front of them, Buddy, the Clintons' brown Labrador retriever, tugged on his leash, which the President twisted nervously in his hand. To the right of the President was his eighteen-year-old daughter, Chelsea, who had abandoned her studies at Stanford University in Palo Alto, California, to rush home and lend support.

The whole country felt sorry for Chelsea. She was the one sympathetic character in the whole degrading Lewinsky mess. Her presence lent a touch of dignity to the long walk across the South Lawn. Chelsea was stationed between her mother and father. She reached out and took her father's hand. Then she joined hands with her mother.

America's favorite daughter was acting as the human bridge between her parents.

CHAPTER TWENTY-THREE

The Wronged Woman

On the flight from Andrews Air Force Base to Martha's Vineyard, Hillary was in a jovial mood, laughing and joking with Chelsea all the way. However, the moment Air Force One touched down at the Edgartown airport, where TV cameras were waiting to record the embattled First Family, Hillary turned into a different person. When she emerged from the plane, she was wearing a pair of dark sunglasses and the grim-faced expression of the Wronged Woman.

At the foot of the ramp, she received a consoling bear hug from Vernon Jordan, who was both an FOH (Friend of Hillary) and an FOB (Friend of Bill). The towering, handsome Jordan was frequently photographed riding with Bill Clinton in the presidential golf cart, puffing on a cigar and laughing at the President's off-color jokes.

The Clintons' friendship with Jordan had a serious dimension as well. Hillary believed that the inside-the-Beltway crowd would never accept her and her husband. That made it hard for the Clintons to govern in a city where relationships were everything, and one hand washed the other. To rectify the situation, Hillary had reached out to Jordan, a respected member of the African American community, a high-powered lobbyist in the nation's capital, and a member of that exclusive group of Washington wheeler-dealers known as "fixers."

As a favor to Hillary and Bill, Jordan had tried to fix the Monica mess by arranging a job for the young woman at Revlon, where he was a director. He managed to line up a $40,000-a-year public-relations job for her, and was later summoned to appear before the Whitewater grand jury to explain his behind-the-scenes role in the Lewinsky affair. But like so many FOHs and FOBs whose reputations were tarnished by their association with the Clintons, Jordan did not allow a little criminal investigation to get in the way of his friendship with the most powerful couple in the United States.

As Vernon Jordan watched from the tarmac of the Edgartown airport, Hillary and Bill worked the rope line. Then they climbed into a bronze-colored Chevy Blazer for the ride to the Oyster Bay compound of Richard Friedman, whose house they were borrowing during their twelve-day stay. A multimillionaire real-estate developer, Friedman was a controversial figure in his own right: he had been accused of using his political connections to help him build a hotel in Boston.[1]

WHILE THE FIRST COUPLE WERE ON MARTHA'S VINEYARD, Hillary's staff held daily briefings for the traveling press corps. And for once, the normally dazed and confused Clintonistas stayed on message.

Hillary, her aides repeated over and over again, was going through a period of "healing." She and the President were "sleeping in separate beds." They were hardly talking to each other. The only one who was giving the President any face time was Buddy the dog.

It was a great tabloid story, but even reporters from the mainstream press swallowed it hook, line, and sinker.

"There was no late evening singing around the piano with Carly Simon and Beverly Sills, no going out every night till all hours, no golf," wrote *Time* columnist Margaret Carlson. "The guest house where the President spent most of his time alone was akin to the woodshed."[2]

About midway through their vacation, the allegedly estranged couple put aside their made-for-the-media differences long enough to go sailing with former CBS anchorman Walter Cronkite and his wife, Betsy, on the Cronkite yacht. Hillary would later claim that the Cronkites had invited the Clintons to go sailing as a gesture of solidarity, but the truth was quite different. In fact, the Clintons arranged the invitation as a public relations gesture—and made sure that photographers were on hand to record them sailing with Cronkite, "the must trusted man in America."[3]

On another occasion, Bill and Hillary attended a dinner party at the West Tisbury home of investment banker Steven Rattner and his wife, Maureen White, who was a major Democratic Party fund-raiser. The guests—the ubiquitous Vernon Jordan; the writer William Styron and his wife, Rose; Beverly Sills; *Washington Post* chairman Katharine Graham; and Miramax honcho Harvey Weinstein—dined on shrimp and lamb kebab with couscous.

"The Clintons were seated at separate tables," said someone who was there that night. "At his table, the subject of Monica Lewinsky came up, and he talked about it. But at Hillary's table, where I was seated, we avoided the subject until the end of dinner, when someone asked her, 'Are you okay?'

"Hillary looked around the table, smiled, and said, 'So where is everyone going on vacation next year?' "[4]

Hillary's decision to avoid talking about Monica and play the Wronged Woman was beginning to pay off. There was an outpouring of sympathy for the First Lady in newspaper columns, magazine articles, and on TV talk shows. Her favorable poll numbers were beginning to inch up.

"In the first administration, when she was running the White House, she was the queen bee, running around, doing whatever the hell she wanted," said David Schippers, chief counsel to the House Managers for the Impeachment Trial of President Clinton. "She was making policy, and things like that. That fell apart, but then she did a complete change.

"She played the poor wife—she'd been betrayed. Instead of being the crook who went down with Whitewater, she suddenly became the object of sympathy. Suddenly, in the public eye, she became the poor wife just moseying around the White House, while people were doing things behind her back. That's absolute bullshit. Within the White House—don't kid yourself—she still ran the show more than ever."[5]

THE ROLE OF VICTIM DID NOT COME EASILY TO HILLARY. IT FLEW directly in the face of the life lessons she had learned from her father and mother. Now, in a major turning point in her life, those lessons had to be updated:

> Lesson No. 1: *Never allow yourself to be a victim* became *Victimhood can be a political plus.*
> Lesson No. 2: *If somebody hits you, hit him or her back harder* became *Being emotionally abused by your husband makes a woman a more sympathetic figure.*
> Lesson No. 3: *Stay in control of your own destiny* became *If*

you're running for office, voters' hearts will go out to the poor, helpless wife.

After Hillary left Martha's Vineyard, she and the President attended two fund-raisers in the Hamptons, the trendy resort community on the east end of Long Island.

"At both shindigs," wrote Michael Tomasky, ". . . applause for Bill was warm; for Hillary, ecstatic. During the applause at one of these events, at the home of Alec Baldwin and Kim Basinger, Bill turned to [New York State Democratic Party chairman Judith] Hope and whispered, 'Wow, they really love her here, don't they?'

" 'Mr. President,' Hope replied, 'Hillary *owns* New York.'

" 'Maybe,' Clinton answered, 'she should run for office from here.' "[6]

"This is the woman who has gone from being what people described as the Democrats' greatest liability to their greatest asset [and then back again] to their greatest liability and to their greatest asset," said Hillary's press secretary, Neel Lattimore. "It's almost like a roller coaster."[7]

That same summer, Hillary launched a "Save America's Treasures" bus tour that took her to four states in four days. Among the national reporters who followed her was NBC News correspondent Maria Shriver, who, as a born and bred Kennedy, knew a thing or two about politics.

"So, for the first time since she stumped for health-care reform, she took to the road on a bus for four days followed by reporters and photographers from the national press," Maria Shriver told the *Today* show audience during an interview with Hillary. ". . . There's so much speculation now about what you're going to do, what Hillary Clinton's life is going to be like after the presidency. Do you find that that takes away from what you're trying to do? Or do you just like slough it off . . . ?"

"I slough it off," Hillary replied. "I mean, you know, everybody else can spend their time speculating about my life. They don't have any more of a clue than I do."[8]

As usual, Hillary was being less than candid about her ambitions.

"The 'America's Treasures' tour got very little publicity," noted Jay Branegan, a former *Time* magazine correspondent who now worked on the Republican staff of the Senate Foreign Relations Committee. "But in my view, that tour planted the seed in her head that she could run for public office. She gave a great speech in apple-knocker country in upstate New York, and she showed great skill in working the rope lines. She really showed a knack for pressing the flesh, speaking high, and speaking low.

"I was there, covering her for *Time*," Branegan went on, "but most of the reporters were women. We rode in the second bus, and during the four days we were on the road, Hillary never came back to our bus. We were a lot of big-time reporters stuck in upstate New York, but she never came back. At that point, I think she was testing her political ability."[9]

PART IV

The Candidate

CHAPTER TWENTY-FOUR

Run, Hillary, Run!

On Friday, November 6, 1998, two venerable New Yorkers sat down to tape a conversation under the scorching lights of a television studio.

One was a swarthy, bantam-sized man with ears that stood out at a sharp angle from his head. This was Gabe Pressman, the veteran WNBC-TV reporter, who had been covering New York politics for as long as anyone could remember.

The other was Daniel Patrick Moynihan, the legendary four-term Democratic senator, who was recognized all over America by his shock of white hair and distinctive singsong style of speaking. The author of eighteen books, and the recipient of sixty-two honorary degrees, Moynihan had been described as "the best thinker among politicians since Lincoln and the best politician among thinkers since Jefferson."[1]

"How do you feel about running again . . . or haven't you made up your mind?" Pressman asked Moynihan.

In posing that question, the TV newsman was aware that

Democratic Party strategists were complaining about Pat Moynihan behind his back. They said he loathed fund-raisers, hated them more than going to the dentist. They said he didn't have a clue who gave and who didn't give him money. They said he had almost no money left in his campaign coffers, and that he did not seem the least bit interested in waging an aggressive effort to raise the vast sums necessary for reelection.

"Gabe," Moynihan replied, "Liz [his wife and campaign manager] made up our mind four years ago. I'll be . . . I've served four terms in the Senate . . . let it stay at that. That's . . . that's the longest term any New Yorker has ever served. . . ."

"You're gonna *retire!*" Pressman said.

The newsman was unable to disguise his excitement. As Pressman knew, there had not been an open Senate seat in New York since 1958. Moynihan's retirement was major political news.

"I am not running for reelection," Moynihan said flatly.

If it had been left entirely up to Moynihan, he probably would have tried for another term in the Senate. But he was turning seventy-two, and his wife felt he was getting too old for the political hustings. She did not want to see him become another Jesse Helms or Strom Thurmond, a decrepit figure lumbering around the hallways of Congress. In addition, Elizabeth Moynihan was concerned about her husband's health. Because of some kind of gag reflex, he had trouble eating, and had begun to lose a lot of weight.[2]

The interview with Moynihan was scheduled to be aired two days later, on Gabe Pressman's Sunday morning show *News4orum*, but given the sensational nature of the news, it was hardly surprising that it leaked out.

THAT SAME NIGHT, REPRESENTATIVE CHARLIE RANGEL, THE Democratic congressman from Harlem, called the White House.

Rangel had been telling Hillary that she would be a natural to fill the Moynihan seat if Pat ever retired from the Senate.[3]

"I'd like to speak to Mrs. Clinton," Rangel told the White House operator in his trademark raspy voice.

The operator immediately patched him through to Hillary.

"I just heard that Senator Moynihan announced he is going to retire," Rangel told the First Lady. "I sure hope you'll consider running, because I think you could win."[4]

From the day Bill Clinton admitted he had had an affair with Monica Lewinsky, the media had wondered: Was Hillary going to divorce him? Would Hillary forgive him? But those turned out to be the wrong questions. Hillary couldn't leave Bill if she wanted to hang on to power. The only relevant question was: Was Hillary going to strike out on her own and run for office?

Hillary promoted the impression that she was consumed with the state of her marriage and the state of Bill's presidency. But in fact she had spent the previous fall barnstorming the country stumping for Democrats in the midterm elections. She had piled up a lot of political chits by making public appearances and radio spots. And not incidentally, her approval ratings kept going up, and were now at a comfortable 56 percent.

She was determined to position herself for a berth in the Senate in 2000, and she did not need convincing by Charlie Rangel, or anybody else. Since her home state of Illinois did not have an open seat (and she wasn't very popular there anyway), she set her sights on New York, where Bobby Kennedy had successfully tried the same carpetbagger strategy.

As one of the first steps in her New Yorkification, she signed on to help the 1998 Senate campaign of Congressman Chuck Schumer, a staunch foe of her husband's impeachment. Schumer needed Hillary's star power to help him defeat a formidable opponent, Senator Al D'Amato, the New York Republican who had embarrassed the Clintons by running lengthy televised hearings on Whitewater. Schumer's upset victory of D'Amato encouraged Hillary in her own ambitions.[5]

After Charlie Rangel spoke to Hillary, he got in touch with his friend Bob Herbert, the only regular African American voice on the Op-Ed page of the *New York Times*. On November 12, just six days after Moynihan's retirement announcement, Bob Herbert wrote a column under the headline AFTER MOYNIHAN. He urged: "Run, Hillary, run!"[6]

To many, Hillary seemed a shoo-in for her party's nomination. As Charlie Rangel noted, "Nobody's going to run against the First Lady."[7]

But Hillary had a gigantic problem to overcome: her penchant for secrecy and concealment would not sit well with New Yorkers.

If she were going to run for office, she would have to get used to the fact that the New York media wasn't going to give her a pass because she was the First Lady. Her life would become an open book. Some Democratic strategists wondered if Hillary was ready for the blood sport of New York politics. Could she handle the press? Did she have anything to hide?

CHAPTER TWENTY-FIVE

The Education of Hillary Clinton

O<small>N S</small>UNDAY MORNING, JANUARY 3, 1999, H<small>ILLARY</small> C<small>LIN</small>-ton sat down with a cup of coffee in front of a TV set in the White House, and turned on *Meet the Press*. In a few days, impeachment proceedings against her husband would move from the House of Representatives, which had already voted in favor of four articles of impeachment, to the Senate, where the President was expected to prevail at trial.* Nonetheless, Hillary wasn't taking anything for granted. She was eager to hear what the Sunday morning pundits had to say about Bill Clinton's prospects.

She was in for a big surprise.

---

*Three months before, C. Vann Woodward, who had compiled a history of presidential misconduct under Hillary's supervision for the Watergate impeachment inquiry, joined some four hundred other historians in signing an open letter denouncing the impeachment proceedings against Bill Clinton.

"Here's a little mini-bombshell," Tim Russert, the moderator of *Meet the Press*, told his guests, journalists Gail Sheehy and David Maraniss, two seasoned Clinton watchers. "Senator Robert Torricelli of New Jersey . . . told me before the program that if he had to guess, he believes that Hillary Rodham Clinton will run for the United States Senate seat being opened by the retirement of Daniel Patrick Moynihan. . . . Gail Sheehy, does that surprise you?"

Not in the least, said Sheehy.

Not at all, Maraniss agreed.[1]

As the panelists continued to talk, the TV screen filled with a clip of Eleanor Roosevelt, the last First Lady whose name was mentioned in the same breath as that of the U.S. Senate. After the death of her husband, Eleanor was urged to run for the Senate by none other than Harold Ickes's father. She declined.

Hillary was speechless. When she had sufficiently recovered from her shock, she picked up the phone and called "the dark prince."

Harold Ickes was the go-to guy in New York, the master of the state's bare-knuckle, anything-goes style of politics. He always seemed to be operating on the edge of the law. There had been charges—never proved—that Ickes illegally backdated a letter regarding a stock sale by one of his clients, former mayor David Dinkins. And the media went into a feeding frenzy investigating Ickes's role in Dinkins's controversial cable television stock transfer to his son.[2]

According to the *New York Post*, it appeared that Ickes had "lied" to federal prosecutors during his grand jury testimony. Criminal charges were never brought against Ickes, the *Post* reported, "because there was insufficient evidence, but [the prosecutors] kept hoping for more."[3]

Ickes had memorized the demographic composition and

voting pattern of nearly every borough, county, city, town, village, and hamlet in the state. He was on a first-name basis with political operatives down to obscure workers at the precinct level. He drank stale beer and ate cold pizza with the leaders of unions, religious organizations, fraternal associations, ethnic groups, immigrant communities, and gay and lesbian clubs.

"Well," Hillary said when Ickes answered the phone, "did you *see* that?"

"Yes," replied Ickes, who had also been watching *Meet the Press*.

"What do you think?" Hillary asked.

"Well, Hillary," Ickes said, "if you don't want to do this, don't fuck around with it. Issue a Shermanesque statement, and that'll be the end of it."

"Well," Hillary said, "that's not where I am with this."[4]

At that moment, Harold Ickes realized for the first time that Hillary was serious about running for the Senate.

THE FOLLOWING MONTH, ON THE VERY DAY THE SENATE WAS TO vote on the articles of impeachment against her husband, Hillary invited Ickes to the White House. He arrived on Friday, February 12, carrying a large portfolio. After a warm greeting from Hillary in the family sitting room, Ickes opened his portfolio and removed a large map of New York State, which he spread out on a table. The sun shone through the arched windows, falling on the map, as Ickes began Hillary's education in the politics of New York State.

"So literally the day that [the senators] were passing judgment on her husband, she was trying to figure out how to join them," said *Washington Post* reporter Peter Baker.[5]

"[Harold] offered a running commentary about the obstacles I would face," Hillary recalled. "He pointed to towns from

Montauk to Plattsburgh to Niagara Falls, and it became clear that to take a campaign to New York's nineteen million citizens, I would have to physically cover a state of fifty-four thousand square miles.

"On top of that I would have to master the intricacies of local politics, of dramatic differences in the personalities, cultures and economies of upstate New York and the suburbs. New York City was its own universe: a cauldron of competing politicians and interest groups. The five boroughs were like individual mini-states, each presenting needs and challenges different from counties and cities upstate and also from the suburbs or neighboring Long Island."[6]

After a couple of hours of this, Hillary and Ickes broke for lunch. They gathered up their maps and took them to the First Family's private dining room, where they continued their conversation against the backdrop of the beautiful antique wallpaper that had been installed thirty-seven years earlier by Jacqueline Kennedy.

At the exact moment the Senate was deciding his fate, Bill Clinton walked into the dining room. He had just finished working out in the White House gym, and his T-shirt was stained with sweat.

"He set out a piece of paper on which he had scratched out a statement in longhand about the Senate verdict, a few carefully chosen words that he planned to deliver in the Rose Garden later in the afternoon," wrote the *Washington Post*'s Peter Baker. "While Hillary Clinton and Ickes chatted about the New York electoral map, the President edited his statement."[7]

Bill Clinton was eager to talk about his impeachment woes, but Hillary and Ickes ignored him. His feelings were hurt, and the President tried to edge into the conversation by pointing out his own strong showing in New York's Herkimer County in the 1992 and 1996 elections.

After the President left, Hillary and Ickes continued to talk for several more hours.

"Why in God's name would you want to do this?" Ickes asked her. "You've been very sheltered from the press, even though you think you haven't been. And you've got to be more open with them. You've got to think of them as people who have a job to do, working stiffs who have to file a story every day. And if they don't, they get laid off."[8]

A FEW DAYS AFTER WINNING THE IMPEACHMENT VOTE, THE Clintons traveled to Buffalo, a solid union town in western New York State at the eastern tip of Lake Erie. Almost twenty thousand people filled the HSBC Arena. Many of those in the crowd had heard that Hillary was thinking of running for the Senate from their state.

Bob McCarthy, the veteran political reporter for the *Buffalo News*, interviewed a number of the cheering Democrats, who told him they had come mainly because of Hillary.

"Why Hillary?" McCarthy asked.

"Because," came the answer, "Hillary is the most famous woman in the world."[9]

CHAPTER TWENTY-SIX

Blowing Them Away

"In the winter of 1999, I was at Camp David with some other major Democratic donors who were close to Hillary, and there was talk of her running for Pat Moynihan's Senate seat," said a prominent Democratic fundraiser. "At one point, Hillary joined us, and the talk started to drift to the subject of her throwing her hat in the ring. We all started to engage her, but she didn't want to be engaged.

"And she explained why," this Friend of Hillary continued.

" 'I've had some pretty tough few years in the White House,' she told us, 'and now that we've won the impeachment battle, I want to do the work I was sent here for.'

"I was impressed, and I figured she had decided not to run. But a couple of months after that conversation at Camp David, it became clear in a number of ways that she wanted financial support. Hillary operates in a different mode than most politicians when it comes to money. Most politicians have to make pilgrimages to people like me, and ask me to help them raise money. Hillary doesn't have to do that. She doesn't have to come begging. She has star power. A lot of rich people are always dying to be near her and give her money."[1]

By late February, Hillarymania was in the air. Both *Newsweek* and *Time* put her on their covers.[2] In early March, she summoned a handful of New York State's top Democratic elected officials and operatives to the White House to sound them out on her getting into the race.

All the people around Hillary—Linda and Harry Thomason, Susan Thomases, Harold Ickes, Maggie Williams, Mandy Grunwald—wanted to see her step out from her husband's shadow and run for office. It was high time she stopped focusing on her husband's political survival, they advised her, and started focusing on her own political future.

That spring, Hillary gathered yet another group of friends and supporters, this time in the Manhattan office of Alan Patricoff, a wealthy venture capitalist who backed liberal Democratic candidates. The subject was money. If Hillary ran for the Senate, the task of raising the money to fund her campaign would fall to the people in the room. Naturally, they wanted some reassurance that Hillary—whose favorability rating was now an astonishing 78 percent in New York City and 65 percent statewide[3]—had thought through the personal implications of running for public office.

"How are you going to handle Monica Lewinsky?" asked one of the women at the meeting.

"I decided because of Kosovo and for the good of the country, I needed to stand by the President of the United States during perilous times," Hillary said, reciting an answer she had committed to memory, and that seemed less than convincing even to her supporters. "And we needed to show that the office of the President was strong and intact. And I had to show that what had gone on was between Bill and me."[4]

* * *

No matter what she said in public about being undecided, Hillary was now privately committed to running. However, she did not want to look like an arrogant interloper, especially in the eyes of New York State's influential Democratic county leaders.

There were sixty-two counties in New York State, and sixty-two county leaders to woo. Ten of those counties had significant voting populations, and Hillary's first order of business was to get the support of the leaders in those counties. These men and women had devoted their lives to the Democratic Party, and they were not eager to welcome a Joannie-come-lately like Hillary. Without their support, however, Hillary had no chance of winning the Senate nomination.

"Before she announced the embryonic stage, her campaign staff did a helluva job with the county leaders," said a Democratic Party activist who was intimately familiar with the state's politics. "Judith Hope, who was then the Democratic Party chairman, went around the state and told the county leaders, 'Listen, you may not like Hillary, and you may not like the idea of her running for the Moynihan seat, but do me a favor and wait and see, and don't say anything yet.' "[5]

Hillary needed to convince the county chairmen that she could beat her likely Republican opponent—New York City's mayor, Rudolph Giuliani—on his home turf in New York City, and hold her own in the Republican suburbs as well as in conservative upstate New York.

That was a big order, and Hillary turned for help to image-maker Mandy Grunwald, a formidable figure both politically and physically. Mandy stood nearly six feet tall and had a booming voice and a thick head of black hair. A bundle of nervous energy, she chain-smoked Marlboros. Some of her Republican counterparts in the political consulting business joked that she looked like the Marlboro man in drag. Mandy didn't take offense. She was a fierce partisan, who could give as good as she got.

Though she grew up in a Republican household (her father, Henry Anatole Grunwald, was the former editor-in-chief of Time-Life), Mandy was a New York liberal to her core. After working on Bill Clinton's first presidential campaign, she stayed on at the Democratic National Committee. But in the wake of the health-care fiasco and the Republican takeover of Congress in 1994, she was fired. Her liberal voice in the White House was replaced by the centrist voice of Dick Morris.[6]

Mandy had been the Harvard roommate of Pat and Liz Moynihan's daughter Maura, and she had made television commercials for three of Moynihan's four campaigns. She had a New York state of mind, and she urged Hillary (who had never lived in New York) to embark on a "listening tour" by traveling all over the state, talking to average New Yorkers about their problems.

It was a sophisticated concept, because it deflected the most potent charge against Hillary—that she was a presumptuous outsider, who knew all the answers and who thought the people of New York owed her a seat in the Senate.

"People wanted to know that it was about *them*, and not about *her*," a campaign aide told *The New Yorker*'s Elizabeth Kolbert.[7]

Mandy set up small, intimate, friendly meetings, where Hillary—in Oprah-like fashion—could sit on a stage with the president of the local hospital, or a union leader, and talk about access to health care and the economy of western New York State. These meetings would give people the opportunity to see that Hillary did not have horns. Many New Yorkers had read that Hillary was cold, mean, and tough. But when they saw her in person, Mandy felt confident they would find someone who smiled, was funny, had boundless energy, and had knowledge of the issues they cared about.

Hillary would blow them away.

But there was a hitch. Before Hillary could embark on her listening tour, she first had to get the blessing of the state's big kahuna: Senator Daniel Patrick Moynihan. And everyone knew that Pat and Hillary did not get along.

CHAPTER TWENTY-SEVEN

"Boob Bait for the Bubbas"

FOR YEARS, PAT MOYNIHAN HAD BEEN SUFFERING FROM BACK pain, and in the spring of 1999, he had surgery to correct his spinal stenosis. The operation was a success, but his recovery was slow, and by May he still did not feel well enough to make an appearance on the floor of the U.S. Senate. However, when Hillary Clinton called to say she would like to drop by for a visit, the gallant senator put on a suit and tie, and personally greeted the First Lady at his front door.[1]

Pat and Liz Moynihan lived on Pennsylvania Avenue in a modern condominium apartment that had prime views of the nation's capital. They also had an apartment in New York City and an eight-hundred-acre farm in Pindars Corners in upstate New York, where the senator had written his eighteen books and many of his thoughtful speeches analyzing the ills of American society. Though Moynihan was often portrayed as an intellectual who was above the political fray—he had served both Republican and Democratic presidents before becoming a senator—he was also a shrewd Irish politician who understood power and its uses.

To break the ice with the Moynihans, Hillary began by chatting about the Dalai Lama, whom Pat and Liz had met when Pat was America's ambassador to India. Hillary said she was deeply moved by the Dalai Lama's spirituality. Moynihan was skeptical. From the icy tone of his voice, it was clear that he did not believe that Hillary "got" the Dalai Lama.[2]

In fact, according to Moynihan's biographer, Godfrey Hodgson, the senator's wife did not hide her impression "that Hillary Clinton 'didn't get it,' meaning that she didn't understand how either the Senate or the Senator worked."[3]

As chairman of the powerful Senate Finance Committee, Moynihan had urged Bill Clinton, after his election in 1992, to tackle the issue of welfare reform, which had many supporters in Congress, before he took on the thorny problem of health care. That way, Moynihan argued, the new president would create a positive legislative record and develop the momentum necessary to push through health-care reform.

The President's decision to ignore this sage advice cost him dearly. In Moynihan's view, the reason for the President's blunder could be summed up in a single word: *Hillary*. She convinced her husband to go for health care first and, what was an even bigger mistake, to put her in charge of the effort. Moynihan believed that Hillary's chief motivation was self-aggrandizement; she was determined to seize the favorable attention of the nation in order to enhance her prospects of succeeding her husband in the White House.[4]

Moynihan had publicly referred to Hillary's health-care plan as a "fantasy" and "boob bait for the bubbas."[5] And he made no secret of the fact that he found both Clintons impossible to deal with. In his eyes, their worst crime was that they and their staffs had displayed a complete lack of decorum, and had ignored him.

"Not a single call," Moynihan complained to *Time* magazine's political columnist Michael Kramer. "Not from the President or any of his top people. I would have thought someone would have gotten in touch by now. I just don't get it."[6]

Not only had the Clintons failed to reach out, but they had also begun as adversaries. The feeling of distrust and animosity was mutual. When it became apparent to Hillary that Moynihan was going to give her a hard time during hearings before his Finance Committee, she sicced one of her aides on the senator.

"Big deal," the aide said. "Moynihan [isn't] one of us, and he can't control Finance like [former Finance Committee chairman Lloyd] Bentsen did. He's cantankerous, but he couldn't obstruct us even if he wanted to. The gridlock is broken. It's all Democrats now. We'll just roll right over him if we have to."[7]

No one rolled over Pat Moynihan, and he never forgot that personal slight. Nor did he forgive the Clintons for failing to support his own proposals to reform Social Security. He told friends that he had a long list of people he disliked in the Clinton administration, and that at the top of the list was Hillary Rodham Clinton.

On a number of occasions, he had caught Hillary shading the truth. For instance, she once told reporters that Moynihan never held hearings on her health-care plan, when in fact he had held thirty such meetings.

Liz Moynihan shared her husband's assessment of Hillary as a liar and dissembler. She and Hillary spent a lot of time together while Hillary was trying to decide whether to run for Pat's Senate seat. Liz told friends that she found Hillary to be one of the strangest people she had ever met. Liz had her own view about what made Hillary that way.

"I believe that she believes that God approves of her, and that therefore she can't do anything wrong," Liz told a friend. "I suppose it's a midwestern Methodist view, the equivalent of Nixon and Quakerism."[8]

The Moynihans were deeply disappointed in Bill Clinton.

They had expected great things from him, and felt that he had squandered an historic opportunity to make a difference. In their opinion, no one in America was better able than Clinton to speak directly to both blacks and whites on the issue of race. Yet, for all his special gifts, Clinton had let the opportunity pass.[9]

What's more, the Moynihans thought that Bill Clinton should have resigned the moment the Lewinsky scandal became public, rather than put the country through the trauma of an impeachment process. And they found Hillary's defense of her husband during the Monica Lewinsky scandal to be nothing short of incomprehensible.[10]

CHAPTER TWENTY-EIGHT

Distortion

WHEN HILLARY HAD THOROUGHLY EXHAUSTED THE subject of the Dalai Lama with Pat and Liz Moynihan, she turned to the real reason for her visit. She had been doing some polling in New York State, she said, and she was sorely disappointed by the lackluster response by the voters to her candidacy.

Liz Moynihan, who had managed all of her husband's Senate campaigns, did not put much store in polls. In fact, she generally commissioned a poll only once every six years, during the middle of Pat's then-current term. The results of the poll were never used to influence how the senator voted, or what he said on any given issue. The results were used purely to make commercials to reach voters who, according to the poll, did not know their senator well.

Hillary found it hard to believe that the Moynihans did not poll as frequently as she and Bill Clinton did—which was as often as twice a week.

"So," Liz Moynihan said, "you're interested in the secret of my success."[1]

"Yes," Hillary said.

"I have a good candidate," Liz said. "People like him and trust him."

"Well . . . ," Hillary began.

"The reason you're not doing well in New York," said the straight-talking Liz, "is because Jews don't like you."

Hillary was taken aback. No one talked to the First Lady like that.

"Is it because of what they say I said about the Palestinians?" Hillary said.

"The thing that is wrong with *that* statement isn't what 'they say' you said," Liz said sternly. "It's what we all *know* you said—that you favor a Palestinian state."

"Well . . . ," Hillary stammered.

"In any case," Liz continued, "it's not what you said about the Palestinians that has disaffected the Jews so much. It's health care."

"Health care?" Hillary said.

"Yes," Liz continued, "health care. New York has a lot of teaching hospitals, and, according to your health-care plan, you want to close them down. New York has lots of Jewish doctors, and those doctors have lots and lots of wives and relatives and patients, and they don't like what you want to do."

"I'm interested in what you say about health care," Hillary said, "because I had a bill that would protect the teaching hospitals—"

"Hillary!" Liz interrupted. "Please! That's *Pat's* bill."

"Oh," said Hillary, "did he have one, too?"

Hillary wasn't an elected official, and yet she was talking as though she had introduced her *own* bill. And she was looking Liz Moynihan in the eye and comparing herself to Pat Moynihan, who had one of the most distinguished records in the history of the U.S. Senate.

At that point, Pat Moynihan had had enough.

"You have to excuse me," he said to Hillary, getting up slowly from his chair, favoring his back. "I told them I would go to the Senate today."

He left the room. But he did not go to the Senate. He went to an adjoining room and waited for Hillary to leave. He later said that he could not stand listening to Hillary avoid giving direct and honest answers.

Liz thought that Hillary would leave as soon as Pat did. But the First Lady stayed on to talk.

"She's duplicitous," Liz later told a friend. "She would say or do anything that would forward her ambitions. She can look you straight in the eye and lie, and sort of not know she's lying. Lying isn't a sufficient word; it's distortion—distorting the truth to fit the case."

CHAPTER TWENTY-NINE

"The Martians Have Landed"

"HILLARY UNDERSTOOD THAT IT WAS VERY IMPORtant to keep Pat on her side," said one of Moynihan's chief political strategists. "Otherwise, Pat could be fatal to her, if he came out and said he didn't back her."[1]

Mandy Grunwald did a masterful job preventing that from happening. She used all the goodwill she had stored up with Liz and Pat to persuade them to support Hillary. Mandy asked for one further favor: would Liz make Pindars Corners, the Moynihans' farm in the rolling hills of New York's Delaware County, available for the kickoff of Hillary's listening tour?

"Liz Moynihan had her doubts about the wisdom of allowing [Hillary] to use her home as the launch pad for a Senate campaign," wrote Godfrey Hodgson. "She drew the line at some of the suggestions made by the First Lady's overly enthusiastic handlers. They wanted a rope line to keep the media at a distance.

" 'No rope line,' Liz said. . . . 'You'll have to find another farm!' Liz went on, 'I've never made a circus for Pat, and I'm not going to make a circus for [Hillary].' Besides, she added shrewdly, you don't want to dilute [Pat's] image. 'It's worth a million votes upstate.' "[2]

Hillary's handlers had no choice but to accept Liz's conditions. Still, Liz was upset by all the pre-event hoopla, including the Secret Service and the additional police. In a moment of indiscretion, she confessed to Thomas Mills, the Delaware County sheriff, that she and her husband did not approve of Hillary's candidacy.

"She's not even from New York," Mills quoted Liz as saying.[3]

In the end, however, Liz relented, and on a hot, sunny day in July, Pindars Corners became the bucolic setting for Hillary's announcement of her listening tour. Gail Collins, the sardonic *New York Times* correspondent assigned to cover the occasion, described it as "the largest press corps ever assembled for a political event held in a pasture."[4]

Some three hundred journalists, some from as far away as Japan, descended on Pindars Corners. As one reporter noted, the journalists spilled more ink and used up more airtime on Hillary "than the presidential race, Kosovo, the stock market, the World Series and Ricky Martin combined."[5]

Television camera crews lined the path that led to a white wooden schoolhouse with a potbellied stove, where Moynihan wrote his books. After a while, the door of the schoolhouse opened, and Hillary and Moynihan emerged. As the cameras rolled, the two politicians strolled down the hill to the microphones, which were set up in front of haystacks. Hillary, dressed in a navy pantsuit, had on her best Mona Lisa smile. Moynihan, in an oxford button-down shirt and khakis, looked gaunt and frail, and not at all enthusiastic about being thrust into the center ring of a three-ring political circus.

"Maybe all of this ceaseless coverage will render the carpetbagger issue irrelevant," noted CNN's astute chief political analyst Jeff Greenfield. "She'll have a year to run around New York. It will be like she's been here forever. It already feels like she's been here for five years."[6]

The deep ambivalence that Moynihan felt toward Hillary became immediately apparent when he stepped in front of the microphones and plunged into a long, rambling discourse about how he had mowed the hay field a week early to accommodate all the satellite dish trucks. Then he caught himself.

"God, I almost forgot," he said with a mischievous grin. "I'm here to say that I hope she will go all the way. I mean to go all the way with her. I think she's going to win. I think it's going to be wonderful for New York."[7]

For Moynihan, apparently it was easier to say "she" than "Hillary."

Hillary tried to use some humor as a way of deflecting tough questions from the press.

"I'm really excited about taking these long, beautiful summer days at a leisurely pace—you know, with a few hundred of you—to travel from place to place and meet people."[8]

Inside the Moynihan farmhouse, Liz stood at a window, marveling over the dozens of TV satellite trucks and buses, the miles of cable, and the local farm kids hawking lemonade to the reporters and onlookers. The scene outside reminded her of the Steven Spielberg sci-fi movie *E.T.*

After a moment, Liz turned to the man standing next to her, Moynihan's chief of staff, Tony Bullock.

"Tony," she said, "look at this! The Martians have landed!"[9]

CHAPTER THIRTY

The Juice

In late June, Harold Ickes convened a top-secret meeting at New York's Sheraton Hotel. The dozen or so people crowded into the conference room comprised a Who's Who of Friends of Bill and Hillary.

The core group included several battle-scarred veterans of past New York political wars, including Samara Rifkin, who was in charge of setting up Hillary's Manhattan office. This New York nucleus was augmented by a number of out-of-staters, who were part of the Clintons' far-flung fund-raising apparatus. Harold Ickes had invited his favorite fund-raising sidekick, Laura Hartigan, who was a partner in the Los Angeles–based consulting firm of Hartigan & Associates.[1]

A tall, strikingly attractive blonde, Laura Hartigan had earned a controversial reputation as the finance director of the 1996 Clinton-Gore campaign. She and her then boss, Terry McAuliffe, who would later become head of the Democratic National Committee (DNC), were questioned after the election by federal prosecutors and Senate investigators about their suspected role in an unlawful fund-raising scheme. It was alleged that McAuliffe and Hartigan had arranged to funnel illegal contributions to Teamsters president Ron Carey's reelection campaign in exchange for more than $1 million in Teamsters contributions to state and local Democratic Party coffers.[2]

According to the *Washington Post*, a memo laying out this money-laundering plan was "sent under the name of Richard Sullivan, who was the DNC's finance director [in 1996]. . . . But the memo was actually written by Laura Hartigan. . . ."[3]

"I made the call as a favor to Laura Hartigan, who for reasons not clear to me was intent on trying to help [the Teamsters' Ron Carey]," Sullivan admitted. "When [a subordinate] came back and said it was not legal . . . I dropped it."[4]

Although Laura Hartigan was never formally charged with any wrongdoing, she did not dispute the existence of an incriminating memo sent out by her campaign office listing specific states where the Teamsters should direct funds.[5] Nor, for that matter, did anyone ever doubt that Laura Hartigan's longtime mentor, Harold Ickes—who had made his mark as a lawyer for some unsavory labor unions—was up to his eyeballs in questionable fund-raising practices during the Clinton-Gore reelection campaign.

These were the dubious credentials of Hillary's top fund-raisers.

Though the Senate election was still nearly a year and a half away—and Hillary had yet to issue a formal declaration of her intent to run—Ickes and company had already signed up Gabrielle Fialkoff, a former fund-raiser for Pat Moynihan and New York City Council speaker Peter Vallone, to aid in the money chase. They had also drafted a month-by-month campaign budget, and were now ready to turn their attention to the crucial matter of creating a campaign war chest.[6]

"It was clear from the way Harold ran the meeting—and the fact that he brought along Laura Hartigan—that he was going to be in total charge of Hillary's Senate campaign," said a New York–based activist who attended the secret meeting. "I found it strange that Hillary, who was going to face the sensitive carpetbagger issue, would choose Harold, who now made his headquarters in Washington, D.C., not in New York, and was seriously contaminated by his alleged connections to so many financial scandals.

"Let's face it," this person continued, "Harold might be a brilliant political strategist, but he's not a good guy. And he hated Bill Clinton for having fired him. True, Hillary had conspired with Bill behind the scenes to fire Harold, but she pretended otherwise, and was able to good-cop Harold back into her camp for the Senate race. That this seriously compromised guy was her guru said an awful lot about the character of Hillary Clinton."[7]

After everyone had a chance to get reacquainted and settle down, Ickes handed out a sheaf of papers labeled "National Fundraising Strategy Plan Working Document/Confidential— Not for Distribution." The room fell silent, except for the rustle of paper.

A quick scan of the document revealed two major surprises. First, the plan set a staggering goal of $25 million in direct contributions, or so-called "hard money," to the candidate. This was an unprecedented amount for a Senate race. Second—and perhaps even more striking—the plan anticipated that more than two-thirds of the money would come from *outside* New York.

As far as Ickes was concerned, this was not going to be a *local* race. From the get-go, it would be treated as a *national* effort. The atmosphere in the room crackled with excitement. Ickes seemed intent on turning Hillary's Senate campaign into a dry run for the White House. He had assembled the members of this group to be in on the ground floor of that bold and daring enterprise.[8]

"Okay," Ickes announced, "let's take a closer look at the plan."

Summary Fundraising Plan/Confidential— Not for Distribution[9]

($ in 000s)

Category	Goal	Expense	Net	Exp%
Political Action Committee	$3,000	$300	$2,700	10%
D.C.; Virginia; Maryland	1,700	306	1,394	18%
N.Y.; N.J.; Connecticut	8,000	1,440	6,560	18%
Boston	500	100	400	20%
Chicago	600	120	480	20%
Los Angeles	900	180	720	20%
Providence	100	20	80	20%
Florida	400	80	320	20%
San Francisco	300	60	240	20%
Las Vegas	200	40	160	20%
Philadelphia	250	50	200	20%
Denver	250	50	200	20%
Texas	300	60	240	20%
Total Events/Committee	$16,500	$2,806	$13,694	17%
Direct Mail	$ 8,500	$4,045	$ 4,455	48%
Total	$25,000	$6,851	$18,149	27%

During the meeting, Ickes got into a nasty argument with Susan Thomases, his old girlfriend. For a time back in the 1960s, Ickes and Thomases had been lovers; they had lived together and worked together on Senator Eugene McCarthy's presidential bid. Like Ickes, Thomases was a bred-in-the-bone leftist, a screamer of obscenities, and a fearless practitioner of the politics of intimidation.[10]

"I have a very strong reality principle, and it's one of the things that gets my mouth in trouble and gets me in trouble—from [the media's] perspective, gets me in trouble," Thomases once told a reporter. "I think, of course, it's the source of my strength."[11]

Others begged to differ. In their view, Thomases's strength derived from her special relationship with Hillary, which had been forged back in Arkansas during Bill Clinton's unsuccessful 1974 campaign for Congress.

During that campaign, Hillary Clinton and Susan Thomases discovered they had a great deal in common. For one thing, they both viewed politics through the same lens: as war by other means. More important, although they were both married, they traced their political ideology to "gender feminism."

Their point of view was summed up by Christina Hoff Sommers in *Who Stole Feminism?*:

"The leaders and theorists of the women's movement believe that our society is best described as a patriarchy, a 'male hegemony,' a sex/gender system in which the dominant *gender* works to keep women cowering and submissive. The feminists who hold this divisive view of our social and political reality believe we are in a gender war, and they are eager to disseminate stories of atrocity that are designed to alert women to their plight. The 'gender feminists' (as I shall call them) believe that all our institutions, from the state to the family to the grade schools, perpetuate male dominance...."[12]

Women like Hillary and Susan Thomases believed that women had to break away from their dependence on powerful men and create an alternative to the "brutal patriarchal system."[13] They did not see any contradiction between their married status and their political philosophy. They could identify with the ideals of gender feminism and political lesbianism without subscribing to its sexual component. Indeed, in the world of national politics, they became the preeminent practitioners of that philosophy.

Over the years, Thomases became Hillary's best friend, alter ego, and chief enforcer. She looked the part. With her frizzy salt-and-pepper hair, frumpy clothes, down-at-the-heel shoes, and expletive-laden vocabulary, Thomases was just the kind of tough, strong-willed, ideologically passionate woman Hillary had always admired. And her admiration was only heightened by the way in which Thomases coped with her medical condition, multiple sclerosis, a progressive and incurable disease.

"They had begun on the same track," noted one of Hillary's biographers. "Both were the only daughters in families of boys, both had strong mothers. Hillary went to Wellesley and Yale, and Thomases attended Connecticut College and Columbia University Law School. But by the 1980s, Thomases was a high-powered New York lawyer making a half million dollars a year, while Hillary's earning power was substantially eroded by her political work for Bill.

"Thomases lived on Park Avenue, had a summer house in Newport, Rhode Island, and was on a first-name basis with the top political figures in New York. She was living in a sophisticated world that Hillary, tied down in Little Rock, could engage with only at a distance. Thomases was anything but the traditional political wife: she kept her own name after marrying a carpenter-turned-artist, William Bettridge, who stayed home and took on many of the child-care responsibilities."[14]

During the 1992 presidential campaign, Hillary appointed Thomases as Bill Clinton's chief scheduler, a role that put her in charge of access to the candidate. Since then, Thomases had become what one observer called "the Clinton administration's

King Kong Kibitzer—whose advice on everything from personnel to politics resounds like a mighty roar through the halls of the West Wing."[15]

Nothing seemed to slow Susan Thomases down—not even her decades-long struggle against multiple sclerosis.

"It's not that she has the juice," said one White House operative. "She *is* the juice. She's the juicer, too. The Braun automatic."[16]

CHAPTER THIRTY-ONE

Hillary's Problem

From the beginning of the campaign, Harold Ickes and Susan Thomases wrestled with a perplexing problem. A must-win demographic group—observant Jews—did not like their candidate. In fact, they despised her.

Normally, a Democratic candidate running a statewide race in New York needed 70 to 75 percent of the Jewish vote to offset the traditional Republican turnout in the suburbs and upstate. But Hillary's likely Republican opponent, Mayor Rudolph Giuliani, was immensely popular with observant Jews. He had reduced crime in Orthodox Jewish neighborhoods and made New York City a cleaner, safer, more civilized place in which to live and earn a living.

Giuliani won the hearts and minds of many Jews by heaping ridicule and contempt on one of their archenemies: Yasser Arafat, the Palestinian Liberation Organization leader. In a wildly popular move, the feisty mayor barred the terrorist leader from city-sponsored events marking the United Nation's fiftieth anniversary, including a concert at Lincoln Center.[1]

Hillary Rodham at Wellesley College in the late 1960s. Her Methodist youth minister planted the seeds of a radical left-wing political philosophy, and those seeds were watered and fertilized at Wellesley.
LEE BALTERMAN/TIME LIFE PICTURES/GETTY IMAGES

Park Ridge, Illinois, in the 1950s. Hillary seemed to come unglued whenever anyone dared to criticize her. When one of her close friends infuriated Hillary by carelessly bumping his bike into hers, she gave him a good punch in the face. Her early combative nature foreshadowed her *Jerry Springer*-style free-for-alls with Bill Clinton.
CLINTON PRESIDENTIAL LIBRARY

A senior at Wellesley. "A lesbian was suddenly not the eccentric old maid of Victorian literature, but a dynamic young woman who had thrown off the shackles of male dominance," said a classmate. "Hillary talked about it a lot, read lesbian literature, and embraced it as a revolutionary concept."
OWEN. R.F./BLACK STAR

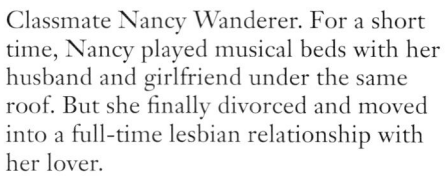

Classmate Nancy Wanderer. For a short time, Nancy played musical beds with her husband and girlfriend under the same roof. But she finally divorced and moved into a full-time lesbian relationship with her lover.
COURTESY WELLESLEY COLLEGE ARCHIVES

Classmate Eleanor "Eldie" Acheson. While Hillary was still in the early stages of exploring her sexual nature, Eldie was already sexually reckless and bawdy. Eldie eventually came out of the closet and moved in with her lesbian partner.
COURTESY WELLESLEY COLLEGE ARCHIVES

With Bill Clinton at Yale in the early 1970s. The normal rules of courtship did not apply. Their romance (if it could be called that) was not based on mutual attraction. Bill frequently found sexual release elsewhere. And Hillary, who had never placed much store in sex, did not seem to mind.

CLINTON PRESIDENTIAL LIBRARY

With Special Counsel John Doar (in glasses) during the impeachment inquiry of President Richard Nixon. Doar treated Hillary Rodham differently from the rest of his staff. She was his favorite. Hillary was hired on the recommendation of Marian Wright Edelman, the founder of the left-leaning Children's Defense Fund, and Burke Marshall, one of Senator Edward Kennedy's closest advisers.
DAVID HUME KENNERLY/GETTY IMAGES

Governor Bill Clinton and Arkansas First Lady Hillary Rodham Clinton visit the White House in 1979. She insisted on keeping her maiden name because she wanted to be "a person in my own right" and not a " 'sacrificial' political spouse." Yet, at the same time, she readily sacrificed her feminist principles and allowed herself to become a doormat to a man who was "ready to go after anything that walks by." BARRY THUMMA/AP

Linda Bloodworth-Thomason and Markie Post jumping for joy in the White House. The Clintons peddled the Lincoln Bedroom to curry favor with big donors and politically connected people. AMERICA MEDIA, INC. REPRINTED WITH PERMISSION.

Hillary's West Wing staff in the Old Executive Office Building, which was dubbed "Hillaryland." Hillary, wrote the historian Paul Johnson, stuck a "feminist finger in the appointment pies, especially of women, sometimes with embarrassing, indeed hilarious, results."
CLINTON PRESIDENTIAL LIBRARY

Harold Ickes and Evelyn Lieberman. Whereas Ickes was Hillary's left-wing political guru, Lieberman (known as Mother Superior) had a different but equally important mission—to keep indiscreet women away from Bill Clinton while allowing "safe" women to be part of his White House harem. DIANA WALKER/TIME LIFE PICTURES/GETTY IMAGES

Above, left: Mandy Grunwald on *Meet the Press*. Mandy used all the goodwill she had stored with legendary New York senator Daniel Patrick Moynihan and his wife, Elizabeth, to persuade them to support Hillary for senator. GETTY IMAGES

Above, right: Susan Thomases takes a coffee break. Hillary and Susan believed that women had to break away from their dependence on powerful men and create an alternative to the "brutal patriarchal system." They became preeminent practitioners of gender feminism. ED LALLO/TIME LIFE PICTURES/GETTY IMAGES

Hillary and Bill dance on the beach in St. Thomas shortly before he was forced to testify in the Paula Jones case, where he was first quizzed about Monica Lewinsky. Though Hillary denied knowing about Monica, she had long been aware of the buxom intern's affair with her husband and allowed this intimate photo opportunity to be staged as a way of deflecting scrutiny of her marriage. PAUL RICHARDS/AFP/GETTY IMAGE

Monica and Bill embrace at a Democratic fund-raiser in Washington in 1996. "The Secret Service knew all about Monica," said a Democratic National Committee official. "Everyone I talked to knew she was obsessed with the President. And when I say everyone, I mean everyone—including *Hillary*." DIRCK HALSTEAD/GETTY IMAGES

First Friend Vernon Jordan gives the President a bear hug as Chelsea and Hillary disembark on Martha's Vineyard in 1998. On the trip from Washington, Hillary was in a jovial mood, joking with Chelsea. But before the plane landed, she put on her "wronged woman" expression for the waiting photographers.
RUTH FREMSON/AP

Pat Moynihan and Hillary Rodham Clinton at Pindars Corners for the kickoff of her 2000 senatorial campaign. The deep ambivalence that Moynihan felt toward Hillary became immediately apparent when he stepped in front of the microphones and failed to even mention her name.
DAVID DUPREY/AP

Hillary in a New York Yankees baseball cap. "I've always been a Yankees fan," Hillary said. After the laughter died down in the saloons and taverns throughout New York City, Hillary looked more like an out-of-touch carpetbagger than ever.
RICHARD ELLIS/GETTY IMAGES

Hillary embraces Yasser Arafat's wife, Suhu. When Hillary realized she had gotten herself into a jam with Jewish voters, she suddenly turned up a long-lost Jewish step-grandfather—an announcement that was dismissed by many cynical New York voters as an example of her pandering.
LAURENT REBOURS/AP

Hillary and Rick Lazio during their first televised debate. When Lazio left his podium, walked across to Hillary, and waved a piece of paper in her face, many women recoiled at his bullying tactics. JAMES ESTRIN/*The New York Times*

Hillary celebrates her Senate victory. After nearly three decades of playing a supporting role for Bill, it was now Hillary's turn to step into the political spotlight. MIKE SEGAR/REUTERS

A twenty-six-foot-long moving van backs up to the White House to cart away valuable furnishings that did not legally belong to Bill and Hillary and take them to their new Chappaqua, New York, home. When the media blew the whistle on the Clintons, they reluctantly agreed to return some of the items to the White House.
STEPHEN CROWLEY/*The New York Times*

Hillary denying that she knew her brother lobbied President Clinton for pardons. No one believed her denials, especially since her own campaign treasurer, William Cunningham, had also lobbied to win pardons from Bill Clinton.
KEVIN LAMARQUE/REUTERS/TIME PIX

Hillary schmoozing her fellow senators. She knew she had to dispel the notion that, as a former First Lady, she would try to dominate the Senate. She also knew that her fellow senators were not going to give her a long honeymoon. Douglas Graham/Polaris

Hillary with presidential candidate John Kerry. Hillary's future depended on George W. Bush's remaining in the White House. But she could not afford to be seen by her fellow Democrats as wobbly or disloyal. She had to *appear* as though she were doing everything in her power to advance the cause of John Kerry. John Gress/Reuters/Landov

Bill Clinton putting the move on a blonde in 2002. In the past, the Clintons' peculiar relationship had been charitably described as a marriage of convenience. But now it was not even that. It was more like a marriage of *in*convenience in which the trajectories of their lives had radically diverged.
ALECSEY BOLDESKUL/ZUMA PRESS

Bill mouth-kissing a supporter. Hillary's aides noticed that Bill seemed to grow even more reckless after his memoir, *My Life*, became a big bestseller. He was rolling in money—and hubris. Throwing caution to the wind, he started a torrid love affair with a divorcée in her early forties. JAY L. CLENDENIN/POLARIS

Hillary visits the troops in Iraq. While she was in the White House, Hillary tried to change the tradition in which military aides wore their uniforms when accompanying the President with the nuclear codes. "She was trying to downplay the military in and around her husband," said the President's former senior military aide. Dusan Vranic./Reuters

Whitehaven, Hillary's White House in exile, near Washington's Embassy Row. Hillary replaced Bill Clinton as her party's most sought-after fund-raiser. The key to her White House strategy was to put Democrats all over America in her debt, building relationships, establishing a firm control over the machinery of the state parties.
Alex Wong/Getty Images

Hillary addresses the political faithful at the 2004 Democratic National Convention. "My two cents' worth," said someone who worked with Hillary on the Clinton administration's health-care reform effort, "is that Hillary Rodham Clinton needs to be kept very far away from the White House for the rest of her life."
Andy Kropa/Redux

Even more alarming in the eyes of Ickes and Thomases was the negative reaction of many college-educated women—and not just Republican women—to Hillary's candidacy. Indeed, her biggest detractors were found among women who resembled Hillary the most—white, professional, upper-middle-class Baby Boomers.

Ellen Chesler, the feminist author of *Woman of Valor*, a biography of birth control pioneer Margaret Sanger, thought she had found an explanation for Hillary's problem.

"Many women who hadn't had it both ways, who gave up either career or family, were confused or resentful of the fact that Hillary did have it both ways," Chesler said. "I think as First Lady maybe she didn't fully understand that."[2]

As Hillary began to gain some political traction, her "woman problem," as it came to be known inside the campaign, continued to bedevil Ickes and Thomases. Finally, after months of dithering, they commissioned a series of focus groups made up of suburban women. Shira Nayman, a psychologist who worked for Strategic Frameworking, a Seattle-based company that specialized in brand marketing strategy, was hired to run the focus groups.[3]

When Ickes and Thomases viewed the tapes from these focus groups, they became deeply alarmed. Asked what they thought of Hillary Clinton, the suburban women said:

"Very controlling."
"Self-serving. She's very cunning, independent."
"She's cold."
"I remember her being on the Today show and her saying that they were framing them, and that really sticks in my head because she thought that everyone was out to get them . . . and when something happens they have to blame it on somebody else instead of looking within."
"You get the sense that she doesn't think like a woman. She thinks like a man."[4]

What did women want from Hillary? Ickes and Thomases weren't sure, but they knew they had to "warm up" their candidate as quickly as possible. That meant Hillary had to appear more maternal, more wifely, and more feminine than she actually was.

They asked Mandy Grunwald to put together a speakers' bureau, whose job was to win over women voters. The bureau was called Hillary's Advocates, and it was run by Ann Lewis, a Democratic Party activist and the sister of Barney Frank, the gay congressman from Massachusetts. Ann Lewis gave Hillary's Advocates a set of talking points, which were aimed in large part at portraying Hillary as a victim of male sexism:

> Probably the most important issue to address can be illustrated by one guest's remark—"Something is stopping me from trusting or supporting [Hillary]." What seems to address this "something" successfully is the realization that more is being asked of her because she is a woman than would be asked of a man in her position—she has to know what it's like to work and change a diaper but he doesn't, she has to justify her marriage, her "realness" but he doesn't. . . .
>
> Typically, a critical mass of positive remarks from the assembled group (not just the speakers) is reached, and the whole room changes. It's possible to see people's faces change from hostility, cynicism, and disbelief to something else—they begin to nod instead of shake their heads.[5]

EVEN AS ICKES AND COMPANY WERE GRAPPLING WITH HILLARY'S "woman problem," they were developing a strategy to attack

Rudolph Giuliani. Opposition researchers were asked to come up with talking points for Hillary and her campaign surrogates that would help them portray Giuliani as an oppressive male bully—the other side of the female-victim coin:

RUDY GIULIANI'S CLAIM TO FAME:
OR, THE EMPEROR'S CLOTHES OR,
THE ROOSTER TAKES CREDIT FOR THE DAWN

Mayor Rudolph Giuliani has pressed his claim to higher office on four specific boasts about his performance in City Hall, in addition to his general claim that he has "turned the city around" by rejecting the failed policies of the past.

Each of his specific claims is demonstrably false. The general acceptance of his claims by much of the public is a tribute to the power of the shouted word, or the bully's ability to silence critics by sheer power of personality. . . .

Beyond the hollowness of his claims to achievement lies Rudy Giuliani's Achilles heel: his arrogance and inability to work with others. . . .[6]

THE WOMEN'S ARM OF THE CAMPAIGN—NEW YORK WOMEN FOR Hillary—scoured Rolodexes and Day Planners for rich donors:

SUBJ: Re: New York Women for Hillary
FROM: Maredaly

Doris Cadoux	Stoneyfield Yogurt
Kim Brassaloria	$$$$$$$
Rena Shulsky	$$$$$$$
Sharon Davis	(let me check her interest in campaign, she is big dollars)

Trudie Styler	(Mrs. Sting; I believe are here in Dec) [phone number] (Trudie is worth a Hillary call. . . . She has lots of friends)
Donna Schinderman	husband is Ann Morris Antiques, has time, beautiful apt money and rich friends
Marilyn Fireman	$$$$$$$$$

Would you like to do a Hillary event in Garrison? I am very wired there and know the richest who would love to host her to raise $$$$$$$. It is the right place for her to do suburban sprawl, environment, etc.[7]

Often, when Hillary addressed women, she appeared wooden and overrehearsed. In one such meeting, which was set up by Ellen Chesler at her husband's law firm in Manhattan, Hillary talked to one hundred committed Democratic women. Yet, during the question-and-answer period, none of the women made a single positive comment about the candidate.

"And this was a meeting of the so-called converted," recalled Eva Moskowitz, a Democratic city councilwoman. "But even at this meeting, one woman asked [Hillary] how she could stay with [her husband]."[8]

At bottom, when all the fancy analysis was stripped away, Hillary's problem seemed to be quite simple: women were far more likely than men to see that all her talk about compassion was an act.

"She's the most unbelievable actress I have ever met," said a woman who worked on Hillary's Senate campaign. "I remember one time at a Woman's Leadership Forum event in New York, thirty of us sat around Hillary, talking about politics. And she said, 'You know, I love this organization, not just because we sit around and talk about politics, but because of the bonds of friendship forming around us.' The way she said it, people were riveted by her performance. But I had gotten to know her, and I could tell she didn't mean it. She has this unbelievable ability to be a liar. She is soulless."[9]

CHAPTER THIRTY-TWO

"A Legend Imploding"

A T SOME POINT IN THE CAMPAIGN, HAROLD ICKES REALIZED that his biggest problem—bigger than women, bigger than Jews—was Hillary Clinton herself.

After years of stumping for her husband, Hillary still had a perverse talent for putting her foot in her mouth. The woman who had once mocked moms who "bake cookies and make tea" and complained of a "vast right-wing conspiracy" was still talking like Mrs. Malaprop.[1]

Ickes's initial instinct was to keep Hillary as far from the press as possible. Her media advisers regularly informed television camera crews to be prepared for "a 70-foot throw"—campaign-speak, as the *New York Post*'s Gersh Kuntzman helpfully pointed out, for "the distance reporters will be kept from the candidate."[2]

"She's been insulated in the cocoon so long that she's definitely uncomfortable," said WNBC's Gabe Pressman, the dean of the New York press corps. "She's not used to hugs and it shows. But she can learn to do it, just like that other alleged carpetbagger, Bobby Kennedy. He was stiff when he started, too."[3]

But "stiff" didn't even begin to describe Hillary Clinton's clumsiness as a candidate. "Ineptness" and "incompetence" were more like it. In fact, Hillary made so many gaffes during her first few months on the campaign trail that people began to wonder if she was cut out for the rough-and-tumble of electoral politics.

When she sat for an interview with a writer from *Talk*, Tina Brown's new celebrity magazine, Hillary indulged in New Age psychobabble. She painted herself as the victim of a cheating husband, and made excuses for Bill Clinton's sexual misbehavior on the ground that he had had an unhappy childhood. The reaction to the Hillary who was portrayed in the article was almost universally negative.

"Another dollop of Clintonspeak," sniffed one newspaper.[4]

When the Yankees won the American League pennant, Hillary lost no time in inviting them to the White House. Manager Joe Torre presented her with a team cap, and she promptly put it on and declared that she had "always been a big Yankees fan."[5] After the laughter died down in the saloons and taverns throughout New York City, Hillary looked more like an out-of-touch carpetbagger than ever.

When President Clinton granted pardons to sixteen imprisoned Puerto Rican terrorists in an obvious bid to help his wife win New York's two million Hispanic votes, Hillary said she had not been involved in the decision—a claim that no one believed. In fact, Hillary's brother Hugh Rodham and her campaign treasurer, William Cunningham, had both lobbied to win pardons from the President.[6]

When Pardongate became yet another Clinton scandal, Hillary spoke out against the clemency offer. But her failure to alert Latino officials in advance of her about-face prompted howls of protest from Fernando Ferrer, the Bronx borough president and the highest-ranking Puerto Rican official in the city. Eventually, Hillary patched up her relations with the Hispanic community—but not without paying a high cost.[7]

When Hillary made the obligatory trip to Israel to win Jewish votes back home, she went to the Palestinian-controlled city of Ramallah. There, she appeared onstage with Yasser Arafat's wife, Suha, who made the outrageously false charge that Israel was poisoning Palestinian women and children with toxic gases. At the end of Mrs. Arafat's speech, Hillary applauded enthusiastically, then gave Suha Arafat a big hug and kiss. The photo of the two women kissing, which was played around the world, sowed serious doubts about Hillary in the minds of many Jewish voters.[8]

When Hillary realized that she had gotten herself in a jam with Jewish voters, she suddenly turned up a long-lost Jewish stepgrandfather—an announcement that was dismissed by many cynical New York voters as an example of her pandering.[9]

When Mayor Giuliani attacked the Brooklyn Museum of Art, which was running an exhibit that featured a painting of the Virgin Mary with breasts made of dried elephant dung, Hillary did not rush forward to defend the museum's First Amendment rights. Trying to have it both ways with voters, she said she found the show "deeply offensive," but believed shutting it down, as Giuliani proposed, was "a very wrong response."[10]

Her response made her look like a woman without any convictions.

When a reporter asked Hillary if she planned to march in the St. Patrick's Day Parade, she promptly responded: "I sure hope to!" Those four words, perhaps more than any others, revealed Hillary's ignorance of New York's convoluted politics. For years, Democratic candidates had avoided the parade because the Ancient Order of Hibernians refused to allow gays and lesbians to march under their own banner. By saying she would march, Hillary offended one of her core constituencies—homosexuals.

"Independently, the mistakes are meaningless," said Democratic political consultant George Arzt. "Cumulatively, I think they are very damaging. . . . She doesn't have the instincts yet of a New York pol. It's like a quarterback not reading the defenses."[11]

"Here's a woman I've admired since '92 for being a strong, smart feminist," wrote Lenore Skenazy. "A woman who knew her own mind—and spoke it. Now I wonder who's at the controls. Every morning I open the papers to find out how she's shot herself in the foot today. With a .38? An Uzi? A small grenade? The gaffes just won't stop."[12]

Others were less generous.

"She'd had about as bad a six months as a candidate can have," wrote one observer. "Her attempt to refashion herself from a distant First Lady into a flesh-and-blood pol was by turns earnest, amateurish, sad, disastrous. The Hillary Clinton of the 70 percent approval ratings and the 172 active fan clubs—the Hillary Clinton whom New York Democrats had begged to enter this race—was scarcely even a memory now."[13]

"That odd sound you hear," wrote Noemie Emery in the *National Review*, "is a legend imploding; the short, saintly stardom of Hillary Clinton, as it sputters to a halt."[14]

CHAPTER THIRTY-THREE

The Turnaround

O<small>N FEBRUARY 4, 2000, BILL CLINTON AND A SMALL GROUP</small> of aides gathered in the White House movie theater to help Hillary rehearse her formal announcement speech. Standing at the podium, shifting uncomfortably from foot to foot, Hillary began reading haltingly from her draft speech.

All of a sudden, the President jumped from his seat.

"You need to say *why* you're running here and now!" he shouted.

"Because I'm a masochist," Hillary shot back, half in jest.

The President looked down at the copy of the draft in his hand, and began rearranging the order of the paragraphs.

"She'll announce," he said. "They'll cheer and dance around. That's fine. . . . Why is she doing it? Why not Illinois, Arkansas, Alaska? Why not rake in some dough? Why ask to be trashed right now? . . . What I wish you could do, Hillary, is a sentence here: 'The overwhelming reason is that I don't want to give up my life in public service.' "

"I'm just a little policy wonk," Hillary joked. "I just want to make life better for little children."

She paused, and then let out a big, heavy sigh.

"I have to memorize too much."[1]

BUT BILL CLINTON REFUSED TO EASE UP ON HIS WIFE. He telephoned Harold Ickes, Susan Thomases, and Mandy Grunwald several times a day, asking for updates on how Hillary was doing. He kibitzed the campaign. He made sure that he was involved in every aspect of decision making, including the most important part of all—fund-raising.

"Past presidents were content selling ambassadorships," the *New York Times*'s Maureen Dowd wrote in September 2000. "The Clintons may as well have listed the Lincoln Bedroom on eBay. Lately, they have packed state dinners with politicians, donors and journalists they hope will boost Mrs. Clinton's Senate campaign. They even put up a circus tent on the lawn for the India state dinner. They have to jam them in fast—only 118 days left to peddle the People's House."[2]

About three-quarters of the way through the campaign, Hillary finally began to get the hang of things. In part, aides attributed the turnaround to Hillary's considerable intelligence. Tony Bullock, Pat Moynihan's chief of staff, found that Hillary displayed an awesome ability to absorb complex information.

"She would call me to discuss the Brookhaven National Lab, the controversial Peace Bridge in Buffalo, and the Lake Onondaga pollution cleanup issue," Bullock said in an interview for this book. "She would get into these details, learn these issues, and then her audiences would be blown away by how she knew more than they did about their local issues."[3]

At the start of the campaign Hillary had come off poorly in small groups. Now, she seemed more at ease schmoozing potential donors.

"I was her table companion at dinner one night," said a committed Democrat. "She takes control as much as she can. She hates the media because she can't control them. But she also listens—she's a good listener, and her responses are thoughtful and discriminating. She doesn't come on with any cuteness, any feminine qualities. She's not taking advantage of being a woman. You could have the very same conversations you have with her with a man."[4]

But there was another explanation for Hillary's dramatic improvement as a campaigner: focus groups.

Ickes and company relied heavily on focus groups to shape the way they marketed their candidate. Gone was the left-wing Hillary, the gender feminist who sounded to many people like a radical bomb-thrower. In her place was the newly minted Hillary, a kinder, gentler, family-oriented candidate who championed such issues as children's mental health.

Elizabeth Moynihan had warned Hillary, "You can't run a campaign that looks and smells like a presidential campaign. You don't provide travel and hotels for the press. Let them fend for themselves. The most important reporter is not from *Time* and the other national media, but from the local New York State newspapers."[5]

Hillary took Liz's advice to heart.

"If she was sitting across the table from the board of editors of a Syracuse newspaper," said Tony Bullock, "she would know what the fuck she was talking about. She took a page out of Chuck Schumer's book, and campaigned like an animal in western New York."[6]

What's more, as part of their campaign strategy, Ickes and company confronted the frequently heard question: Why do people dislike Hillary so much?

Their answer: *a strong woman threatens men.*

Of course, it wasn't only men who disliked Hillary; she had

even more trouble winning the trust and support of white, suburban, college-educated women. Still, the notion advanced by Ickes and company that Hillary threatened *insecure men* was an effective ploy. It resonated with many successful women, who secretly worried that they, too, might intimidate their husbands, boyfriends, and male coworkers. Such women identified with Hillary, because they knew how hard it was to juggle career, family, and femininity.

Furthermore, Hillary's campaign managers accused her critics of using a double standard when they criticized her for being overly ambitious. Why should ambition be considered a virtue in men, but a vice in women? they asked. Why were boys encouraged to dream of growing up to become president, but girls were not? Why was ambition in Hillary any different than, say, ambition in Rudy Giuliani or, for that matter, in any male candidate?

These were all legitimate questions. But they totally missed the point. The objection that people had to Hillary was not that she was ambitious, or that she pursued power. Nowadays, people applauded powerful women in every field of endeavor—from Texas senator Kay Bailey Hutchison to Secretary of State Condoleezza Rice. Such women had *earned* their place in the sun.

Hillary, on the other hand, behaved as though she was *entitled* to power. She had been brought up by parents who taught her to believe that she was stronger, smarter, and better than everyone else. Her Methodist youth minister, Don Jones, reinforced her grandiose self-image by convincing her that she was doing God's work. It was Hillary's exaggerated sense of her own importance and her feelings of superiority—*not her gender*—that turned people off. People hesitated to vote for a woman like Hillary not because she was a woman, but because she acted as though she had a divine right to rule.

CHAPTER THIRTY-FOUR

"Pure Hollywood"

"**W**HERE'S PAT?"

That question—repeated over and over by the political reporters covering Hillary—became a constant refrain of the campaign.

"Why isn't Pat here supporting Hillary?" the reporters asked.

"He's coming," Hillary's press spokesman replied. "He's coming."

But Senator Daniel Patrick Moynihan didn't come. In fact, with the exception of one campaign commercial on Hillary's behalf, Pat Moynihan had been virtually invisible since the satellite trucks and television cameras left his farm at Pindars Corners several months before.

That did not come as much of a surprise to those who knew of Pat and Liz Moynihan's standoffish attitude toward Hillary. And yet, Ickes and company reacted to the Moynihan snub with panic. They had been counting on Moynihan to act as a counterweight to Hillary's opponent, Rudolph Giuliani. After all, Moynihan was popular with some of the same groups that made up Giuliani's base, especially Irish Americans and Italian Americans.

Even more important, Jews adored Pat Moynihan, and Hillary needed all the help she could get with Jewish voters. Indeed, when it was revealed that she had attended secret fund-raisers sponsored by Muslim groups, some of which were dedicated to the destruction of Israel, Hillary realized she had painted herself into a corner.[1]

Astute political observers detected the fingerprints of Bill Clinton on the campaign's Muslim strategy. They pointed out that one Muslim donor, Hani Masri, who helped raise $50,000 for Hillary's campaign, was simultaneously lobbying her husband the President for a $60 million government loan.[2]

That Hillary was courting radical Muslim groups did not remain secret for long. And when she showed up to march in the annual Israel Day Parade, the crowds roundly booed her. Worse, she was booed off the stage during a "Solidarity for Israel" rally at the Israeli consulate in New York.[3]

ON THE MORNING OF MAY 19, SHORTLY AFTER SHE WAS FORMALLY nominated as her party's standard-bearer, Hillary woke to discover that Pat Moynihan's usefulness had been radically diminished. For on that day—and with just six months to go until the election—Rudy Giuliani announced he had prostate cancer, and was bowing out of the race.

In Rudy's place, the Republican Party turned to a young Long Island congressman by the name of Rick Lazio. Though he was likable and telegenic, Lazio was never able to mount a campaign to match Hillary's.

"She'd fly into these little upstate towns aboard an Air Force plane, with this Secret Service entourage, and out steps the reigning First Lady," Lazio complained. "It was pure Hollywood."[4]

Nor did Lazio have time to develop an effective ground

game. He failed to show up at county fairs in upstate New York, and completely ignored direct mail. Instead, he spent all his resources on TV commercials and raising hard money.

Many of Lazio's managers came from out of state, and seemed more intent on running a hate campaign than a political campaign. They spent a lot of money running negative commercials against Hillary, even though her negative poll numbers were already as high as they were going to get. They did little to present a positive image of Lazio himself.

What's more, they seemed obsessed with Hillary's ready access to soft money. But instead of trying to keep up with her on the soft-money front, they attempted to shame Hillary into agreeing to bar soft money in the campaign.

Of course, Hillary made all the appropriate noises about the toxic effects of soft money on politics. Meanwhile, her Machiavellian campaign manager, Harold Ickes, was raising soft money as fast as he could.

Hillary's aides were not above dealing in some underhanded tactics. In June, one of Harold Ickes's closest political cronies in New York, Comptroller H. Carl McCall, used his official letterhead to write to the Securities and Exchange Commission to request an investigation of a stock transaction by Rick Lazio. Simultaneously, McCall released the letter to the *New York Times*. (Lazio was subsequently cleared of any wrongdoing.)[5]

Thrown on the defensive, Lazio entered the first of three candidates' debates with an ill-conceived plan to embarrass Hillary. When it came his turn to answer moderator Tim Russert's question, Lazio left his podium, walked across to Hillary Clinton, and waved a piece of paper in her face.

"You say you are against soft money," Lazio said. "Will you sign this pledge not to use soft money in this campaign?"

Hillary refused, and many of the women watching the debate on television recoiled at Lazio's bullying tactics, which reminded them of their husbands' or boyfriends' overbearing behavior during a fight. Lazio, they felt, had invaded "Hillary's space."

After that debate, Hillary's transformation from political troublemaker into sympathetic victim was complete. Her supporters flocked to the polls, and on election night in November 2000, she won by a landslide—55 percent to Lazio's 43 percent.

She was now *Senator-elect* Hillary Rodham Clinton. Her husband was soon to be *former president* Bill Clinton. After nearly three decades of playing a supporting role for Bill, it was now Hillary's turn to step into the political spotlight.

PART V

The Road Back to the White House

CHAPTER THIRTY-FIVE

The "Phenom"

THE REVEREND DON JONES, A HEAVYSET, BALDING MAN now well into his sixties, peered down from the packed gallery of the U.S. Senate. Below, he spotted Hillary Rodham Clinton, his onetime Methodist youth group student, being escorted by New York's senior senator, Chuck Schumer, from her seat in the back row of the chamber to the well of the Senate.[1]

She was dressed for the occasion in a turquoise pantsuit, which made her a conspicuous figure (as if she wasn't already one) in the sea of dark-suited men.[2] She raised her right hand, and took the oath administered by the presiding officer of the Senate, Vice President Al Gore, who was still bitter over his loss of the White House to George W. Bush, a defeat that he blamed in no small part on Hillary.*

---

*Actually, Gore reproached both Bill and Hillary. He blamed Bill because the lingering stench of the Lewinsky scandal had turned off many people who might otherwise have voted for the Gore-

"Congratulations, *Senator*," Gore told Hillary.

In the gallery, Don Jones and Dorothy Rodham beamed with pride. Hillary's father, who had died several years before, wasn't around to wisecrack that the Senate must be an easy place to get into if it admitted his daughter.

Only three years before, at the height of the Monica Lewinsky scandal, many people had predicted that Hillary and her husband were washed up politically. But rather than allow that near-death experience to destroy her, Hillary had turned it to her advantage by casting herself as a sympathetic victim and national martyr.

"Hillary's gone from a completely derivative role to nonderivative role," said a former White House staff member. "In Washington, 'First Lady' has never really been taken that seriously. 'Senator' has. She's not trying to construct something from nothing."[3]

BUT SOME THINGS NEVER CHANGED. AND EVEN AS SHE WAS RECITING the oath of office, Hillary was once again at the center of an ethical storm. Just weeks before she became a senator, she had signed a controversial $8 million book contract with Simon & Schuster.

The deal dismayed even her most enthusiastic fans. It was, said the *New York Times*'s editorial page, "an affront to common sense. No lawmaker should accept a large, unearned sum from a publisher whose parent company, Viacom, is vitally interested in government policy on issues likely to come before Congress—for example, copyright or broadcasting legislation."[4]

Greed seemed to be the only explanation for the outlandish

Lieberman ticket. He faulted Hillary for siphoning off millions of dollars in contributions from outside New York State, which, he felt, should have gone to his campaign.

book deal. And greed was a motivating factor behind two other ill-considered moves by Hillary—to register like a bride for gifts for her newly acquired homes in Chappaqua, New York, and Washington, D.C., and to strip the White House of hundreds of thousands of dollars' worth of furniture.

A twenty-six-foot-long moving van was backed up to the White House and loaded with valuable furnishings—two sofas, an iron-and-glass coffee table, an ottoman, a painted TV armoire, a custom wood gaming table, and a wicker center table with a wood top. Much of the furniture had been acquired by Hillary's interior decorator, Kaki Hockersmith, for the 1993 redecoration project, and therefore legally belonged to the government, not the Clintons. When the media blew the whistle on the Clintons, they reluctantly agreed to return some of the items to the White House.[5]

No sooner had Hillary finished taking the oath and signed her name in the Senate register than she was approached by an unlikely pair—Senate Republican leader Trent Lott of Mississippi, who had helped lead the effort to impeach her husband, and Strom Thurmond, the randy, ninety-eight-year-old southern segregationist, who was the Senate's senior member.

"Can I hug you?" Thurmond asked.

Before Hillary could reply, Thurmond had enveloped her in a bear hug, and was slobbering nonagenarian kisses on her cheek.[6] Other senators followed suit, and soon Hillary was the center of a crowd of lawmakers, many of them Republicans, thumping her on the back, pumping her hand, and kissing her.

"Yes," wrote Alison Mitchell in the *New York Times*, "there have been Senate celebrities before: Bill Bradley, the Rhodes scholar who played for the Knicks; John Glenn, the modest astronaut. But Mrs. Clinton is a phenom the likes of which the staid Senate has rarely if ever seen. . . ."[7]

Along with the President, Chelsea, Dorothy Rodham, and Don Jones, Hillary trooped over to the Old Senate Chamber for a reenactment of the swearing-in ceremony. This was a hallowed tradition, permitting the recently elected and reelected senators to pose for photos that were not allowed in the Senate chamber.

As a junior senator ranked ninety-seventh out of one hundred in seniority, Hillary would normally have had to wait her turn. But she was the only senator who had a full-time Secret Service escort, and as a result, she was whisked to the head of the line for the photo op with Chelsea, who held a Bible as the flashbulbs lit up the plush, velvet-draped chamber.

That afternoon, there was a reception for Hillary in the Dirksen Senate Office Building, followed by a party at Washington's Mayflower Hotel, which was sponsored by none other than Walter Kaye, the New York insurance mogul who had used his influence to get Monica Lewinsky an intern's job at the White House.

"In a way, it felt like the last of the '90s," wrote a journalist who was present at the Mayflower shindig. "There were really smart young women, interesting New Yorkers, loud liberals, fashionable eyewear, gay guys, Harry Connick songs piped in—you know, that jazzy, idealistic hyperdiversity-land where we all used to live—and lots of juicy salmon on serving trays. . . . Walter Kaye . . . took the podium and pronounced the crowd to be 'bigger than my bar mitzvah.' "[8]

"It was a wonderful round of parties," recalled Don Jones. "My old student Rick Ricketts [Hillary's grammar school playmate] was there as well. He told me he was staying in the Lincoln Bedroom. . . .

"I said, 'What's the deal with that?' or something to that effect," Don Jones continued, unable to disguise his feelings of jealousy. "The remark was apparently overheard by one of Hillary's staffers, because a few minutes later I was told I'd be staying in the Queen's Bedroom, which while not as famous as the Lincoln, is actually quite a bit better."9

Commenting on Hillary's first day as a senator, another Clinton insider said: "Hillary's mother, Dorothy, had one of the pithiest takes on what Hillary had been through. She commented, 'You can never trust a man with an erection.'

"As to the question of whether Bill will continue to have sexual relations—or whatever he wants to call them—with another woman, I believe that if it happened again and became public, Hillary would leave him.

"Look, let's not kid ourselves. Hillary is aware that some of her base supporters were very disappointed that she chose to stay with Bill. And she doesn't want to be seen as a doormat. That would be devastating to her image."10

Given Hillary's White House ambitions, that seemed like a reasonable conclusion. But then, one had to ask: when had Hillary ever acted reasonably when it came to Bill Clinton?

No one could predict how the relationship between *Senator* Clinton and soon-to-be *ex-president* Clinton would differ, if at all, from their previous relationship. As a result, the gossip regarding their arrangements started all over again.

Would Bill and Hill live mostly together or mostly apart?

Would Bill's new freedom encourage him to indulge his sexual appetites more than before?

Would Hillary rely on private detectives—instead of Evelyn Lieberman—to keep an eye on Bill?

Could Hillary leave Bill and still become president?

CHAPTER THIRTY-SIX

"The Perfect Student"

"Hillary walks across the room—and the cameras go *click, click, click*," Representative Anthony Weiner, a Brooklyn Democrat, told a reporter. "Hillary pours herself coffee—*click, click, click*. She sits down again—*click, click, click*. It was a sign of what she was up against, and she knew it. There were a lot of people who wanted to say she was in too much of a hurry...."[1]

These people predicted that Hillary would repeat the bullheaded blunders in the Senate that she had made in the White House. Even her supporters were worried; they wondered if she could adjust to the courteous, collegial atmosphere of the Senate, which was run like a men's club.

Hillary, they said, using the jargon of politics, did not have "soft hands."

What these skeptics failed to take into account, however, was that Hillary had been reared in a household where her parents and brothers treated her like one of the boys. The men's club atmosphere of the Senate would not feel unfamiliar to a woman who had been playing with males—and beating them at their own game—all her life.

Nor did Hillary's friends and enemies understand that she had been tested and tempered by the hardships of the White House. They overlooked the fact that the Monica Lewinsky scandal and Bill Clinton's impeachment in the House of Representatives had taught Hillary a valuable lesson: in order to survive in public life, she had to build political coalitions.

Contrary to expectations, therefore, Hillary had no intention of charging into the Senate as if she owned the place. She knew she had to dispel the notion that, as a former First Lady, she would try to dominate the Senate. She also knew that her fellow senators were not going to give her a long honeymoon.

SHE PREPARED FOR HER NEW ROLE IN HER USUAL METHODICAL manner. To begin with, she asked a number of White House aides to conduct tutorials for her on the customs and practices of the Senate.

"During the White House years, West Wing staffers who worked for her husband were known by her staff as the 'White Boys,' and she treated them with cool distance," wrote John F. Harris of the *Washington Post*. "Starting last winter, she called those same West Wingers, the ones with knowledge of the Senate, into the White House residence for skull sessions."[2]

Her principal tutor was White House chief of staff John Podesta, an old hand on Capitol Hill, where he had worked as counselor to Senator Thomas Daschle, the Democratic leader. Podesta's tutorials were supplemented by his chief of congressional relations, Pat Griffin, who had learned the Senate ropes as an aide to Robert C. Byrd of West Virginia, widely considered to be the greatest living student of Senate procedures and protocol.

With the assistance of Podesta and Griffin (and with some kibitzing from the sidelines from her politically savvy husband),

Hillary devised a plan for her first couple of years in the Senate. In her personal conduct, she decided to model herself after Lyndon Baines Johnson, whose rapid ascent in the Senate was smoothed by his deference to such powerful mentors as Georgia's Richard Russell.

In her legislative role, Hillary modeled herself after Massachusetts's Edward Kennedy. Despite his outmoded liberalism, which had pushed him to the margins of American politics, Kennedy was respected by his colleagues for the work of his top-flight staff.

TO THE SURPRISE OF MANY, HILLARY TURNED OUT TO BE MORE than equal to the task of winning friends on both sides of the aisle. Like a major-league pitcher, she kept a mental playbook on the strengths and weaknesses of each of her ninety-nine Senate colleagues, and she pitched each of them in a unique way.

Republicans Orrin Hatch, Kay Bailey Hutchison, and Don Nickles all fell under Hillary's spell during prayer breakfasts conducted by the Senate chaplain, Dr. Lloyd Ogilvie, an evangelical Presbyterian minister.[3] But her biggest catch was a Democrat, Senator Robert Byrd, who was no friend of Bill Clinton, and had once referred to the President's actions as "malodorous."[4]

"After a decisive vote," wrote Gail Sheehy, "[Hillary] makes a beeline for Robert Byrd, the white-domed icon of the Senate, who inevitably will be standing with one arm tucked into his silk vest and the other planted on his desk, Daniel Webster–style. The former First Lady will bow her head and virtually genuflect before him."[5]

"I had seen her a few times through a glass darkly, as the Scripture says," Byrd told a reporter. "I would say she did not necessarily start out as one of my favorites, if I might use that term. But she is one of my favorites now, because I like her approach. I like her sincerity. I like her convictions . . . I think she has been the perfect student."[6]

Senators liked working with Hillary's staff, which did not big-foot around.[7] Her top aide was Chief of Staff Tamera Luzzatto, a savvy Senate insider who had fifteen years of experience working for Senator Jay Rockefeller as his legislative director and chief of staff. The new senator earned kudos from all quarters, even from those conservative Republicans, like South Carolina's Lindsey Graham, who had been in the forefront of the House impeachment of her husband, and who eventually replaced the deceased Strom Thurmond in the Senate.

"People will attribute motives to her on anything she does," Graham said. "I feel sympathetic to her situation as a junior member with such a high-profile status. It's hard because people get jealous. She has handled this better than I think anyone expected."[8]

"Hillary has demonstrated a stunning flair for bipartisanship," wrote the political reporter Jennifer Senior in *New York* magazine. "In just four years, she's managed to co-sponsor a bill with nearly every legislator who, at one time or another, professed to hate her guts.

"With Tom DeLay . . . she collaborated on an initiative concerning foster children. With Don Nickles, the former Oklahoma senator who breezily speculated in 1996 that Hillary would be indicted, she worked on a bill to extend jobless benefits. With Mississippi senator Trent Lott, who wondered aloud whether lightning might strike her before she arrived at the Senate, she worked on legislation to help low-income pregnant women. A Reuters story from April 2003 noted she'd already sponsored bills with more than 36 Republican senators."[9]

Some senators professed to detect the emergence of a kinder, gentler Hillary. They noted that she never criticized President

George W. Bush. She even gushed over the inspiring leadership of her New York archenemy, former mayor Rudolph Giuliani.

During her first year in the Senate, no one saw the other side of Hillary Clinton's face, which she kept carefully hidden behind a mask of collegiality. That other face belonged to the combative pugilist from the suburban streets of Park Ridge, Illinois.

"Giuliani will screw you *every time!*" she hissed in private, even as she was lauding the ex-mayor in public.[10]

Asked by a reporter how she thought the American people would react to the attack on the World Trade Center and the Pentagon now that they were on "the receiving end of a murderous anger,"[11] Hillary let her façade slip, and gave vent to all her self-pity and narcissism.

"Oh, I am well aware that it is out there," she said. "One of the most difficult experiences that I personally had in the White House was during the health-care debate, being the object of extraordinary rage. I remember being in Seattle. I was there to make a speech about health care. This was probably August of '94. Radio talk-show hosts had urged their listeners to come out and yell and scream and carry on and prevent people from hearing me speak. There were threats that were coming in, and certain people didn't want me to speak, and they started taking weapons off people, and arresting people. I've had firsthand looks at this unreasoning anger and hatred that is focused on an individual you don't know, a cause that you despised—whatever motivates people."[12]

As always with Hillary, it was all about her.

CHAPTER THIRTY-SEVEN

Where's Waldo?

S HE HARDLY SAW BILL ANYMORE.
The former president dismissed gossip that he and his wife were, for all intents and purposes, leading separate lives. He insisted that they usually spent three or four nights a week together—one night at their $2.85 million Georgian mansion off Washington's Embassy Row, and weekends at their $1.7 million New York residence in Chappaqua.

But since they were rarely seen—and almost never photographed—together, no one bought Bill's story of togetherness. Not even Hillary.

Once, during an appearance before a gay rights group, Hillary was asked what she thought of her husband's sexy new slimmed-down look.

"The next time you see him," she quipped, "tell him I noticed."[1]

"He's not here [in Washington] very often," confessed one of her aides. "*Her* scheduler stays in contact with *his* scheduler."[2]

There was talk inside Hillary's camp that Bill was up to his old tricks. He certainly had plenty of opportunity. While Hillary was mastering the Senate, he was on the road, traveling an average of twenty-five days a month, giving speeches at up to $300,000 a pop and plugging his book, *My Life*. For the first time since Bill's disastrous first term as governor of Arkansas, Hillary was too busy with her own career to play housemother to her bad-boy husband.

"It's like that game Where's Waldo?" Hillary said when questioned about her husband's whereabouts. "Let's see. It's 11:20 A.M. on a Thursday morning. You know where he is right now? He's in Africa."[3]

In the past, the Clintons' peculiar relationship had been charitably described as a marriage of convenience. But now it was not even that. It was more like a marriage of *inconvenience* in which the trajectories of their lives had radically diverged.

After months of following the former president around for a story in *Vanity Fair*, Robert Sam Anson reported what many people had suspected: Bill Clinton was up to no good. Wrote Anson:

"He's ... chatted up the openly bisexual British beauty Saffron Burrows at the bar of the Hudson Hotel in Manhattan (she said he was amused to learn that she once fancied Hillary); lunched with model Naomi Campbell at a mountaintop restaurant in Austria ... ; had a late-night encounter with former New Zealand talk-show host Charlotte Dawson in Aukland ... ; taken in the Preakness with blonde billionaire Canadian businesswoman Belinda Stronach ... ; and, according to the *Globe*, been a reputed cause for the split of Seagram heir Matthew Bronfman from Canadian heiress Lisa Belzberg. ..."[4]

It was not only the supermarket tabloid *Globe* that linked Bill Clinton to the Bronfman split-up; so did Nigel Dempster, the gossip columnist of the London *Daily Mail*; Blair Golson in the *New York Observer*; George Rush and Joanna Molly in the *New York Daily News*; the *New York Post*; and *Newsweek*.[5]

Bill spent as much time as he could in Los Angeles, and Hillary grew concerned that he was hanging out with the wrong people in La La Land. One of his new buddies was Jason Binn, the thirty-six-year-old publisher of such glossy upscale magazines as *Hamptons* and *Los Angeles Confidential*. Binn always seemed to be surrounded by a fast crowd of starlets and models, including Heidi Klum. Another pal was Jeffrey Epstein, a money manager with his own custom-fitted 727, a private island off St. Thomas, and an endless supply of Victoria Secret–grade models to go around.[6]

Hillary's aides noticed that Bill seemed to grow even more reckless after his memoir, *My Life*, became a big best seller. Thanks to his record-shattering $12 million book advance plus another $10 million in speaking fees, he was rolling in money—and hubris.

Throwing caution to the wind, he started a torrid affair with a stunning divorcée in her early forties, who lived near the Clintons in Chappaqua. There was nothing discreet about the way he conducted this illicit relationship; he often spent the night at his lover's home, while his Secret Service agents waited in a car parked at the end of her driveway.[7]

"It's one thing to go out to California with his wild buddies and do stuff there," said someone with intimate knowledge of the former president's philandering. "But being indiscreet with a woman in Chappaqua steps over the line. That's the place Hillary calls home."[8]

Though it was an open secret among reporters that Bill was sexually out of control, the mainstream media stayed clear of the story. Perhaps it was Clinton Fatigue. Perhaps it was liberal bias. Whatever it was, the spotlight had shifted away from Bill to Hillary.

CHAPTER THIRTY-EIGHT

The 800-Pound Gorilla

SHE LOOKED DIFFERENT NOW—MORE THE WAY SHE DID WHEN she was a frumpy Yale Law student than when she was a glammed-up First Lady.

She stopped wearing pastel pantsuits and adopted black as her noncolor color. Her hair, which Isabelle Goetz used to tease into a mighty blonde helmet, à la Britain's Maggie Thatcher, hung limp around her temples. She was too intent on servicing her constituents back home and too focused on fetching coffee for her male colleagues in the Senate to take time out for such frivolous matters as personal grooming.

She put in twelve- to fourteen-hour days.[1] She trudged along the broad hallways on Capitol Hill, her low-heeled shoes echoing off the hard marble floor, a cell phone stuck in her ear, a sheaf of documents tucked under her arm. She attended one interminable committee meeting after another, stifling yawns of boredom. She was willing to take on any assignment, and won the Senate's Golden Gavel Award for presiding over that body (usually when it was nearly empty) more than one hundred hours.[2]

She was a woman in perpetual motion. All of this activity exacerbated her chronic lymphedema, and the swelling in her legs, ankles, and feet grew worse, and sometimes made it painful for her to walk. According to people who visited her in her office, she looked like a zombie—baggy-eyed, gray-skinned, zoned out for lack of sleep.

Her large L-shaped suite on the fourth floor of the Russell Senate Office Building had once belonged to her predecessor, Daniel Patrick Moynihan. Now, the furniture, wallpaper, carpeting, and curtains all reeked of Kaki Hockersmith.

One day, Pat Moynihan dropped by for a visit. He had lost more weight and looked sickly. (He would be dead by the spring of 2003.) He glanced around his old office, and remarked wryly:

"The place looks a lot more yellow."[3]

YELLOW WAS ALSO THE DOMINANT COLOR SCHEME AT Whitehaven, the stately brick mansion near Washington's Embassy Row that served as Hillary's White House in exile. For the job of decorating Whitehaven, Hillary passed over Tacky Kaki and picked the firm of Brown-Davis Interiors, which had recently renovated the British embassy. *Architectural Digest* ranked Brown-Davis as among the top one hundred interior designers and architects in America.[4]

When guests arrived at Whitehaven for one of Hillary's fund-raisers, they stepped through a red door into a foyer with stenciled floors. There, they were greeted by a battalion of neatly dressed staffers and escorted directly outdoors to a tent in the garden, where they joined other donors and white-coated waiters. No one was allowed to wander around the house; if they had, they might have noticed that, among all the silver-framed photos, there were no recent pictures of Hillary with Bill.[5]

Hillary sometimes produced back-to-back fund-raisers on

the same night. In her first twenty-two months in office, she held forty-six fund-raisers at Whitehaven, an unheard-of pace.[6]

Donors who were rich enough to pony up $25,000 were treated to private little dinners with Hillary herself. Several couples were ushered into Whitehaven's large dining room, where they were seated in yellow chairs with pink backs.[7] Hillary—usually the only married person at the table without a spouse—presided from the head of the table.

These dinners reminded some old-timers of the days back in the 1980s and early 1990s when the late Pamela Harriman held court at *her* Washington mansion. Like Pamela, Hillary turned her home into the Democratic Party's Fund-Raising Central.

Of course, she had the perfect teacher: Bill Clinton had brought political fund-raising to an art form. The excesses perpetrated by Harold Ickes in the President's name had led to the campaign-finance scandals of the 1996 election. But Hillary kept Ickes on as her fund-raiser-in-chief.

Despite the effort she and Ickes put into fund-raising, money was really never a problem for Hillary. Thanks to an organization called Friends of Hillary, she could easily raise all the funds she needed for her own 2006 Senate reelection campaign. Hillary and Ickes spent most of their energy raising money for *other* Democrats.

"She can give $10,000 to a candidate through her multimillion-dollar leadership political action committee, HILLPAC," noted a leading expert on the campaign-finance laws, "but if she has a fund-raiser at her home, she can raise hundreds of thousands of dollars in one night for a Democratic candidate. No one can do that as effectively as she can. Who isn't going to show up if Hillary Clinton invites you to her home?

"That's what makes Hillary different from other Democrats," this person continued. "And that's the key to her strategy over the next few years. She's putting Democrats all over America in her debt, building relationships, establishing a firm control over the machinery of the state parties outside New York."[8]

By 2003, Hillary had replaced Bill Clinton as her party's most sought-after fund-raiser.[9] And she accomplished that by imitating Bill's three-pronged approach to raising money: Hollywood celebrities, liberal businessmen, and female activists.[10]

"She's more of a star than the other 99 of us combined," said Senator Mark Dayton of Minnesota, a Democratic recipient of Hillary's generosity.[11]

The fine hand of Harold Ickes could be detected behind Hillary's money-raising activities. As Eliza Newlin Carney wrote in the *National Journal*:

"The ethical problems that earned the Clintons such notoriety at the White House may come to dog Hillary Clinton's massive fundraising operation, particularly as it attracts more scrutiny. As a candidate in 2000 and as a senator, Clinton has moved vast sums of money around in a complicated array of interlocking and sometimes controversial campaign accounts—leadership PACs, nonfederal accounts, joint committees with the Democratic Senatorial Campaign Committee. . . .

"The 2002 campaign finance law has unquestionably drained the major party committees of both cash and influence. The new power centers are now outside interest groups and individual officeholders, such as [Hillary] Clinton, who can motivate low-dollar donors by virtue of their ideological appeal or their celebrity. With its vast staff budget, and campaign coffers, Clinton's political organization has begun to assume a quasi-party status."[12]

THUS, HILLARY EMERGED AS THE 800-POUND GORILLA IN HER party. A Quinnipiac University poll put her ahead of the entire field of candidates for the 2004 Democratic presidential nomination.

"If she even let herself be talked about seriously, she'd be the one to beat among the Democrats [in 2004] and she could raise zillions of dollars," said Quinnipiac pollster Maurice Carroll. "I can't figure out who in the bunch of them could beat her."[13]

Bill Clinton was eager for Hillary to throw her hat into the ring, and he used all his powers of persuasion to make his wife run for the nomination in 2004. They argued about it endlessly, but Hillary decided to pass on *that* race in the belief that a) she needed more time to establish a record, and b) George W. Bush was unbeatable as a wartime president. Instead, she decided the time had come for her to move into the second stage of her Senate career.

"She spent the first two years in a learning process . . . not only the rules of the Senate, but the traditions of how things should be handled here," said Senator John Breaux of Louisiana, a moderate Democrat. "She was very careful and more restricted. Now she's moving into a second stage, being more out front, more visible and more available to articulate issues."[14]

CHAPTER THIRTY-NINE

"So Hillary"

"It must have been springtime, because I remember not wearing a coat when we flew down to Washington to see Hillary."[1]

The speaker was a stylish New York woman in her late fifties. A lifelong do-gooder, she had brought a group of ten Latina women activists to the nation's capital to lobby Senator Clinton on behalf of minority children.

The women expected a sympathetic hearing. After all, Hillary had once chaired the left-leaning Children's Defense Fund, and she was still on friendly terms with the organization's militant founder, Marian Wright Edelman.

When the women were ushered into the senator's private office, they found her sitting there with an aide. She looked like the old Hillary. As part of her new higher-profile strategy, she had discarded her somber black pantsuit look in favor of a brighter, more telegenic color. Judging from her chic hair-do, Isabelle Goetz, the stylist from Salon Cristophe, was back on the case. The skin on Hillary's face was pulled tight, as though she had recently had a Botox treatment. As indeed she had.

"She's been Botoxed to the hilt," said a New York physician who had knowledge of such matters.[2]

Most of the women in the delegation had voted for Hillary because they believed her when she had promised during the Senate campaign to take care of poor inner-city children. True, the women knew you couldn't always count on the Clintons' keeping their word. For instance, they had been bitterly disappointed when then-president Clinton announced he was going to sign a welfare-reform bill requiring people on assistance to go out and find work. Up until the last moment, the women had been optimistic that Marian Wright Edelman could convince Hillary—her protégée from Yale and the Children's Defense Fund—to stop her husband from signing the bill into law.

"Hillary," Marian Wright Edelman had said at the time, "will never let this happen."[3]

But not only did Hillary let it happen; she even refused to meet with her mentor, Marian Wright Edelman. Instead, Hillary used George Stephanopoulos to carry word to welfare advocates all over America that the First Lady could do nothing to change her husband's mind.

Nonetheless, after Hillary became a senator—with all the power that implied—Marian Wright Edelman recognized the need to patch up their friendship. To those who inquired about the new senator's intentions, Marian Wright Edelman assured them not to worry; Hillary was still a committed liberal.

"Hillary's heart," said Marian Wright Edelman, "is in the right place."[4]

THAT, HOWEVER, REMAINED TO BE SEEN.

Hillary offered the women a choice of coffee, tea, or water, and then opened the floor for discussion. The well-dressed leader of the group was the first to speak up.

"From the time you were chair of the board of the Children's Defense Fund," she said, "we were led to believe that you would do anything in your power to push through legislation to help children. And we were encouraged when you introduced legislation to reauthorize the Child Care Bill. But then you backed off it, and we are having a difficult time with that."

"The reason I backed off," Hillary replied a bit testily, "is that the bill was never going to pass."

"All the bill asks for is $11 billion, over a five-year period, for child care across America," one of the women pointed out. "That's lunch money in the federal budget. Right now, one out of seven children is covered. We're only asking to increase that to two out of seven."

"It's not going to fly," Hillary said firmly. "I'm not going to spend my political capital on something that's doomed before it starts."

"We *want* you to spend your capital whether you win or not," the leader of the group said. "That's how you'll get this into the public arena so people can understand there is a problem. If it was Ted Kennedy, he'd stand on what he believes."

Hillary bristled at the invidious comparison between her and Ted Kennedy. And as the conversation grew more heated, the women began to suspect that Hillary's agenda was not what Marian Wright Edelman had led them to expect.[5]

"If Hillary's only ambition was to be a liberal senator from New York," one of the women recalled, "she would gladly have gone down in defeat. But that wasn't her only ambition. She was clearly taking care of her legislative record so that, when she runs for president, no one could accuse her of being a crazy leftist."[6]

What had happened to that "crazy leftist"—the Hillary of yore?

Where had Miss *motive* Magazine of 1965 gone?

What about Miss Black Panther of 1971?

Not to mention Miss Health-Care Reform of 1993?

The answer came crashing down on the women as they realized that Hillary had turned her back on her past—*and them*—and was feverishly repositioning herself as a moderate centrist.

All the signs were there.

Hillary had persuaded Tom Daschle, the Democratic Senate leader, to appoint her as head of the party's steering and coordination committee, a position that gave her a role in shaping the party's message.

Hillary was instrumental in starting a think tank called the Center for American Progress, a "New Democratic" version of the conservative Heritage Foundation. The center would function as Hillary's instrument to help move the Democratic Party toward the center.

Hillary gave up her seat on the powerful Senate Budget Committee in exchange for a less prestigious one on the Senate Armed Services Committee. As a woman and a notoriously left-wing Democrat, she needed all the credentials she could get to prove she was solid on military matters and national security.

Hillary voted to authorize the war in Iraq, and, in the words of William Safire, she "startled her conservative detractors by emerging as a congenital hawk."[7]*

The delegation of New York women was startled, too.

"I think Hillary's ambition simply got the better of her," the leader of the group said, "and that she will do anything to get to the White House, including dropping child care."[9]

---

*Safire was playing on words; he had once called Hillary a "congenital liar."[8]

Suddenly, in the middle of the conversation, Hillary got up from her chair.

"If you don't understand my position," she told the women, "there is nothing more to say. I have other people waiting.... *Good-bye!*"[10]

And with that, she strode out of the room in a huff.

"We had supported her, raised money for her, and there we were with our jaws on our toes," said the group's leader. "It was so high-handed, so arrogant . . . so Hillary."[11]

CHAPTER FORTY

Hillary from Chappaqua

IT WAS SHORTLY AFTER TEN O'CLOCK ON A COLD DECEMBER morning, and Hillary Clinton was just finishing a late breakfast in the glassed-in sunroom of her home at 15 Old House Lane in Chappaqua. She was drinking a cup of decaffeinated coffee and listening to *The Brian Lehrer Show* on public radio station WNYC.

Hillary knew that Lehrer planned to devote most of his popular call-in talk show to her emergence as the most popular figure in the Democratic Party. The previous month, she had emceed a Democratic dinner in Iowa, the site of the first-in-the-nation presidential caucuses, and she had blown away all nine of her party's presidential wannabes.

To drive home the point that she was a political giant in a party of midgets, she invited a small army of print and television reporters to accompany her on her first overseas trip as a U.S. Senator. She flew to Afghanistan to share Thanksgiving dinner with American servicemen and -women and, while on tour, met with prime ministers, generals, and diplomats. She then returned home to a public-relations trifecta—appearing on all three Sunday morning network television news shows on the same day.

"In the last several weeks," the *New York Times* noted, "it has been all Mrs. Clinton almost all the time."[1]

Almost—but not quite.

As things turned out, while Hillary was in Afghanistan, President Bush upstaged her with his own unannounced Thanksgiving trip to Iraq. When she was informed by an aide traveling with her in Kabul that the President had unexpectedly turned up in Baghdad, Hillary snapped: "Son of a bitch!"[2]

But George W. Bush was the least of Hillary's worries. Her decision not to run for the 2004 nomination left a power vacuum in the Democratic Party that had been filled by her least-favorite candidate—Howard Dean. Almost overnight, the former governor of Vermont had become the darling of the antiwar wing of the party. As the 2004 primary season approached, Dean had taken a commanding lead in the polls and was poised to capture the nomination.

It was Hillary's firm belief that an antiwar candidate like Dean had about as much chance of winning the White House as had George McGovern, who was buried in a Republican landslide in 1972. Most political analysts assumed that Hillary would be pleased by a Dean defeat, since that would give her an unobstructed shot at the presidency in 2008.

But Hillary did not see it that way. In her view, Howard Dean's very *nomination* posed a major threat to her power over the Democratic Party. Unlike John Kerry and the other candidates, Dean was not dependent on the traditional Democratic money pool controlled by Bill and Hillary Clinton. His financial base was on the Internet, where he raised funds from hundreds of thousands of small donors.* If Hillary was going to hold on to the reins of the Democratic Party for the next four years, she had to stop Dean and his army of young, Internet-savvy volunteers from capturing the nomination.

With that in mind, she huddled with Bill Clinton and her other top advisers and devised a two-pronged strategy aimed at maintaining her claim to the future leadership of the party. On the one hand, she would do everything in her power to prop up John Kerry or some other Democrat as an alternative to Dean. At the same time, she would position herself as representing a broad spectrum in the party—from left to right.

To outflank Dean on the left, Hillary launched a withering attack on the Bush administration for its "ruinous policies":[4] alienating traditional allies in Europe; granting "no-bid contracts to the likes of Halliburton";[5] failing to put enough boots on the ground in Iraq; supporting Israel's security fence; running up a huge national deficit; underfunding public schools; and stinting on unemployment benefits.

At the same time, she appealed to the moderates in her party by emerging as a full-fledged hawk, who favored a "tough-minded and muscular foreign and defense policy."[6]

"When Tim Russert on *Meet the Press* gave her the opening to say she had been misled when she voted for the Senate resolution authorizing war," wrote William Safire, "Senator Clinton countered with a hard line: 'There was certainly adequate intelligence, without it being gilded and exaggerated by the administration, to raise questions about chemical and biological programs and a continuing effort to obtain nuclear weapons.' . . .

"Her range of expressed opinions urging us to 'stay the

---

*As of November 30, 2004, Howard Dean had received 97 percent of his campaign contributions from individual contributors.[3]

course,'" Safire concluded, "can only be characterized as tough-minded."[7]

Not everyone agreed.

Indeed, even as Hillary was finishing her breakfast of bran flakes, a listener to *The Brian Lehrer Show* was impugning her credibility as a hawk.

FORTY MILES SOUTH OF CHAPPAQUA, BRIAN LEHRER SAT IN A windowless studio in the Municipal Building in lower Manhattan. It was from these same studios that Fiorello La Guardia, the legendary mayor of New York City, had famously read the funnies during a newspaper strike in the midst of the Great Depression.

Lehrer was a veteran broadcaster, who had hosted his own show for the past fifteen years. Under his big, padded earphones, he was the picture of casual composure in an open-necked shirt and a closely cropped salt-and-pepper beard.

Each week, Lehrer did a segment called "Monday Morning Politics," in which he and a guest journalist analyzed the previous Sunday's network talk shows. Today, his guest was Jodie Allen, the managing editor of *U.S. News and World Report*.

He and Jodie Allen had just taken a call from a listener who complained that Tim Russert had failed to ask Hillary an important question on *Meet the Press*: how could anyone take Hillary seriously as a hawk when she had established a policy barring military personnel from wearing their uniforms in the White House?

". . . And the . . . no, wait a minute, I'm getting a flash from the screening room here," Lehrer told his listening audience.

His producer, Nuala McGovern, was talking in his earphone.

"You're not going to believe this," McGovern said into Lehrer's earphone, "but Hillary Clinton is on the phone."

In his fifteen years on the air, this had never happened to Lehrer. Neither Senator Pat Moynihan nor Senator Alfonse D'Amato nor Senator Chuck Schumer had ever called into his show in response to something that someone had said about them.

"Guess what?" Lehrer told his listeners once he had recovered from his shock. "After a half hour of talking about Senator Hillary Clinton, she's calling in. So let's welcome her. Senator Clinton, are you there?"

"I am there, Brian," said Hillary. "How are you?"

"Okay, thank you for calling," Lehrer said. "Were you listening?"

"I always listen whenever I can," Hillary replied, "and I was listening, and I want to say 'Hello' to Jodie Allen as well as you, and I also wanted a chance to respond to the gentleman who called in and said, Oh, he wished someone had asked me that question about some alleged policy in the beginning of the Clinton Administration. So I thought I would take him up on his offer and call in and respond to the charges that he made."

"All right now," Lehrer said, "we're coming to a break. We have to take sixty seconds. But why don't you go ahead and start, and then we'll finish after the break? Did you ban uniforms on people from the military in the White House?"

"Of course not," Hillary said. "Now I know that there were some stories that circulated early in the administration that some young staffer had said something critical to someone in uniform. We tried to chase that down. I never could, to my satisfaction, determine who had done it, if it had indeed been done. And I also think part of it was, as you recall, my husband's efforts, very early on in the administration, to lift the ban on gay military service people. . . ."

"Senator," Lehrer interrupted, "hold it right there. We have to take that break. And we'll finish up with you after that."[8]

* * *

"I WAS SURPRISED THAT SHE WAS CALLING IN TO TAKE ISSUE WITH the caller," Lehrer recalled in an interview for this book. "I thought it was a relatively small-bore thing that she was calling about.... And I thought that one of the things that she was trying to do in that phone call was to set herself up as the ecumenical Democrat, who was above the fray in that political year, because she had her eye on 2008.

"She was trying to walk the line of distancing herself from Howard Dean's position on the war, while still calling him a patriot," Lehrer continued. "And not endorsing anybody else, or any other wing of the party. And I thought that was consistent with Bill Clinton's approach—what helped to make Bill Clinton successful, which was that he was able to unite the various factions in the party behind him.... She was going for the same thing as Bill Clinton—the triangulated common interest."9

"WELL, BRIAN," HILLARY SAID AFTER THE SHOW RETURNED TO THE air, "I have been always trying to figure out where that [story about banning military uniforms in the White House] got started. And, again, I can't speak for the hundreds and hundreds of people who worked in the White House, and perhaps someone, in a moment of what I would consider a terrible lapse of judgment, said something or did something that then became a wild fire of rumor and innuendo . . . but I certainly had nothing to do with it, and I know my husband didn't."

"At the risk of being accused of lobbing you a soft ball," Lehrer said, ". . . how do you deal with that constant, constant harassment?"

"Well, Brian," Hillary said, segueing into her vast right-wing conspiracy mode, "you know, I have obviously thought a lot about it, because literally I have been accused of everything from murder on down. And it is hurtful and personally distressing when it first happens. But when it continues to, you know, come from the radio talk-show people and, you know . . . untrue books about us, on and on, you know, I've concluded that there is some other purpose at work here."[10]

DESPITE HILLARY'S REPUTATION FOR SHADING THE TRUTH, BRIAN Lehrer believed her explanation. And no wonder. After all, it seemed incredible that a First Lady would attempt to ban the wearing of military uniforms in the White House.

And yet, that is exactly what Hillary had tried to do in the spring of 1996. At that time, all military personnel serving in the White House wore business suits, except for the one day a week on which they were required to don their uniforms. There were only two exceptions to this rule: junior officers who served at White House social events wore dress uniforms; and military aides who carried the nuclear "football" containing the top-secret codes the President needed in case of nuclear war wore their service uniforms.

"Hillary tried to change the tradition where military aides wore their uniforms when accompanying the President with the nuclear football," said air force lieutenant colonel Robert "Buzz" Patterson, who served as President Clinton's senior military aide. "There were five military aides—from the air force, army, navy, marines, and coast guard—and she wanted us to wear business suits when we were carrying the football.

"The directive came down from Hillary through the President's chief of staff, Leon Panetta," Patterson continued. "Secret Service agents opposed her plan, because they wanted us to be easily identifiable by our uniforms in the event that something critical went down. We military aides were not just responsible for the nuclear codes, but also for evacuating the President and accompanying him to safe houses.

"Eventually, Hillary relented. My opinion is she was trying to downplay the military in and around her husband. It's ridiculous for her to claim that the story was the result of some young staffer who, in a lapse of judgment, said something critical to someone in uniform. It was all Hillary's doing from beginning to end."[11]

CHAPTER FORTY-ONE

Shut Out?

CHARLES GIBSON,
co-host of *Good Morning America*[1]
(Off Camera) We're going to turn now to the woman who is helping kick off the Democratic convention tonight [Monday, July 26, 2004] by introducing her husband, Bill Clinton. Hillary Clinton first came to national attention as a political wife, but she is now one of the undisputed stars of the Democratic Party. So here's a look at Hillary Clinton at center stage at conventions over the years.

SENATOR HILLARY RODHAM CLINTON
(film clip of Hillary Clinton) You know, I suppose I could have stayed home and baked cookies and had tea, but what I decided to do was to fulfill my profession which I entered before my husband was in public life. . . .

SENATOR HILLARY RODHAM CLINTON

(second film clip of Hillary Clinton) I am overwhelmed. In October, Bill and I will celebrate our 21st wedding anniversary. Thank you for supporting my husband. What an eight years it has been.

CHARLES GIBSON

(Off Camera) And joining us from [Boston's FleetCenter] convention hall is Senator Hillary Clinton. Back at the Democratic convention. Senator, good to have you with us.

SENATOR HILLARY RODHAM CLINTON

Thank you, Charlie. I'm glad to be back.

CHARLES GIBSON

Let me ask you about your role in this convention. Because a lot has been made, as you know, in the political pages about the fact that you were not on the original speaking schedule for the convention. Was that an oversight, or do you think it was [a] deliberate [snub] by the [John] Kerry people?

SENATOR HILLARY RODHAM CLINTON

Oh, you know, I have no reason to think either. I think that a convention is an evolving kind of event. And I'm just delighted to be part of supporting John Kerry and John Edwards....

CHARLES GIBSON

(Off Camera) There's something I've wanted to ask you about ever since I had a chance to talk to your husband when [his memoir, *My Life*] came out. You have been very circumspect about your own presidential ambitions, and I asked President Clinton about it in our interview. And I just want to play the clip.

PRESIDENT WILLIAM JEFFERSON CLINTON
(film clip of Bill Clinton) She's now where I was in 1988. When I didn't run [for president] in 1988, I thought I'd never get another chance to run, because I really thought the Democrats were going to win. . . .

CHARLES GIBSON
(Off Camera) Now, that was his comparison. And I thought it was really interesting. We know he thought about running in 1988. Decided against it. And acknowledges that if [Michael] Dukakis had won, he'd have been shut out for some period of time. He made the comparison. Do you, this time, if John Kerry wins, are you shut out for some period of time?

SENATOR HILLARY RODHAM CLINTON
You know, I don't know, and I really don't care. . . .

CHAPTER FORTY-TWO

Hedging Her Bets

"**D**OES SHE REALLY THINK WE'RE STUPID ENOUGH TO believe she doesn't care about the presidency?" said a Democratic political analyst who had followed Hillary's career closely. "Listen, we're talking about a woman who says she doesn't know what her next move is going to be, but she's known her next move since the eighth grade."[1]

Hillary's words could never be taken at face value; whenever she was questioned about her political ambitions, she avoided giving a direct and honest answer. She reserved her true feelings for a small group of people who comprised her kitchen cabinet: Bill Clinton (whom she trusted when it came to politics, if not to personal matters); Don Jones (personal matters, not politics); Harold Ickes (her bag man); Susan Thomases (her staffing dominatrix); Ann Lewis (her Democratic Party commissar); and Patti Solis Doyle (her top fund-raiser and, some said, closest confidant).

Many of the members of her kitchen cabinet, including Bill Clinton, had wanted her to run in 2004. And for a period of about six weeks in the spring of 2003, they thought they had converted her to their way of thinking. But she hemmed and hawed, dropped a few encouraging hints, and then backtracked.[2]

It didn't help when Bill reminded her of what she already knew—that in politics, timing was all-important, and that she might not get another chance at the White House. After she let the nomination slip from her grasp (and it was hers practically for the asking in 2004), Bill could hardly disguise his disappointment. As far as he was concerned, she had blown it.

Not everyone agreed.

One who didn't was Bernard Nussbaum, an attorney who had served with Hillary on the Nixon impeachment inquiry and who, eighteen years later, had been appointed as White House counsel. After Vincent Foster's suicide, Nussbaum had denied the FBI and other law enforcement agencies access to Foster's office for nearly two days, while he allegedly supervised the removal of potentially incriminating files. For his role in that cover-up, he became Bill Clinton's scapegoat, and was fired by the President from his job.[3]

Nussbaum was still on good terms with Hillary, however, and continued to speak with her quite often. He believed that the terrorist attacks on 9/11 had turned George W. Bush instantly into a wartime president, making him virtually unbeatable.[4]*

Bernie Nussbaum advised Hillary to save her best shot for 2008. She was doing the right thing by building a strong record in the Senate.

This was exactly what Hillary wanted to hear. As a perfectionist and control freak, she was deathly afraid of making a mis-

---

*Hillary agreed with Nussbaum's assessment. After the election, she told Fox News's Greta Van Susteren: "We've never unseated an incumbent president during wartime. That's just a given."[5]

step. Her meteoric rise to a position of leadership in the Senate had been remarkably error-free. Her popularity among the party faithful was unmatched by any other Democrat. Still, she knew that she had a long way to go before she could hope to overcome the visceral hatred she provoked in large swaths of the country.

Searching for any excuse *not* to run until 2008, Hillary pointed to a poll that was conducted at the 2004 Democratic National Convention. The delegates were asked whom they would choose in 2008 if John Kerry lost. Twenty-six percent of them said Hillary Clinton. The runner-up was John Edwards, with only 17 percent.[6]

HILLARY'S FUTURE DEPENDED ON GEORGE W. BUSH REMAINING IN the White House. But she could not afford to be seen by her fellow Democrats as wobbly or disloyal. On the contrary, she had to *appear* as though she was doing everything in her power to advance the cause of John Kerry.

This balancing act was not as difficult as it might appear. Hillary had always subscribed to the view that perception trumped truth. With a great show of magnanimity, she announced that she and her husband would cancel their plans to hold a book-signing party during the 2004 Democratic National Convention, lest they be accused of stealing the spotlight from John Kerry (which they did anyway).

When Kerry had to cancel an appearance at the annual convention of the National Education Association—a powerful teachers' lobby whose legions of left-wing activists were vital to the Democrats' fortunes at the ballot box—Hillary agreed to fill in for him at the last moment.

"If anyone was disappointed by the switch [from Kerry to Hillary], it was hard to tell as Mrs. Clinton took the stage," the *New York Times* reported. "People jumped to their feet with a sudden burst of applause, hoots and cheers, as confetti rained down on the convention floor. 'Hillary for President,' someone shouted."[7]

Hillary plunged into a blistering attack against George W. Bush, which the delegates ate up.

"If he was one of your students, you would be sending notes to his mother: 'Dear Mrs. Bush, he never admits he's wrong,' " she told the audience of nine thousand teachers, to roars of laughter.[8]

Hillary offered some obligatory words of praise for the Kerry-Edwards ticket. But she spoke mostly about *herself*—how *she* was interested in education, and how much *she* had done for children and teachers. By the end of the speech, the teachers had all but forgotten John Kerry, and were wondering why Hillary wasn't running for president.

For the next several weeks, Hillary campaigned for herself under the guise of campaigning for Kerry.

"I have two overwhelming priorities," Hillary told reporters. "To elect Kerry-Edwards and to elect a Democratic Senate."[9]

She instructed her advisers to draw attention to the fact that she was giving John Kerry's staff access to her valuable donor list and top fund-raisers.[10] The Hillary publicity machine left the impression that she was engaged in a full-court press on behalf of the nominee.

The truth was quite different. Hillary spent most of her time on the road raising money and campaigning for Democratic *senatorial* and *congressional* candidates, not for the *presidential* ticket. And she made numerous appearances in states, like South Dakota, where John Kerry did not have the slightest chance of winning.

"We know how hard Hillary can campaign when she wants to win," said a Democratic political analyst. "Think of how fiercely she campaigned on behalf of her husband. Think of that famous line of hers from the New Hampshire primary of 1992. She said she'd campaign 'until the last dog dies.' Well, the dogs were still alive and barking when she stopped campaigning for John Kerry."[11]

One of Hillary's overwhelming priorities was to prevent Kerry from taking over the Democratic Party. A key part of her strategy was to strengthen her hold on the party's fund-raising machinery through Terry McAuliffe, the Clintons' handpicked chairman of the Democratic National Committee.

"McAuliffe dominates the party's fund-raising efforts," wrote Dick Morris. "Democrat fat cats give when they are told, and to whom they are instructed by the smoothly oiled national fund-raising operation. Despite Howard Dean's now-legendary Internet-driven fund-raising success, the big checks still do the talking—and the Clintons control the process."[12]

However, in the event that Kerry won the election and was able to seize control of the Democratic National Committee, Hillary hedged her bets. She encouraged Harold Ickes to join with billionaire George Soros in setting up a group called Americans Coming Together. The goal of this group was to raise several hundred million dollars in soft money and, in effect, strip the Democratic National Committee of its main role as a fund-raising machine for candidates and causes.[13]

One way or another, Hillary was going to be ready for 2008.

CHAPTER FORTY-THREE

Gearing Up

WITHIN DAYS OF KERRY'S DEFEAT, SHE MADE HER FIRST move.

Hillary had been scheduled to deliver the annual Issam M. Fares Lecture on the Middle East at Tufts University the previous spring, but had postponed her appearance until one week after the presidential election in order to achieve the maximum possible impact.[1]

It was the opening salvo of her 2008 presidential campaign, and she did not squander the opportunity. In her remarks, she deftly dispatched her likely baby-faced competitors for the 2008 Democratic nomination—John Edwards of North Carolina and Evan Bayh of Indiana—and set out to seize the leadership of the party for herself. Then she tackled the questions in the mind of the audience about her qualifications:

How was she going to handle the issue of moral values?
Could a woman be elected president?
Would Hillary make red-state voters see more red?[2]

In her speech, Hillary portrayed herself as a God-fearing, church-going, Bible-reading Democrat from a southern state (Arkansas), not some soulless, canapé-nibbling, Chablis-sipping northeastern liberal.

"I don't think you can win an election or even run a successful campaign if you don't acknowledge what is important to people," she told the partisan crowd of 2,300 people jammed into the Tufts University gym. "No one can read the New Testament of our Bible without recognizing that Jesus had a lot more to say about how we treat the poor than most of the issues that were talked about in this election."[3]

Jesus was on her side.

But what about flesh-and-blood voters?

It was an immutable fact of electoral politics that men were from Mars and mostly Republican, and women were from Venus and often felt more comfortable voting for Democrats. In fact, as John Kerry had just demonstrated to his dismay, a Democratic candidate for president could not win without attracting a sizable majority of women.

Would that pattern hold if a woman ran for president? Put another way: men might not be ready for a woman presidential candidate, but were *women* ready for a *woman?*

Hillary thought so.

A woman, she told the Tufts audience, had been on the ballot in Afghanistan's recent elections—"a feat that puts Afghanistan women ahead of American women!"[4]

Human progress was on Hillary's side, too.

SOME OF THE SHREWDEST POLITICAL HANDICAPPERS IN THE BUSIness thought that Hillary was on to something, and the public was ready for a woman president.*

---

*With four years to go until the next presidential election, Hillary-

"Her approval rating in New York went from 38 percent in February 2001 to a high of 61 percent last month, suggesting she has expanded her appeal beyond Democratic diehards," wrote Jill Lawrence in *USA Today*.[5]

SportingbetUSA.com, an online gambling site, made Hillary its odds-on favorite in 2008. The site offered odds of seven to one that Hillary would be the next Democratic presidential nominee—well ahead of the runner-up, Senator John Edwards, who was twelve to one.[6]

Not long after the election, Dick Morris appeared on the Fox News Network's popular program *Hannity and Colmes*, where Sean Hannity, brandishing a red-and-blue electoral map of the United States, sought to persuade Morris that Hillary Clinton could not hope to win a single red state.

"Well," replied Morris, "it's [an evolving] map, Sean. Let me give you an example. Texas is now 49.5 percent minority. By 2008, it'll be 53 or 54 percent minority."

"But that didn't answer the question," Hannity pressed on. "Can she win a single red state that you see?"

"Oh," said Morris, "I think that she would have a very good chance of carrying Ohio. I think it's going to become much more Democratic and black and Hispanic. . . . I think she would have a good chance in Missouri. I think she'd have a good chance in a number of those [red] states."[7]

BUT DID HILLARY HAVE A *SERIOUS* CHANCE OF BECOMING OUR NEXT president?

Many people still doubted it. They clung to the notion that a blue-state woman couldn't possibly conquer the red-state world.

---

mania swept the Internet, where surfers bought shirts, hats, coffee cups, and bumper stickers promoting her candidacy.

And it was true that Hillary's negative poll numbers were nosebleed high across broad swaths of the country. Millions of people said they wouldn't vote for her under any circumstances.

And yet, the political experts who handicapped such things thought she would make a strong candidate. They reminded us that George W. Bush won reelection in 2004 even though he, too, was reviled by millions of his fellow countrymen. Indeed, looked at from Hillary's point of view, her positives far outweighed her negatives.

More than any other figure in her party, she had universal name recognition, control over the party's powerful money machine, the advice of the smartest politician in the party—Bill Clinton—and the support of millions of liberals, gays, lesbians, feminists, young people, teachers, journalists, trial lawyers, African Americans, and poor Hispanics and other minorities.

What's more, as a U.S. Senator, Hillary had developed into a cunning and crafty politician. She wisely swallowed her pride and made friends with her onetime Republican enemies in the Senate. Through sheer determination and hard practice, she honed her oratorical skills to the point where she was now one of the best public speakers in America. In the eyes of many of her fellow liberals, she even managed to acquire a quality that her husband possesses in great abundance: *charisma*.

Because she dominated her party, some people were willing to concede that Hillary was in a strong position to capture the Democratic presidential *nomination*. But they were quick to argue that she was too much of a northeastern elitist liberal to win the *general election*.

Hillary and her closest political advisers strongly disagreed.

They were optimistic that in a campaign for the White House, she would begin with tremendous advantages. They were counting on carrying New York, California, Florida, New

Jersey, and Massachusetts—five critical states whose combined 140 electoral college votes amounted to more than half the 270 required for victory.

And that was just for starters. As a result of demographic changes favoring Democrats in the 2008 election, Hillary would be viable in such red states as Texas, Ohio, Iowa, and Missouri, which could add another 72 electoral votes to her 140, and put her within 58 electoral votes of winning the White House. Throw in Michigan, Illinois, and Pennsylvania—and she was over the top.

Still, the skeptics persisted.

They pointed to the scarlet letter—*L* for liberal—that was emblazoned on Hillary's forehead. How, they asked, was she going to disguise *that?*

They seemed to forget that, like Madonna, her sister in blonde ambition, Hillary was a master of reinvention. She would simply invent a "new Hillary." In fact, she had already begun to do just that by positioning herself as a centrist on domestic policy and a hawk on foreign affairs.

Of course, this "new Hillary" was an illusion, for if she was elected president, it would be *déjà Clinton* all over again. Bill Clinton would return with Hillary to the White House for a third and fourth term.

"She would make an excellent President," Bill said, "and I would always try to help her."[8]

And along with Bill would come Harold Ickes, Susan Thomases, James Carville, the pollster Stan Greenberg, and the usual Clinton suspects. The culture of concealment and deception that had infected the American presidency during the years of Bill Clinton's administration would be back in full swing.

"With the Clintons, like it or not—and I do not, much—we are in the middle of a primal American saga and the important part is yet to come," wrote *Time* magazine's Lance Morrow. "Bill Clinton may be merely the prequel, the President of lesser moment—except, so to speak, as the horse she rode in on. Do not underestimate Hillary Clinton's ambition, or her destiny. It is no small thing."[9]

Eight years as copresident was not enough to satisfy Hillary's ambition, or her destiny. Hillary wanted *eight more years*, which would give her a total of sixteen years in the White House—the longest incumbency since Franklin Delano Roosevelt.

HILLARY THOUGHT HER CHANCES WERE GOOD ENOUGH TO BEGIN assembling her Old Girl feminist network. She created a national political operation—not in her home state of New York, but in Washington, D.C. Her most impressive hire was Ann Lewis, the former White House communications director and political director of the Democratic National Committee.

"While Mrs. Clinton lost some of her feminist edge in the White House," wrote Ben Smith in the *New York Observer*, "she's kept it behind the scenes, and the women around her, like Ms. Lewis, remain sharply aware that men continue to dominate politics."[10]

But not for long if Ann Lewis had anything to say about it.

"If you think of politics as a sport," she said, "it is likely to be male-dominated. Politics is: Can you get the job done. Do you understand how important this is to people's lives? It's not running across an end zone and doing a little victory dance."[11]

Without fanfare, Hillary set up a below-the-radar campaign headquarters in the offices of the Glover Park Group, a powerhouse political consulting firm that had been founded by two longtime Clintonistas, Carter Eskew and Joe Lockhart. Hillary dispatched three of her most trusted advisers to work at Glover Park: Gigi Georges, who previously served as state director for

Hillary's Senate campaign; Howard Wolfson, who served as communications director of that campaign; and Patti Solis Doyle, who was national political director of HILLPAC.

But despite all the presidential talk, Hillary stayed focused on her next big hurdle—the Senate reelection campaign in 2006. Her fellow New York senator, Chuck Schumer, had recently won reelection by an astounding 71 percent, and Hillary hoped to match that number, or do even better.

Republican leaders had conflicting views about how to deal with Hillary in 2006. Most of them wanted to knock her out of the political ring once and for all. But they were not convinced there was a candidate who could beat her in New York, which had become a solid blue state—and, thanks to a huge influx of minorities, was getting bluer by the day.

Some conservative Republican analysts toyed with an intriguing idea. Since they were not so sure that defeating Hillary in 2006 was the best strategy for 2008, perhaps they should give her a bye in New York. Their reasoning went as follows:

Nobody was more reviled in Republican circles than Hillary Rodham Clinton. Allowing her to win an easy reelection to the Senate would grease the skids for her presidential prospects. And if Hillary became the Democratic presidential nominee, she would be the *perfect instrument* to rally the Republican base, and fill Republican coffers.

For their part, Democrats saw other dangers for Hillary lurking in the shadows of 2006.

"If she is our best hope for a woman to be President some day—and I believe she is—another run for the Senate from New York is not necessarily the best way to get there," said Hilary Rosen, former president of the Recording Industry Association of America, and an influential Democrat. "She's just going to have to keep talking about all of the issues of the [liberal base] for the next two years, whereas if she weren't running, she would be able to dictate the agenda."[12]

Hillary and her kitchen cabinet did not agree with this assessment. Hillary had three goals in 2006: first, to win reelection by the biggest possible margin as a way of establishing her vote-getting potential; second, to use the Senate campaign to test her presidential themes; and third, to burnish her image in the American heartland.[13]

"Upstate [New York]—that's [like] the Midwest," said one Clinton backer. "That's Cleveland and Detroit. The themes that will be tested in [New York], we'll see how they work also on a national level."[14]

Charles Cook, the head of the highly respected nonpartisan report that bore his name, thought Hillary could use a couple of more years of seasoning. For one thing, she needed some serious political dermabrasion in order to remove the scar tissue that had accumulated during the Clinton presidency.

"Hillary is still a polarizer," Cook said. "There is a big chunk of people who would never vote for her under any circumstances. The people who will never listen to her or give her a chance are still 30 to 40 percent of the electorate. . . .

"But in this highly polarized environment," he continued, "Hillary has the advantage that she can hold onto 45 percent of the Democratic voters better than any other Democrat. That means she only has to target 5 to 6 percent of the swing vote."[15]

Joseph Mercurio, a veteran Democratic political consultant, believed that Team Hillary had one of the best ID (voter identification) and GOTV (get out the vote) operations in the country.[16]

"The National Committee for an Effective Congress (NCEC) is now one of those unheralded groups, from the Democratic-left-labor perspective, that 'brings you the government, or topples it,' as political consultants like to joke," wrote Mercurio.

"NCEC has analyzed every election district, every precinct, in every neighborhood in the country. They analyze for candidates the history of voting patterns in minute detail, e.g., which voters turn out and how various Democrats did in each election in every district. This is the kind of vital information you need for hard-core field operations that turn an election. . . .

"[In 2000], the Democrats' coordinated campaign used an updated version of this plan, with new data from NCEC. Gigi Georges brilliantly employed those statistics to mount this . . . field operation. They ID'd Hillary's favorables and tagged voters who were 'hostile' to her. Consequently, Team Hillary had the ability to surgically communicate with targeted voters with the message they needed to hear. It was a top-of-the-line direct mail and phone campaign that worked."[17]

CHAPTER FORTY-FOUR

Nixon's Disciple

Hillary Clinton didn't invent the art of political packaging; it came into vogue well before she appeared on the scene.

Starting with the presidential campaign of 1960, the new medium of television radically transformed politics, and made it easier than ever to market a candidate like a product. John. F. Kennedy, a shameless adulterer, was sold to the public as a scrupulous family man. And in 1968, after losing to Kennedy and failing in his bid to become governor of California, Richard Nixon underwent an extreme makeover at the hands of advertising executives and public relations specialists.

In his obituary of Richard Nixon, the *New York Times*'s R. W. Apple Jr. recalled the former president's protean quality.

"Again and again," wrote Apple, "Mr. Nixon reinvented himself—so much so that people talked and wrote about 'the new Nixon' and 'the new, new Nixon.' "[1]

Now, as Hillary gathered her forces for an assault on the presidency in 2008, she was prepared to adopt the strategy that had been used so brilliantly by Richard Nixon. She was going to reinvent herself as "the new, new Hillary."

"The supreme irony," noted Barbara Olson, "is that this 1960s liberal . . . has become ever more darkly Nixonian in her outlook and methods—though without Nixon's knowledge, statesmanlike substance, and redemptive Quaker conscience. . . ."[2]

"President's Nixon's 'enemies list' ignited a political firestorm when it became public," Olson went on. "But . . . Hillary's creation of a taxpayer-funded political database created scarcely a ripple from watchdogs of civil liberties. . . . Such an idea—no less than the raid on Vince Foster's office or the accumulation of FBI files for a White House blackmail database—could only come from the mind of someone who thinks like Nixon. And it apparently did—from Hillary Rodham Clinton, Nixon's disciple of hardball politics."[3]

What will the "new, new Hillary" look like?

Just as "the new, new Nixon" emerged sunny and smiling from the dark, brooding larva of his former self, so Hillary will metamorphose into the opposite of "the old Hillary."

Was "the old Hillary" a congenital liar who misled the country about everything from Whitewater to Monica?

"The new, new Hillary" will come across above all as . . . sincere.

Was "the old Hillary" a hypocrite who disguised her arrogance and ambition under a cloak of moral sanctimony?

"The new, new Hillary" will give the impression of being . . . the genuine article.

Did "the old Hillary" favor massive retaliation against her enemies?[4]

"The new, new Hillary" will behave as though she is . . . forbearing and open-minded.

Did "the old Hillary" frequently explode in fear-induced furies, and curse her friends for not fighting hard enough to defend her?

"The new, new Hillary" will appear as (shades of Richard Nixon!) ... sunny and smiling.

Was "the old Hillary" identified with abortion rights and gay marriage?

"The new, new Hillary" will talk about ... God, prayer, and the need to be tolerant of people who are opposed to abortion and gay marriage.

Did "the old Hillary" look upon Howard Dean as her most serious rival for control of the Democratic Party?

"The new, new Hillary" did nothing to block Dean's election as chairman of the Democratic National Committee ... because Dean's high-decibel left-wing rhetoric makes Hillary seem more like a centrist, and allows her to run against the Democratic Party's discredited establishment.

Like all such political makeovers, however, Hillary Clinton's will be only skin deep. Beneath the surface will be the same controlling, combative Park Ridge little girl who bloodied Jim Yrigoyen's nose for disobeying her and giving away one of her baby rabbits.

THE COMPARISON BETWEEN HILLARY CLINTON AND RICHARD Nixon can be pushed only so far. Whereas Nixon sought power in large part to overcome his *low* self-esteem, Hillary seeks power because she has unrealistically *high* self-esteem. With Hillary, we are dealing with a woman whose need for dominance is far more pathological than Nixon's.

What does that say about the kind of president Hillary might make?

A useful framework for evaluating Hillary's temperament as a predictor of her presidential performance is provided by Stanley

Renshon, the author of a classic study, *The Psychological Assessment of Presidential Candidates*.

Ambition, Renshon says, is a form of "healthy narcissism," and the key to achievement. "Some children, however," he points out in a passage that seems especially relevant to Hillary Clinton, ". . . retain their sense that they are different, special, entitled and ultimately not to be limited by conventional boundaries.

"These are people whose . . . *ends therefore justify any means*. Often this leads to a tendency to cut corners, to be less than forthcoming, to portray things always in the best light (in keeping with their own high views of themselves and their motives) and to be ready to bend the rules when it comes to their convenience. Such persons are vulnerable to getting into legal trouble."[5]

Psychologists aren't the only ones who can provide us with useful clues to the kind of president Hillary would make. There is also the testimony of those who have had the opportunity to see her in action up close and personal.

"My two cents' worth—and I think it is the two cents' worth of everybody who worked for the Clinton Administration health care reform effort of 1993–1994—is that Hillary Rodham Clinton needs to be kept very far away from the White House for the rest of her life," writes Bradford DeLong, deputy assistant secretary of the Treasury during the first Clinton administration. "Heading up health-care reform was the only major administrative job she ever tried to do. And she was a complete flop at it. She had neither the grasp of policy substance, the managerial skills, nor the political smarts to do the job she was then given. . . .

"Hillary Rodham Clinton," he continues, "has already flopped as a senior administrative official of the executive branch—the equivalent of an Undersecretary. Perhaps she will make a good senator. But there is no reason to think that she would be anything but an abysmal President."[6]

EPILOGUE

March 1993

What is morally wrong can never be politically right.
—Abraham Lincoln

During his long years of exile, Richard Nixon had been to the White House several times. But neither Ronald Reagan nor the first George Bush ever saw fit to put the disgraced president's name on the official list of White House visitors that was distributed to the media, or to release a photograph of Nixon revisiting his old haunt. As far as the public was concerned, Nixon was still persona non grata in the President's House.

At age eighty and in declining health, Nixon had no reason to believe that his official banishment would end during his lifetime. Now that Hillary Clinton, his old nemesis from the House impeachment inquiry, had taken up residence in the White House, Nixon did not expect the Clinton administration to reach out to him.

But he was wrong.

After Nixon returned from a trip to Russia, President Clinton phoned him. They had a cordial forty-minute talk, which Nixon later described as "the best conversation with a president I've had since I was president."[1] Then, Clinton invited Nixon to the White House, in his official capacity as a former president, to continue their discussion about the number-one issue on Clinton's foreign policy agenda: Russia.

And so on a blustery March day in 1993, Nixon found himself being ushered into the White House, where he had once tearfully bid farewell to his staff. He was kept waiting by Bill Clinton, who finally appeared and escorted the former president to the second-floor family residence.

The elevator door opened, and the first person Nixon saw when he stepped off was Hillary Clinton.

"Your health care reform legislation in 1973–74 was so good that we are using it as a blueprint for our own package," Hillary said.[2]

This struck Nixon as an incredibly strange, wonkish greeting from the First Lady. But then, Hillary managed to top even that by adding:

"Had you survived in office, you would have been light-years ahead of your time."[3]

Had I survived in office! Nixon later remembered thinking. *Maybe I could have if she hadn't been working to impeach me.*[4]

The two presidents made their way to the West Sitting Room, passing the Cézanne, the de Kooning, the Cassatt, and the Tiny Tim. After they were comfortably seated, they began to discuss Russian president Boris Yeltsin. Nixon respected Clinton's intelligence, but not his foreign policy experience or his leadership. He saw Clinton as a Hamlet-like figure who couldn't make up his mind.

"All of this . . . deliberating over Bosnia makes [Clinton] look weak," Nixon would later say. "We've got to get our allies, the Congress, and the people to go along. Instead of *telling* them what we are going to do, [Clinton is] looking for their permission! This isn't leadership! He doesn't *scare* anybody. . . ."

Then Nixon added, as though he had a sudden insight:

"*Hillary* inspires fear."[5]

After a while, Chelsea Clinton joined the group.

"The kid ran right to [Clinton] and never once looked at her mother," Nixon remarked. "I could see that she had a warm relationship with him, but was almost afraid of [her mother]. Hillary is ice-cold. You can see it in her eyes. She is a piece of work. She was very respectful to me, and said all the right things. But where he was very warm with Chelsea—he's touchy-feely, anyway—she wasn't at all. . . ."[6]

Hillary slid along the sofa to be closer to her daughter, and the young girl involuntarily jerked her arm away from her mother.

"Hillary," Nixon concluded, "inspires fear!"

ACKNOWLEDGMENTS

IT WAS MY GOOD FORTUNE to work on this book with several first-rate people. One who deserves to be singled out is Leon Wagener, a veteran journalist and author of *One Giant Leap: Neil Armstrong's Stellar American Journey*. Leon was particularly helpful in providing insights into Hillary's years in Park Ridge, Wellesley, and Yale.

Others who stood by my side from beginning to end: my agent, Daniel Strone; my editor, Bernadette Malone; Adrian Zackheim, the publisher of Sentinel; Will Weisser, the head of marketing and publicity at Sentinel; and my wife, Dolores Barrett, who read the manuscript several times and provided invaluable suggestions.

I also owe a debt of gratitude to the following people: Ronald Kessler, Melissa Goldstein, Dick Morris, Steven Hirsch, David Schippers, Christopher Emery, Charles Cook, Juanita Broaddrick, Dolly Kyle Browning, Kathleen Willey, Mickey Kaus, Lucianne Goldberg, Maurice Carroll, Richard Lambert, Tony Bullock, Monica Crowley, and Christopher Hitchens.

SELECTED BIBLIOGRAPHY

Anderson, Christopher. *Bill and Hillary*. New York: William Morrow, 1999.

———. *American Evita: Hillary Clinton's Path to Power*. New York: HarperCollins, 2004.

Baker, Peter. *The Breach*. New York: Berkley Books, 2000.

Barone, Michael, with Richard E. Cohen, *Almanac of American Politics*. New York: National Journal Group, 2003.

Blumenthal, Sidney. *The Clinton Wars*. New York: Farrar, Straus and Giroux, 2003.

Brock, David. *The Seduction of Hillary Rodham*. New York: The Free Press, 1996.

Clinton, Hillary Rodham. *It Takes a Village*. New York: Touchstone, 1996.

———. *Living History*. New York: Simon & Schuster, 2003.

Crowley, Monica. *Nixon off the Record*. New York: Random House, 1996.

Faderman, Lillian. *To Believe in Women: What Lesbians Have Done for America*. New York: Mariner Books, 1999.

Goldman, Peter, Thomas M. DeFrank, Mark Miller, Andrew Murr, and Tom Mathews. *Quest for the Presidency 1992*. College Station, TX: Texas A&M University Press, 1994.

Hodgson, Godfrey. *The Gentleman from New York*. New York: Houghton Mifflin, 2000.
Horn, Miriam. *Rebels in White Gloves*. New York: Anchor Books, 1999.
Isikoff, Michael. *Uncovering Clinton: A Reporter's Story*. New York: Crown, 1999.
Johnson, Paul. "42. William Jefferson Clinton" in *Presidential Leadership: Rating the Best and Worst in the White House*, edited by James Taranto and Leonard Leo. New York: The Free Press, 2004.
Klein, Joe. *The Natural*. New York: Broadway Books, 2002.
Kurtz, Howard. *Spin Cycle*. New York: The Free Press, 1998.
Lasky, Victor. *It Didn't Start with Watergate*. New York: Dial Press, 1977.
McCormick, Naomi B. *Sexual Salvation: Affirming Women's Sexual Rights and Pleasures*. Westport, CT: Praeger, 1994.
Maraniss, David. *First in His Class*. New York: Touchstone, 1995.
Milton, Joyce. *The First Partner: Hillary Rodham Clinton, A Biography*. New York: Perennial, 2000.
Morris, Dick, with Eileen McGann. *Because He Could*. New York: HarperCollins, 2004.
———. *Rewriting History*. New York: HarperCollins, 2004.
Morris, Roger. *Partners in Power*. New York: Henry Holt, 1996.
Olson, Barbara. *Hell to Pay*. Washington, DC: Regnery Publishing, 1999.
Renshon, Stanley A. *The Psychological Assessment of Presidential Candidates*. New York: Routledge, 1998.
Rothblum, Esther D., and Kathleen A. Brehony, editors. *Boston Marriages: Romantic but Asexual Relationships among Contemporary Lesbians*. Amherst: University of Massachusetts Press, 1993.
Sheehy, Gail. *Hillary's Choice*. New York: Random House, 1999.
Sommers, Christina Hoff. *Who Stole Feminism?* New York: Touchstone, 1994.
The Starr Report: The Findings of Independent Counsel Kenneth W. Starr on President Clinton and the Lewinsky Affair, with analysis by the Staff of the Washington Post. New York: Public Affairs, 1998.
Stephanopoulos, George. *All Too Human*. Boston: Little, Brown, 1999.

Tomasky, Michael. *Hillary's Turn*. New York: The Free Press, 2001.
Toobin, Jeffrey. *A Vast Conspiracy*. New York: Random House, 1999.
U.S. Congress. House. Committee on the Judiciary. *Impeachment of Richard M. Nixon, President of the United States*. 93rd Congress, 2nd session, 1974. House Report 93-1305.
Zeifman, Jerry. *Without Honor: The Impeachment of President Nixon and the Crimes of Camelot*. Emeryville, CA: Thunder's Mouth Press, 1995.

NOTE ON SOURCES

As a general rule, perfectionists who have a compelling need to be seen as right all the time, and who exert an iron control over their public image, do not get along well with the media. And Hillary Rodham Clinton is no exception to that rule.

She has had an adversarial relationship with the press for more than thirty years—from the moment she got involved in electoral politics in Arkansas. Her fear and loathing of the media was obvious to everyone in the press corps who covered the Clinton White House. And although she has been forced to soften her public relationship with the press since she became a U.S. senator, her genuine dislike has not changed.

Thus, when I set out to write this book, I did not find it surprsing that my repeated requests for an interview with Senator Clinton were greeted by a shattering silence from her staff. Nor did it come as a shock that many sources, fearing Hillary's power to exact retribution, asked to remain anonymous.

The discerning reader will find many references to such

anonymous sources in the notes that follow. Because I could not name these sources, I felt an extra obligation to the reader to redouble my efforts to verify the fairness and accuracy of all their statements.

NOTES

Prologue

1. **"He had this big fiftieth birthday"**: "The Testing of the President: Lewinsky's Testimony on Love, Friend and Family," *New York Times*, September 22, 1998.
2. **". . . I don't even know if he *remembers*,"**: Ibid.
3. **"I like it when you wear my ties"**: Monica Lewinsky quoted in Toobin, *A Vast Conspiracy*, p. 308.
4. **Tonight's extravaganza:** Jeannie Williams, "The stars come out for Clinton's big 50th," *USA Today*, August 19, 1996.
5. **"I had an emergency phone call"**: Interview with an official of the Democratic National Committee, who requested anonymity, March 11, 2004.
6. **"spearheaded"**: *The Starr Report: The Findings of Independent Counsel Kenneth W. Starr on President Clinton and the Lewinsky Affair, with analysis by the Staff of the* Washington Post, p. 69.
7. **"Hey, Handsome"**: "The Testing of the President: Lewinsky's Testimony on Love, Friend and Family," *New York Times*, September 22, 1998.
8. **That same night:** Ibid.
9. **"[Bill] and I talk about everything"**: Hillary Rodham Clinton

quoted in Alex Massie, "How Hillary brought Bill to book," *Scotsman*, June 8, 2003.
10. **"The estrangement was vital":** Morris, *Rewriting History*, p. 228.
11. **"The great irony of [Hillary's] life":** Tomasky, *Hillary's Turn*, p. 37.

PART I: THE BIG GIRL

Chapter One: The Impossible Dream

1. **In the pantry:** Interview with a member of the Clintons' personal White House staff, who wished to remain anonymous.
2. **As a rule:** Ibid.
3. **which was adorned:** Marian Burros, "A Visit to the White House," *House Beautiful*, March 1994.
4. **"It's hurting so bad":** Arianna Huffington, "Hillary the Enabler Stands By Her Man," *Chicago-Sun Times*, January 28, 1998.
5. **"[Hillary] kept her eye on":** Johnson, "42. William Jefferson Clinton" in *Presidential Leadership*, p. 205.
6. FOOTNOTE: **"She doesn't want":** Bill Clinton quoted in Maki Becker with Veronika Belenkaya, "Bill: Hil Eyes Run for Prez," *Daily News* (New York), June 24, 2004.

Chapter Two: Hillary's Bubble

1. **"stupid motherfucker":** Anderson, *Bill and Hillary*, p. 258.
2. **"Where's the miserable cocksucker?":** Interview with David Schippers, chief counsel to the House Managers for the Impeachment Trial of President Clinton, March 7, 2004.
3. **Until her ill-conceived decision:** Martha Sherrill, "The Man Hillary Ushered Out," *Washington Post*, March 23, 1994.
4. **During the day:** Interview with former White House usher Christopher Emery, April 5, 2004.
5. **When she first arrived:** Sheehy, *Hillary's Choice*, p. 227.
6. **She had the White House pressroom sealed off:** Stephanopoulos, *All Too Human*, p. 112.
7. **This obsession with privacy:** Interview with former White House usher Christopher Emery, April 5, 2004.

8. **"Bill learns from his mistakes"**: Morris, *Because He Could*, p. 153.
9. **"The mood inside the West Wing"**: Michael Isikoff and Evan Thomas, "Clinton and the Intern," *Newsweek*, February 2, 1998.

Chapter Three: Tacky Kaki

1. **Kaki had a weakness for the Victorian period**: Jura Koncius, "Present at the Transition: The Clinton Decorator Looks Back on Eight Years of Change," *Washington Post*, January 18, 2001.
2. **When she was through**: Joyce Saenz Harris, "Kaki Hockersmith: First Designer to the First Family," *Dallas Morning News*, July 17, 1994. See also Michael Kilian, "First Patron: As Usual, Hillary Clinton's Taste Is on the Cutting Edge of Art," *Chicago Tribune*, June 12, 1997.
3. **She had replaced the eighteenth century–style hand-painted wallpaper**: Clair Whitcomb, "Two Centuries of Changing Taste," *House Beautiful*, March 1994.
4. **"When Barbara Bush"**: Richard L. Berke, "The Transition: The Other Clinton Helps Shape the Administration," *New York Times*, December 14, 1992.
5. **Christopher Emery, a White House usher**: Interview with former White House usher Christopher Emery, April 5, 2004.
6. **Several Arkansas state troopers**: David Brock, "Living with the Clintons: Bill's Arkansas Bodyguards Tell the Story the Press Missed," *American Spectator*, January 1994.
7. **"Within the small circle"**: Interview with Michael Galstar, March 12, 2005.
8. **When Michael Galster**: Ibid.
9. **She sent two of her most trusted**: Olson, *Hell to Pay*, pp. 267–69.
10. **In addition, a White House staffer**: Ibid.
11. **"The Usher's Office plotted"**: Patria Leigh Brown, "A Redecorated White House, the Way the Clintons Like It," *New York Times*, November 24, 1993. See also Ian Brodie, "Clintons Pay Own Way in White House Decoration," *Times* (London), August 20, 1993.

12. **Thanks to her pals:** Cathy Horn, "The Look of Hillary Clinton: Fashion Designers Await Selection of First Clothes," *Washington Post*, December 22, 1992.
13. **According to her friends:** Interviews with anonymous sources close to the Clintons.
14. **She had not always been that way:** Interview with Wellesley College classmate who requested anonymity.
15. **However, after giving birth to Chelsea:** Interview with anonymous medical authority.
16. **might have explained her onetime neglect:** Morris, *Partners in Power*, p. 139.

Chapter Four: First Lovebirds

1. **"CLINTON ACCUSED":** Susan Schmidt, Peter Baker, and Toni Locy, "Clinton Accused of Urging Aide to Lie," *Washington Post*, January 21, 1998.
2. **Four days earlier:** Peter Baker and Ruth Marcus, "Clinton Intends to Say He Didn't Harass Jones; President Deposition Set Today," *Washington Post*, January 17, 1998.
3. **The federal judge presiding:** Ibid.
4. FOOTNOTE: **Among the unions:** "Ickes: Dirty Harry," *Hotline*, October 26, 2000.
5. **"From the unions to Whitewater":** Micah Morrison, "Who Is Harold Ickes? A Look at the Mastermind of Hillary's Senate Campaign," *Wall Street Journal*, October 26, 2000.
6. **her main concern:** Toobin, *A Vast Conspiracy*, p. 48.
7. FOOTNOTE: **"Shortly after Jones":** Toobin, *A Vast Conspiracy*, p. 50. In the interest of full disclosure Ruth Shalit is the author's daughter-in-law.
8. **"This is an election year":** This and the account of Bennett's hiring that follows are from an interview with Robert S. Bennett, March 3, 2004.
9. **His advice to the Clintons was simple:** Toobin, *A Vast Conspiracy*, p. 118.
10. **"We know things at many different levels":** Interview with a psychotherapist who requested anonymity.
11. **"Hillary had put the hammer on":** Paul Fray quoted in Maraniss, *First in His Class*, p. 320.

12. **"went through Bill Clinton's desk"**: Olson, *Hell to Pay*, p. 68.
13. **Later, in the early 1980s:** Interview with Ivan Duda, March 5, 2005.
14. **"Hillary learned about private investigators"**: Olson, *Hell to Pay*, p. 87.
15. **Betsey Wright "said that he was having a serious affair"**: Maraniss, *First in His Class*, p. 450.
16. **"The hired hands still felt queasy"**: Hillary Clinton quoted in Goldman, *Quest for the Presidency 1992*, p. 127.
17. **"The wife who deludes herself"**: Michael Kelly, "Blame Hillary," *Jewish World Review*, July 15, 1999.
18. **"Buddy"**: Hillary Rodham Clinton quoted in Karen Tumulty and Nancy Gibbs, "The Better Half: During Her Husband's Greatest Crisis, Hillary Has Come into Her Own," *Time*, January 4, 1999.
19. **"When Bill Clinton"**: Interview with David Schippers, March 8, 2004.
20. **"After the deposition was over"**: Isikoff, *Uncovering Clinton*, pp. 332–36.
21. **At 2:32 A.M. Sunday morning:** Matt Drudge, *Drudge Report*, January 17, 1998.
22. **"I talked to the White House this morning"**: Transcript of *Good Morning America*, ABC News, January 21, 1998.

Chapter Five: Celestial Ambitions

1. **As a teenager in the early 1960s:** Interview with Don Jones, May 17, 2004.
2. **"From an early age"**: Ibid.
3. **"If she comes to Arkansas"**: Bill Clinton quoted in Maraniss, *First in His Class*, p. 326.
4. **Nonetheless, Hillary hitched her star:** Louise Branson, "The Truth about HRC," *Scotsman*, August 12, 1998.
5. **According to the Reverend Don Jones:** Interview with Don Jones, May 17, 2004.
6. **"What Mrs. Clinton seems"**: Michael Kelly, "Saint Hillary: Hillary Rodham Clinton and the Politics of Virtue," *New York Times Magazine*, May 23, 1993.

7. **The cadre of feminists:** Interview with White House source who requested anonymity, March 18, 2004.
8. **"Hillary never wanted to be a wife":** Ibid.

PART II: THE BOOK OF LIFE

Chapter Six: Toughening Up

1. **"Hillary and I were both standouts in our class":** Interview with classmate Jim Yrigoyen, May 27, 2004.
2. **"If Suzy hits you":** Clinton, *Living History*, p. 12.
3. **"Hillary immediately":** Interview with Jim Yrigoyen, May 27, 2004.
4. FOOTNOTE: **The quick and easy:** Sheehy, *Hillary's Choice*, p. 310.
5. **He idolized Gene Tunney:** Martha Sherrill, "Education of Hillary Clinton; Growing Up in a Chicago Suburb: A Good Girl Getting Better All the Time," *Washington Post*, January 11, 1993.
6. **"rougher than a corn cob, as gruff as could be":** Paul Fray quoted in Maraniss, *First in His Class*, p. 320.
7. **"That must be an easy school":** Clinton, *It Takes a Village*, p. 22.
8. **Some biographers believed:** Paul Lowinger, "Bill Clinton Meets the Shrinks," http://www.zpub.com/un/un-bc9.html, July 1998.
9. **"Among both relatives and friends":** Morris, *Partners in Power*, p. 115.
10. **"For all his grouchiness":** Milton, *The First Partner*, p. 15.
11. **One of her closest friends:** Interview with Jim Yrigoyen, May 27, 2004.
12. **"We were in a snowball fight":** Ibid.

Chapter Seven: The Great Debate

1. **When she was sixteen years old:** Interview with Don Jones, May 17, 2004.
2. **"I was really stupid":** Clinton, *Living History*, p. 24.
3. **"It's incredible":** Interview with Timothy Sheldon, May 20, 2004.

4. **"The reason Hillary still makes excuses"**: Interview with a classmate who requested anonymity.
5. **"in an act of counter-intuitive brilliance"**: Clinton, *Living History*, p. 24.
6. **"more than dramatic fervor"**: Ibid.
7. **"Hillary's version of the debate"**: Interview with Jerry Baker, January 11, 2005.

Chapter Eight: The Radical

1. **"When Hillary left Park Ridge"**: Interview with Penny Pullen, May 2004.
2. **"highly politicized, left-wing ideology"**: Collections of the North Alabama Conference, United Methodist Church. August 18, 2004.
3. **"our sexist, racist"**: Charlotte Bunch and Rita Mae Brown, "What Every Lesbian Should Know," *motive*, vol. 32, no. 1, 1972.
4. **"At this time"**: Editorial, "Motive Comes Out," *motive*, vol. 32, no. 1, 1972.
5. **"Male society"**: Charlotte Bunch and Rita Mae Brown, "What Every Lesbian Should Know," *motive*, vol. 32, no. 1, 1972.
6. **"I still have every issue"**: Hillary Rodham Clinton quoted in Kenneth L. Woodward, "Soulful Matters," *Newsweek*, October 31, 1994.
7. **In one of the college's most degrading traditions**: Horn, *Rebels in White Gloves*, p. 9.
8. **"The buttocks"**: Ibid., p.10.
9. **The freshmen were warned**: Ibid., p. 9.
10. **Much of the Wellesley curriculum**: Ibid.
11. **"the Bolshevik women's auxiliary"**: *Boston Herald* quoted in Horn, *Rebels in White Gloves*, p. 18.
12. **"Theirs was a generation"**: Horn, *Rebels in White Gloves*, p. xvi.
13. **When she and Alison**: Ibid., p. 20.
14. **"I wasn't surprised"**: Interview with Penny McPhee, April 5, 2004.
15. **There was a long tradition**: Faderman, *To Believe in Women*, pp. 189–92.

16. **In those early days:** Ibid., pp. 184, 189–92.
17. **"The notion of a woman being a lesbian":** Interview with Penny McPhee, April 5, 2004.
18. **"That all depends on what":** "The President's Grand Jury Testimony," *Washington Post*, September 22, 1998.
19. **"This question has the potential":** Rothblum and Brehony, *Boston Marriages*, p. 10.
20. **"Female bisexuality and lesbianism":** McCormick, *Sexual Salvation*, p. 2.
21. **During her last three years:** Sheehy, *Hillary's Choice*, pp. 62–69.
22. **"I never stated a burning desire to be president":** Ibid., p. 74.
23. **"People who claim that they were born asexual":** Interview with Dr. Claudia Six, a clinical sexologist, September 2004.
24. **Most of the members of her Wellesley class:** From Horn, *Rebels in White Gloves*, pp. 260–77, 308.
25. **"Maybe":** Ibid., p. 308.

Chapter Nine: The Intern

1. **Some of her best friends at Wellesley College:** *Wellesley News*, May 16, 1968.
2. **"By this time":** Interview with Sarah Calvedt, May 2, 2004.
3. **"We all stayed at the Fountainebleau Hotel":** Interview with one of Hillary's classmates who requested anonymity. June 10, 2004.

Chapter Ten: Grooving at Cozy Beach

1. **In her remarks:** "Edelman Calls for Redirection," *Yale Daily News*, September 20, 1971.
2. **"The country was tired":** Marian Wright Edelman quoted in Brock, *The Seduction of Hillary Rodham*, p. 115.
3. **"requires that":** Mickey Kaus, "The Godmother: What's Wrong with Marian Wright Edelman, Children's Defense Fund Founder," *New Republic*, February 15, 1993.
4. **"Bill's pattern":** Interview with Yale Law School classmate who requested anonymity, May 18, 2004.
5. **In fact, Bill:** Ibid.

6. **In its debut issue:** Evan Gahr, "Will the Real Hillary Please Stand Up?" *American Enterprise*, July 1, 2000.
7. **"the purpose of gaining political control":** *Yale Review of Law and Social Action* quoted in Daniel Wattenberg, "The Lady Mac-Beth of Little Rock," *American Spectator*, August 1992.
8. **In a later special double issue:** Evan Gahr, "Will the Real Hillary Please Stand Up?" *American Enterprise*, July 1, 2000.
9. **"Jeff Rogers and Kris Olson":** Interview with Yale Law School classmate who requested anonymity, May 18, 2004.
10. **During their remaining time at Yale:** Horn, *Rebels in White Gloves*, p. 92.
11. **Bill frequently found:** Interview with Yale Law School classmate who requested anonymity, May 18, 2004.

Chapter Eleven: The Other "Smoking Gun"

1. **She was twenty-six:** Morris, *Rewriting History*, p. 37.
2. **"The women in this office":** Maraniss, *First in His Class*, p. 312.
3. **John Doar kept his window shades drawn:** Zeifman, *Without Honor*, pp. 95–96.
4. **Among other things:** Ibid.
5. FOOTNOTE: **"a single intelligence unit":** Ibid.
6. **"The fact that underlay the [impeachment] ordeal":** Renata Adler, "Searching for the Real Nixon Scandal," *Atlantic Monthly*, December 1976.
7. **"Doar fixes":** Maraniss, *First in His Class*, p. 309.
8. **As part of Richard Nixon's defense:** Interview with Jerome Zeifman, March 4, 2004.
9. **"When Nixon entered office":** Interview with Geoffrey Shepard, December 27, 2004.
10. **The answer was contained:** Zeifman, *Without Honor*, pp. 95–96.
11. **While Hillary was at Yale:** Brock, *The Seduction of Hillary Rodham*, p. 47.
12. **Now, as the attorney-general-in-waiting:** Zeifman, *Without Honor*, p. 11.
13. **From his professor's perch:** Ibid.

14. **"Don Edwards of California"**: Ibid., p. 48.
15. **Among those who agreed:** Ibid., p. 110.
16. **They argued that a president:** Ibid., pp. 122–23.
17. **The Doar irregulars further:** Ibid.
18. **After Doar finished reading:** Ibid., p. 214.
19. FOOTNOTE: **In fact, all the internal memoranda:** Interview with Geoffrey Shepard, December 27, 2004.
20. **"When Congressman Charles Wiggins"**: Renata Adler, "Searching for the Real Nixon Scandal," *Atlantic Monthly*, December 1976.
21. **"Now with our inquiry as a precedent"**: U.S. Congress, House, *Impeachment of Richard M. Nixon*, 1974, p. 296.

Chapter Twelve: The Misfit

1. **While Hillary was still in Washington:** Maraniss, *First in His Class*, p. 319.
2. **"I'm Hillary's dad"**: Ibid., pp. 319–20.
3. **"One of the worst-kept secrets"**: Ibid.
4. **"That's exactly what he did"**: Paul Fray quoted in Sheehy, *Hillary's Choice*, p. 113.
5. **"You should have seen her!"**: Interview with Dolly Kyle Browning, February 27, 2004.
6. **"Virginia loathed Hillary then"**: Mary Lee Fray quoted in Maraniss, *First in His Class*, p. 326.
7. **"Listen,"** . . . **"I don't need to be married"**: Bill Clinton quoted in Sheehy, *Hillary's Choice*, p. 119.
8. **"You have to remember"**: Morris, *Partners in Power*, p. 151.
9. **"If you looked at her in that day"**: Paul Fray quoted in Sheehy, *Hillary's Choice*, p. 112.
10. **"This rumor has to be faced"**: Paul Fray and Hillary Rodham quoted in Sheehy, *Hillary's Choice*, p. 112.
11. **"I know he's ready"**: Hillary Rodham quoted in Morris, *Partners in Power*, p. 186.
12. **"was capable of understanding"**: Jim Guy Tucker quoted in Morris, *Partners in Power*, p. 100.
13. **"Hillary's keeping"**: Bill Clinton and Virginia Kelley quoted in Morris, *Partners in Power*, p. 187.
14. **"a person in my own right" and not a " 'sacrificial' political**

spouse": Hillary Rodham quoted in Morris, *Partners in Power*, p. 188.
15. **"all the women":** Interview with Juanita Broaddrick, February 18, 2005.
16. **"He turned me around":** Ibid.
17. **"I felt responsible":** Ibid.

Chapter Thirteen: A Night to Remember

1. **"I'm going back to my cottage":** Bill Clinton quoted in interview with an anonymous source who was with the Clintons in Bermuda.
2. **"The next morning":** Interview with an anonymous source who was with the Clintons in Bermuda.
3. **"One time,"** . . . **"Billy told me":** Interview with Dolly Kyle Browning, February 21, 2005.

Chapter Fourteen: All the Governor's Women

1. **"At times,"** . . . **"he flirted outrageously":** Milton, *The First Partner*, pp. 115–16.
2. **"He had two levels of women":** Nancy "Peach" Pietrefesa quoted in Sheehy, *Hillary's Choice*, pp. 149–50.
3. **was rumored:** Milton, *The First Partner*, p. 104.
4. **"He knows human nature":** Nancy "Peach" Pietrefesa quoted in Sheehy, *Hillary's Choice*, pp. 149–50.
5. **"One Saturday morning":** Maraniss, *First in His Class*, p. 394.
6. **"Bill was like a kid":** Connie Bruck, "Hillary the Pol," *New Yorker*, May 30, 1994.
7. **People in small towns:** Morris, *Partners in Power*, p. 242.
8. **And to drive the point home:** Ibid., p. 245.
9. **"I was her worst critic":** Richard Herget quoted in Brock, *The Seduction of Hillary Rodham*, p. 133.
10. **"It shook both of them":** Connie Bruck, "Hillary the Pol," *New Yorker*, May 30, 1994.
11. **"The experience of watching":** Ibid.
12. **"She conformed":** Morris, *Partners in Power*, p. 278.
13. **"I don't have to change":** Hillary Rodham Clinton quoted in Sheehy, *Hillary's Choice*, p. 145.

14. **"Did you change"**: Ibid.
15. **" 'No,' came the ice cold answer"**: *Times-News* (McGehee, Alabama) quoted in Maraniss, *First in His Class*, p. 400.
16. **"The deal was"**: Nancy "Peach" Pietrefesa quoted in Sheehy, *Hillary's Choice*, p. 146.
17. **She telephoned Dick Morris:** Sheehy, *Hillary's Choice*, p. 146.
18. **"Hillary was intrigued"**: Dick Morris quoted in Sheehy, *Hillary's Choice*, p. 146.
19. **"Wright wasn't romantically interested"**: Brock, *The Seduction of Hillary Rodham*, p. 139.
20. **"She asked to see me"**: Interview with Ivan Duda, March 5, 2005.
21. **"Hillary made her trade-offs"**: Jan Piercy quoted in Sheehy, *Hillary's Choice*, p. 151.

PART III: THE WHITE HOUSE YEARS

Chapter Fifteen: Her Husband's Keeper

1. **"After Monica admitted to an affair"**: Louise Branson, "The Truth about HRC," *Scotsman*, August 12, 1998.
2. **"Whenever I go out and fight"**: Stephanopoulos, *All Too Human*, p. 389.
3. **No sooner:** "Don't Call Me," *American Spectator*, March 1998.
4. **"I got a call from Walter Kaye"**: Interview with former official of the Democratic National Committee who requested anonymity, March 11, 2004.
5. **"Monica started working"**: Interview with former White House official who requested anonymity.
6. **"We never saw her in the East Wing"**: Interview with former White House employee Kathleen Willey, January 22, 2005.
7. **"Hillary gave an ideological edge"**: Johnson, "42. William Jefferson Clinton," in *Presidential Leadership*, p. 204.
8. **"Vote for Hillary's Husband"**: Irene Sege, "Hillary & Company; Spirit of '69: The Wellesley Connection Pays Off," *Boston Globe*, September 3, 1992.
9. **"In Clinton's cabinet"**: Andrew Sullivan, "Counter Culture:

Not a Straight Story," *New York Times Magazine*, December 12, 1999.
10. **"Evelyn was a force for order"**: Interview with former White House speechwriter who requested anonymity, April 5, 2004.
11. **"She called one day"**: ": Interview with former White House official who requested anonymity, April 5, 2004.
12. **"Bill couldn't have possibly"**: Interview with a U.S. senator's wife who requested anonymity, April 5, 2004.
13. **"Sexual snobs"**: Tina Brown, "The bookworm and the Viking," *salon.com*, June 13, 2003.

Chapter Sixteen: "Bill Owes Me"

1. **"graduates"**: Isikoff, *Uncovering Clinton*, p. 135.
2. **"Bill's girlfriend from our hippie days"**: Marsha Scott quoted in Karen Tumulty, "Who Is Marsha Scott? Another Arkansas Transplant Becomes Mired in Questionable White House Activities," *Time*, March 24, 1997.
3. **"The assumption among the women"**: Interview with former White House official who requested anonymity, March 18, 2004.
4. **The President had other rumored girlfriends:** Milton, *The First Partner*, p. 265.
5. **"She is so shrewd"**: Jan Piercy quoted in Connie Bruck, "Hillary the Pol," *New Yorker*, May 30, 1994.
6. **"I'm not sure how many"**: Interview with Clinton campaign donor who requested anonymity, April 2, 2004.
7. **"Watching [Bill Clinton] was very much like"**: David Gergen quoted in "The Clinton Years," a *Frontline* special anchored by Chris Bury, WNET, January 16, 2001.
8. **"A Secret Service officer"**: *The Starr Report: The Findings of Independent Counsel Kenneth W. Starr on President Clinton and the Lewinsky Affair, with analysis by the Staff of the* Washington Post, p. XII.
9. **By that time, however, rumors about Monica:** Interview with a former fund-raiser for the Democratic National Committee, March 11, 2004.

Chapter Seventeen: Payback Time

1. **"She was upset"**: "Don't Call Me," *American Spectator*, March 1998.
2. **"In the spring of 1992"**: Interview with a former White House official, March 18, 2004.
3. **"We were using these dial meters"**: Paul Begala, George Stephanopoulos, and James Carville quoted on "The Clinton Years," a *Frontline* special anchored by Chris Bury, WNET, January 16, 2001.
4. **"We found out from those focus groups"**: Interview with a former White House official, March 18, 2004.
5. **In late April:** Michael Kelly, "The Transition: Packaging the Candidate; The Making of a First Family: A Blueprint," *New York Times*, November 14, 1992.
6. **"DRAFT/CONFIDENTIAL"**: Campaign memorandum published in Goldman, *Quest for the Presidency 1992*, pp. 657–64.
7. **"What is most striking"**: Michael Kelly, "The Transition: Packaging the Candidate; the Making of a First Family: A Blueprint," *New York Times*, November 14, 1992.
8. **Hillary suddenly became a kinder:** Interview with a former White House official, March 18, 2004.
9. **"I told [the President] that he was terribly out of position"**: David Gergen quoted on "The Clinton Years," a *Frontline* special anchored by Chris Bury, WNET, January 16, 2001.
10. **"Some in the White House"**: "The Clinton Years," a *Frontline* special anchored by Chris Bury, WNET, January 16, 2001.

Chapter Eighteen: Hibernation

1. **As Hillary sat on the stage:** Author's observation.
2. **"I am a product of my own experience"**: Ibid.
3. **"After health care"**: Interview with former White House official who requested anonymity.
4. **"And the public liked very much"**: Dick Morris quoted on "The Clinton Years," a *Frontline* special anchored by Chris Bury, WNET, January 16, 2001.
5. **"Although she was less visible now"**: Stephanopoulos, *All Too Human*, pp. 387–88.

6. **"I made my speech at Goucher's winter convocation"**: Clinton, *Living History*, pp. 442–43.
7. **"Certainly I believe they are false"**: Ibid.

Chapter Nineteen: Hillary's Brain

1. **"heated exaggeration"**: Richard Hofstadter, "The Paranoid Style in American Politics," *Harper's*, November 1964.
2. **"Since what is at stake"**: Ibid.
3. **"perhaps the most partisan"**: Toobin, *A Vast Conspiracy*, p. 241.
4. **"vast, obscure Manichean fantasies"**: Klein, *The Natural*, p. 106.
5. **His enemies list**: Kurtz, *Spin Cycle*, p. 87.
6. **Blumenthal was also behind**: Toobin, *A Vast Conspiracy*, p. 280–81.
7. **"[Hillary] explained"**: Blumenthal, *The Clinton Wars*, p. 339.

Chapter Twenty: "This Is War"

1. **"The whole room seemed to hold its breath"**: Sandra Sobieraj, "Clinton's Denial a Stern 20 Seconds," Associated Press, January 26, 1998.
2. **"We've had a slow-motion assassination"**: Harry Thomason quoted in Toobin, *A Vast Conspiracy*, p. 248.

Chapter Twenty-one: "Screw 'Em"

1. **The next day**: Deborah Orin, "It's a Right-Wing Plot—She Goes on *Today* Show to Defend Prez," *New York Post*, January 28, 1998.
2. **"She was very relaxed"**: Melanie Verveer quoted in David Maraniss, "First Lady Launches Counter Attack; Prosecutor Called 'Politically Motivated' Ally of 'Right-Wing Conspiracy,'" *Washington Post*, January 28, 1998.
3. **"I suggested that she say"**: Blumenthal, *The Clinton Wars*, p. 373.
4. **"There has been one question"**: Toobin, *A Vast Conspiracy*, pp. 254–56.
5. **Later, Hillary's attorney**: Clinton, *Living History*, p. 445.
6. **"I heard your words of wisdom"**: Ibid.

Chapter Twenty-two: The Human Bridge

1. **One of Starr's lieutenants:** Toobin, *A Vast Conspiracy*, p. 307.
2. **"I had some conversations":** Interview with a source close to the Whitewater investigation who requested anonymity, May 8, 2004.
3. **"I could hardly breathe":** Clinton, *Living History*, p. 466.
4. **"come out and hammer Ken Starr":** Anderson, *Bill and Hillary*, p. 27.
5. FOOTNOTE: **Shrum has the draft:** Ken Auletta, "Kerry's Brain: Bob Shrum is one of the biggest names in the campaign business—but is he prepared to take on Bush?" *New Yorker*, September 20, 2004.
6. **"Hillary's not naïve":** Jesse Jackson quoted in Melinda Hennenberger, "Testing of a President," *New York Times*, August 18, 1998.
7. **"She had no good options":** Interview with former White House official who requested anonymity, April 5, 2004.
8. **"It was his digging in his heels":** Dick Morris quoted on "The Clinton Years," a *Frontline* special anchored by Chris Bury, WNET, January 16, 2001.
9. **"It was the President":** Blumenthal, *The Clinton Wars*, p. 465.

Chapter Twenty-three: The Wronged Woman

1. **As Vernon Jordan watched:** William Mills and Mark Merchant, "Clintons Can't Wait to Get to Vineyard," *Cape Cod Times*, August 18, 1998.
2. **"There was no late evening singing":** Margaret Carlson, "The Shadow of Her Smile," *Time*, September 21, 1998.
3. **Hillary would later claim:** Interview with an anonymous source close to Walter Cronkite, March 8, 2005.
4. **"The Clintons were seated at separate tables":** Interview with an anonymous source who attended the Rattner dinner, April 2, 2004.
5. **"In the first administration":** Interview with David Schippers, chief counsel to the House Managers for the Impeachment Trial of President Clinton, May 8, 2004.
6. **"At both shindigs":** Tomasky, *Hillary's Turn*, p. 34.
7. **"This is the woman":** Neel Lattimore quoted in Ellen O'Brien

and Alfred Lubrano, "A More Popular Clinton, On the Defense—Hillary/Americans Admire Her Courage and Resolute Dignity, Polls Show," *Philadelphia Inquirer*, December 20, 1998.
8. **"So, for the first time"**: *Today* show, NBC, July 16, 1998.
9. **"The 'America's Treasures' tour"**: Interview with Jay Branegan, March 30, 2004.

PART IV: THE CANDIDATE

Chapter Twenty-four: Run, Hillary, Run!

1. **"the best thinker"**: *The Almanac of American Politics*.
2. **If it had been left entirely up to Moynihan:** Interview with a source close to the Moynihans who requested anonymity, April 5, 2004.
3. **That same night:** Clinton, *Living History*, p. 483.
4. **"I'd like to speak to Mrs. Clinton"**: Rep. Charlie Rangel quoted in Clinton, *Living History*, p. 483.
5. **As one of the first steps:** Blumenthal, *The Clinton Wars*, p. 678.
6. **After Charlie Rangel spoke to Hillary:** Bob Herbert, "After Moynihan," *New York Times*, November 12, 1998.
7. **"Nobody's going to run"**: Tomasky, *Hillary's Turn*, p. 40.

Chapter Twenty-five: The Education of Hillary Clinton

1. **"Here's a little mini-bombshell"**: *Meet the Press*, January 3, 1999.
2. **Harold Ickes was the go-to guy:** Wendy Lin, "Ickes Nixes Job with Clinton," *Newsday* (New York), January 7, 1993.
3. **"because there was insufficient evidence"**: "White House Staff: Sounds Like It's Done but Not Official," *New York Post*, January 15, 1993.
4. **"Well," . . . "did you *see* that?"**: Hillary Rodham Clinton and Harold Ickes quoted in Tomasky, *Hillary's Turn*, p. 19.
5. **"So literally the day"**: Peter Baker quoted on *Fresh Air*, National Public Radio, September 28, 2000.
6. **"[Harold] offered a running commentary"**: Clinton, *Living History*, p. 497.
7. **"He set out a piece of paper"**: Baker, *The Breach*, p. 413.

8. **"Why in God's name"**: Ibid., p. 44.
9. **"Why Hillary?"**: Interview with Bob McCarthy of the *Buffalo News*, March 15, 2004.

Chapter Twenty-six: Blowing Them Away

1. **"In the winter of 1999"**: Interview with Democratic donor who requested anonymity, May 17, 2004.
2. **Both *Newsweek* and *Time***: See cover stories of *Time*, March 1, 1999, and *Newsweek*, March 1, 1999.
3. **whose favorability rating**: Romesh Ratnesar, "A Race of Her Own," *Time*, March 1, 1999.
4. **"How are you going to handle Monica Lewinsky?"**: Interview with anonymous source who was present at the meeting, May 10, 2004.
5. **"Before she announced"**: Interview with source active in New York Democratic politics who requested anonymity.
6. **But in the wake**: Elizabeth Bumiller, "A Top Adviser to a Much-Advised First Lady," *New York Times*, July 20, 1999.
7. **"People wanted to know"**: A campaign aide quoted in Elizabeth Kolbert, "The Student: How Hillary Clinton Set Out to Master the Senate," *New Yorker*, October 13, 2003.

Chapter Twenty-seven: "Boob Bait for the Bubbas"

1. **For years, Pat Moynihan had been suffering from back pain**: Interview with anonymous source close to Senator Moynihan, April 5, 2004.
2. **To break the ice with the Moynihans**: Ibid.
3. **"that Hillary Clinton 'didn't get it' "**: Hodgson, *The Gentleman from New York*, p. 5.
4. **Moynihan believed that Hillary's chief motivation**: Interview with anonymous source close to Senator Moynihan, April 5, 2004.
5. **Moynihan had publically**: Adam Nagourney and William M. Welch, "Moynihan an ally, a tormentor as well," *USA Today*, January 14, 1994.
6. **"Not a single call"**: Senator Daniel Patrick Moynihan quoted

in Michael Kramer, "The Political Interest: Still Waiting for Bill's Call," *Time*, February 1, 1993.
7. **"Big deal"**: Clinton aide quoted in Michael Kramer, "The Political Interest: Still Waiting for Bill's Call," *Time*, February 1, 1993.
8. **"I believe that she believes"**: Interview with source close to Elizabeth Moynihan who requested anonymity, April 5, 2004.
9. **The Moynihans were deeply disappointed:** Ibid.
10. **What's more, the Moynihans thought:** Ibid.

Chapter Twenty-eight: Distortion

1. **"So" . . . "you're interested in the secret"**: This conversation is from an interview with an anonymous source close to Senator and Mrs. Moynihan, April 5, 2004.

Chapter Twenty-nine: "The Martians Have Landed"

1. **"Hillary understood"**: Interview with former employee of Senator Moynihan who requested anonymity, April 5, 2004.
2. **"Liz Moynihan had her doubts"**: Hodgson, *The Gentleman from New York*, p. 5.
3. **"She's not even from New York"**: Thomas Mills quoted in Brian Blomquist, "Pol's Wife Hasn't Got Hill Story Down Pat," *New York Post*, July 10, 1999.
4. **"the largest press corps ever assembled"**: Gail Collins, "Making Political Hay on Mr. Moynihan's Farm," *New York Times*, July 8, 1999.
5. **"than the presidential race"**: Howard Kurtz, "Grabber Strikes Again," *Washington Post*, July 12, 1999.
6. **"Maybe all of this"**: Jeff Greenfield quoted in Howard Kurtz, "Grabber Strikes Again," *Washington Post*, July 12, 1999.
7. **"God, I almost forgot"**: Senator Moynihan quoted in Joel Siegel, "Hil Begins Senate Campaign, Travels to Pat's Farm to Start Upstate Tour," *Daily News* (New York), July 8, 1999.
8. **"I'm really excited"**: Hillary Rodham Clinton quoted in Robert Hardt Jr., "The Silly Campaign Is Just Getting Started," *New York Post*, July 11, 1999.

9. **"Tony," ... "look at this!":** Elizabeth Moynihan quoted in interview with Tony Bullock, Senator Moynihan's former chief of staff, March 11, 2004.

Chapter Thirty: The Juice

1. **In late June:** Interview with an anonymous source who worked on fund-raising for the Senate campaign, May 4, 2003.
2. **She and her then boss:** Susan Schmidt, "Teamsters Contributions to Clinton Effort Probed," *Washington Post*, October 9, 1997.
3. **"sent under the name of Richard Sullivan":** Ibid.
4. **"I made the call as a favor":** Richard Sullivan quoted in "Reno 'Mad' about Tape Release Delay," *USA Today*, credited to Associated Press, October 9, 1997.
5. **she did not dispute:** Susan Schmidt, "Teamsters Contributions to Clinton Effort Probed," *Washington Post*, October 9, 1997.
6. **They had also drafted:** Interview with an anonymous source who worked on fund-raising for the Senate campaign, May 4, 2003.
7. **"It was clear from the way Harold ran the meeting":** Ibid.
8. **As far as Ickes was concerned:** Ibid.
9. **Summary Fundraising Plan:** Confidential documents provided to the author by a campaign employee who was involved with fund-raising.
10. **Like Ickes:** Lloyd Grove, "The Clintons' Bad Cop," *Washington Post*, March 2, 1993.
11. **"I have a very strong reality principle:** Susan Thomases quoted in Lloyd Grove, "The Clintons' Bad Cop," *Washington Post*, March 2, 1993.
12. **"The leaders and theorists of the women's movement":** Sommers, *Who Stole Feminism?*, p. 16.
13. **"brutal patriarchal system":** Faderman, *To Believe in Women*, p. 334.
14. **"They had begun on the same track":** Brock, *The Seduction of Hillary Rodham*, p. 222.
15. **"the Clinton administration's King Kong Kibitzer":** Lloyd Grove, "The Clintons' Bad Cop," *Washington Post*, March 2, 1993.

16. **"It's not that she has the juice"**: James Carville quoted in Lloyd Grove, "The Clintons' Bad Cop," *Washington Post*, March 2, 1993.

Chapter Thirty-one: Hillary's Problem

1. **In a wildly popular move:** David Firestone, "In Mayor's Arafat Snub, a Hint of Strategy," *New York Times*, October 26, 1995.
2. **"Many women who hadn't had it both ways":** Ellen Chesler quoted in Tomasky, *Hillary's Turn*, p. 88.
3. **Finally, after months of dithering:** Tomasky, *Hillary's Turn*, pp. 190–92.
4. **Asked what they thought:** Ibid.
5. **"Probably the most important issue":** Confidential documents provided to the author by a source involved in the Senate campaign.
6. **"RUDY GIULIANI'S CLAIM TO FAME":** Ibid.
7. **"Subj: Re: New York Women for Hillary":** Ibid.
8. **"And this was a meeting of the so-called":** Eva Moskowitz quoted in Tomasky, *Hillary's Turn*, p. 93.
9. **"She's the most unbelievable actress":** Interview with an anonymous source who worked on Hillary's Senate campaign, November 8, 2004.

Chapter Thirty-two: "A Legend Imploding"

1. **The woman who had once mocked moms:** Gersh Kuntzman, "Why Hillary Is a Bad Campaigner," *New York Post*, June 10, 1999.
2. **Her media advisers:** Ibid.
3. **"She's been insulated in the cocoon":** Gabe Pressman quoted in Gersh Kuntzman, "Why Hillary Is a Bad Campaigner," *New York Post*, June 10, 1999.
4. **"Another dollop of Clintonspeak":** "Psychobabbling over Tomcat Spouse," *Arizona Republic*, August 5, 1999.
5. **"always been a big Yankees fan":** Hillary Rodham Clinton quoted in Peter Botte and Joel Siegel with Michael Finnegan, "Hil: 'Go Yanks! Go Knicks!' " *Daily News* (New York), June 11, 1999.

6. **When President Clinton:** For background see Don Van Natta Jr. and Marc Lacey, "Access Proved Vital in Last Minute Race for Clinton Pardons," *New York Times*, February 25, 2001.
7. **When Pardongate:** For background see Elizabeth Bumiller, "Clemency, from Bronx Leader to First Lady," *New York Times*, September 15, 1999.
8. **When Hillary made:** For background see Thomas J. Lueck, "Mrs. Clinton Explains Kiss in Middle East," *New York Times*, July 14, 2000.
9. **When Hillary realized:** For background see "Hillary's Jewish Roots—Rooted in Political Pandering," *New York Post*, August 8, 1999.
10. **When Mayor Giuliani:** Adam Nagourney, "First Lady Assails Mayor over Threat to Museum," *New York Times*, September 28, 1999.
11. **"Independently, the mistakes are meaningless"**: George Arzt quoted in Joel Siegel with Thomas M. DeFrank, "Hillary's Missteps Worrying Her Followers," *Daily News* (New York), November 13, 1999.
12. **"Here's a woman I've admired"**: Lenore Skenazy, "When Hillary Goofs, I Wince," *Daily News* (New York), November 17, 1999.
13. **"She'd had about as bad a six months"**: Tomasky, *Hillary's Turn*, pp. 84–85.
14. **"That odd sound you hear"**: Noemie Emery, "Hillary's Meltdown; or, the Death of a Legend," *National Review*, August 30, 1999.

Chapter Thirty-three: The Turnaround

1. **On February 4, 2000:** Blumenthal, *The Clinton Wars*, pp. 686–87.
2. **"Past presidents were content"**: Maureen Dowd, "Tin Cup Couple," *New York Times*, September 24, 2000.
3. **"She would call me to discuss"**: Interview with Tony Bullock, March 11, 2004.
4. **"I was her table companion"**: Interview with a prominent foundation head who requested anonymity, May 9, 2004.

5. **"You can't run a campaign":** Elizabeth Moynihan quoted in an interview with an anonymous source, April 5, 2004.
6. **"If she was sitting across the table":** Interview with Tony Bullock, March 2, 2004.

Chapter Thirty-four: "Pure Hollywood"

1. **Indeed, when it was revealed:** John Podhoretz, "Israel in the Balance," *New York Post*, October 26, 2000.
2. **Astute political observers:** Eli Lake, "Hillary Fattening Campaign War Chest at Secret Sit-Down with Arafat Cronies," *Forward*, May 26, 2000.
3. **That Hillary was courting radical Muslim groups:** Eric Lipton, "Divisiveness at Parade as Mrs. Clinton and Lazio Salute Israel," *New York Times*, June 5, 2000. See also Michael Grunwald, "First Lady Is Booed at Pro-Israel Rally," *Washington Post*, October 13, 2000.
4. **"She'd fly into these little upstate towns":** Rick Lazio quoted in Anderson, *American Evita*, p. 196.
5. **In June:** Interview with anonymous source at the SEC, March 17, 2004.

PART V: THE ROAD BACK TO THE WHITE HOUSE

Chapter Thirty-five: The "Phenom"

1. **The Reverend Don Jones:** Interview with Don Jones, May 2004.
2. **She was dressed for the occasion:** Shannon McCaffrey, "Hillary Clinton Sworn in as Senator," Associated Press, January 3, 2001.
3. **"Hillary's gone from a completely derivative role":** White House official quoted in John F. Harris, "Hillary's Big Adventure," *Washington Post*, January 27, 2002.
4. **"an affront to common sense":** "Mrs. Clinton's Book Deal," *New York Times*, December 22, 2000.
5. **A twenty-six-foot-long moving van:** See George Lardner Jr., "Clinton's Shipped Furniture Years Ago; White House Usher

Doubted Ownership," *Washington Post*, February 10, 2001; "First Lady Starts to Move to New York," Associated Press, January 5, 2000; Marian Burros and John Leland, "Clintons Return Household Gifts of Uncertain Ownership," *New York Times*, February 8, 2001.

6. **"Can I hug you?"**: Strom Thurmond quoted in Shannon McCaffrey, "Hillary Clinton Sworn in as Senator," Associated Press, January 3, 2001.
7. **"Yes," . . . "there have been Senate celebrities"**: Alison Mitchell, "The Freshman: Starring Hillary Clinton," *New York Times*, January 7, 2001.
8. **"In a way, it felt like the last of the '90s"**: Hank Stuever, "Multi-Party System: On Their First Day, the Newest Senators Got a Hearty Reception," *Washington Post*, January 4, 2001.
9. **"It was a wonderful round of parties"**: Interview with Don Jones, May 2004.
10. **"Hillary's mother"**: Interview with an anonymous source close to the Clintons, April 3, 2004.

Chapter Thirty-six: "The Perfect Student"

1. **"Hillary walks across the room"**: Rep. Anthony Weiner quoted in John F. Harris, "Hillary's Big Adventure," *Washington Post*, January 27, 2002.
2. **"During the White House years"**: John F. Harris, "Hillary's Big Adventure," *Washington Post*, January 27, 2002.
3. **Republicans Orrin Hatch:** Gail Sheehy, "Hillary's Solo Act," *Vanity Fair*, August 2001.
4. **But her biggest catch:** Ibid.
5. **"After a decisive vote"**: Ibid.
6. **"I had seen her a few times through a glass darkly"**: Sen. Robert Byrd quoted in Elizabeth Kolbert, "The Student: How Hillary Set Out to Master the Senate," *New Yorker*, October 13, 2003.
7. **Senators liked working:** Interview with Steve Jarding, adjunct lecturer in public policy at the Kennedy School of Government, past executive director of the South Dakota Democratic Party, and former communications director in Bob Kerrey's U.S. Senate campaigns in Nebraska. He also served as communications

director of the national Democratic Senatorial Campaign Committee and has run leadership PACs for Senators John Kerry and John Edwards.
8. **"People will attribute motives"**: Sen. Lindsey Graham quoted in Nedra Pickler, "Clinton, a Popular Pick for President, Sticks to Senate," Associated Press, May 31, 2003.
9. **"Hillary has demonstrated a stunning flair"**: Jennifer Senior, "President and Mr. Clinton," *New York Magazine*, February 21, 2005.
10. **"Giuliani will screw you"**: Sen. Hillary Rodham Clinton quoted in John F. Harris, "Hillary's Big Adventure," *Washington Post*, January 27, 2002.
11. **"the receiving end of a murderous anger"**: Nicholas Lemann, "The Hillary Perspective: Government Suddenly Looks Good Again," *New Yorker*, October 8, 2001.
12. **"Oh, I am well aware"**: Sen. Hillary Rodham Clinton quoted in ibid.

Chapter Thirty-seven: Where's Waldo?

1. **"The next time you see him"**: Sen. Hillary Rodham Clinton quoted in Robert Sam Anson, "Bill and His Shadow," *Vanity Fair*, June 2004.
2. **"He's not here [in Washington] very often"**: Aide to Sen. Hillary Rodham Clinton quoted in John F. Harris, "Hillary's Big Adventure," *Washington Post*, January 27, 2002.
3. **"It's like that game Where's Waldo?"**: Sen. Hillary Rodham Clinton quoted in Robert Sam Anson, "Bill and His Shadow," *Vanity Fair*, June 2004.
4. **"He's ... chatted up"**: Robert Sam Anson, "Bill and His Shadow," *Vanity Fair*, June 2004.
5. **It was not only the supermarket tabloid**: See Nigel Dempster, "More trouble Brews for Bill," *Daily Mail* (London), June 28, 2002; Blair Golson, "Seagram's Heir to Sell Townhouse for $27 Million," *New York Observer*, August 5, 2002; George Rush and Joanna Molloy, "Stylish Power Struggle on 42nd St.," *Daily News* (New York), November 3, 2002; "Splitsville," *New York Post*, February 27, 2002; Jonathan Alter, "Citizen Clinton Up Close," *Newsweek*, April 8, 2002.

6. **One of his new buddies:** Robert Sam Anson, "Bill and His Shadow," *Vanity Fair*, June 2004.
7. **Throwing caution to the wind:** Interview with Clinton biographer who requested anonymity, March 4, 2004.
8. **"It's one thing to go out to California":** Ibid.

Chapter Thirty-eight: The 800-Pound Gorilla

1. **She put in twelve- to fourteen-hour days:** John F. Harris, "Hillary's Big Adventure," *Washington Post*, January 27, 2002.
2. **She attended one interminable committee meeting:** Alexander Bolton, "Workhorse or Senatorial Stalking Horse? When Clinton Was Elected in 2000, Her First Task Was to Tame a Senate Lion," *Hill*, March 31, 2004.
3. **"The place looks a lot more yellow":** Pat Moynihan quoted in Elizabeth Kolbert, "The Student: How Hillary Set Out to Master the Senate," *New Yorker*, October 13, 2003.
4. **For the job of decorating:** Donna Gehrke-White, "Designing Men: Decorators of the Political Stars Gave Up Beltway Stress for South Florida Breeze," *Miami Herald*, May 11, 2002.
5. **When guests arrived at Whitehaven:** Gail Sheehy, "Hillary's Solo Act," *Vanity Fair*, August 2001.
6. **In her first twenty-two months:** Interview with Dick Morris, October 3, 2002.
7. **Donors who were rich enough:** Adam Nagourney and Raymond Hernandez, "For Hillary Clinton, a Dual Role as Star and Subordinate," *New York Times*, October 21, 2002.
8. **"She can give $10,000 to a candidate":** Interview with an anonymous expert on campaign finance and ethics, November 9, 2004.
9. **By 2003, Hillary had replaced Bill:** Eliza Newlin Carney, "Hillary, Inc.," *National Journal*, October 18, 2003.
10. **And she accomplished that:** Ibid.
11. **"She's more of a star than":** Sen. Mark Dayton quoted in Eliza Newlin Carney, "Hillary, Inc.," *National Journal*, October 18, 2003.
12. **"The ethical problems":** Eliza Newlin Carney, "Hillary, Inc.," *National Journal*, October 18, 2003.
13. **"If she even let herself be talked about":** Maurice Carroll

quoted in Deborah Orin, "Hillary Romps in Dems' Prez Poll," *New York Post*, February 7, 2003.
14. **"She spent the first two years"**: Sen. John Breaux quoted in James VandeHei, "Clinton Develops into a Force in the Senate; Growing Role in Policy, Fundraising Fuels Talk of '08 Campaign," *Washington Post*, March 5, 2003.

Chapter Thirty-nine: "So Hillary"

1. **"It must have been springtime"**: Interview with a member of the board of the Children's Defense Fund who requested anonymity, October 7, 2003, and November 11, 2004.
2. **"She's been Botoxed"**: Interview with anonymous medical source, October 5, 2004.
3. **"Hillary" . . . "will never"**: Marian Wright Edelman quoted in interview with a member of the board of the Children's Defense Fund who requested anonymity, October 7, 2003, and November 11, 2004.
4. **"Hillary's heart"**: Ibid.
5. **"From the time you were chair"**: Interview with a member of the board of the Children's Defense Fund who requested anonymity, October 7, 2003 and November 11, 2004.
6. **"If Hillary's only ambition"**: Ibid.
7. **"startled her conservative detractors"**: William Safire, "Hillary, Congenital Hawk," *New York Times*, December 8, 2003.
8. FOOTNOTE: **"congenital liar"**: William Safire, "Blizzard of Lies," *New York Times*, January 8. 1996.
9. **"I think Hillary's ambition simply"**: Interview with a member of the board of the Children's Defense Fund who requested anonymity, October 7, 2003, and November 11, 2004.
10. **"If you don't understand my position"**: Hillary Rodham Clinton quoted in ibid.
11. **"We had supported her"**: Interview with a member of the board of the Children's Defense Fund who requested anonymity, October 7, 2003, and November 11, 2004.

Chapter Forty: Hillary from Chappaqua

1. **"In the last several weeks"**: Raymond Hernandez, "For Mrs. Clinton, Listening Subsides; Her Talk Is Louder," *New York Times*, December 23, 2003.
2. **"Son of a bitch!"**: Anderson, *American Evita*, p. 259.
3. FOOTNOTE: **As of November 30, 2004:** www.opensecrets.org.
4. **"ruinous policies"**: Hillary Rodham Clinton quoted in Raymond Hernandez, "For Mrs. Clinton, Listening Subsides; Her Talk Is Louder," *New York Times*, December 23, 2003.
5. **"no-bid contracts to the likes of Halliburton"**: Hillary Rodham Clinton quoted in Ira Stoll, "Hillary Spreads Both Her Wings," *New York Sun*, December 16, 2003.
6. **"tough-minded and muscular"**: Ibid.
7. **"When Tim Russert"**: William Safire, "Hillary, Congenital Hawk," *New York Times*, December 8, 2003.
8. **". . . And the . . . no, wait a minute"**: Transcript of *The Brian Lehrer Show*, December 8, 2003.
9. **"I was surprised that she was calling in"**: Interview with Brian Lehrer, January 20, 2005.
10. **"Well, Brian"**: Transcript of *The Brian Lehrer Show*, December 8, 2003.
11. **"Hillary tried to change the tradition"**: Interview with retired air force lieutenant colonel Robert "Buzz" Patterson, February 2, 2005.

Chapter Forty-one: Shut Out?

1. **Charles Gibson, co-host of *Good Morning America*:** Transcript of *Good Morning America*, ABC, July 26, 2004.

Chapter Forty-two: Hedging Her Bets

1. **"Does she really think we're stupid"**: Interview with a Democratic political analyst who requested anonymity, December 10, 2004.
2. **Many of the members:** Interview with Robert Sam Anson, March 4, 2004.
3. **After Vince Foster's suicide:** Susan Schmidt, Sharon La-

Fromiere, "Senators Hear 2 Stories On Foster Office Search," *Washington Post*, July 27, 1995. See also William Safire, "3 Scandals and Out," *New York Times*, June 24, 1996.
4. **Nussbaum was still on good terms:** Interview with anonymous source close to the Clintons, March 12, 2003.
5. FOOTNOTE: **"We've never unseated":** Transcript of *On the Record with Greta Van Susteren*, Fox News Network, November 17, 2004.
6. **The delegates were asked:** Richard Cohen, "The Once and Future Hope," *Washington Post*, November 4, 2004.
7. **"If anyone was disappointed by the switch":** Raymond Hernandez, "Looking at Democrats' 2008 through 2004 Eyes," *New York Times*, July 7, 2004.
8. **"If he was one of your students":** Hillary Rodham Clinton quoted in Raymond Hernandez, "Looking at Democrats' 2008 through 2004 Eyes," *New York Times*, July 7, 2004.
9. **"I have two overwhelming priorities":** Hillary Rodham Clinton quoted in Raymond Hernandez, "Kerry's Choice Could Limit Hillary Clinton's Options in '08," *New York Times*, July 10, 2004.
10. **She instructed her advisers:** Raymond Hernandez, "Kerry's Choice Could Limit Hillary Clinton's Options in '08," *New York Times*, July 10, 2004.
11. **"We know how hard Hillary can campaign":** Interview with a Democratic political analyst who requested anonymity, December 10, 2004.
12. **"McAuliffe dominates":** Morris, *Rewriting History*, p. 261.
13. **However, in the event that Kerry won:** Dick Morris, "The Front," *New York Post*, November 25, 2003.

Chapter Forty-three: Gearing Up

1. **Hillary had been scheduled to deliver:** Patrick Gordon, "Clinton Recommends U.S. Foreign Policy Shift," *Tufts Daily*, November 11, 2004.
2. *Would Hillary make red-state voters:* Richard Schwartz, "She's Not the One. Democrats Need Someone Else for '08," *Daily News* (New York), November 4, 2004.
3. **"I don't think you can win an election":** Hillary Rodham

Clinton quoted in David R. Guarino, "Hill at Tufts: Use Bible to Guide Poverty Policy," BostonHerald.com, November 11, 2004.
4. **"a feat"**: Ibid.
5. **"Her approval rating in New York"**: Jill Lawrence, "Field's Wide Open for Next Election," *USA Today*, November 5, 2004.
6. **SportingbetUSA.com:** Albert Eisele and Jeff Dufour, "Ante Up for the 2008 Race, Already," *Hill*, December 1, 2004.
7. **"Well," . . . "it's [an evolving] map, Sean":** Transcript of *Hannity and Colmes*, Fox News Network, November 4, 2004.
8. **"She would make an excellent President":** "Clinton says Hillary would make excellent first U.S. female president," Associated Press, February 28, 2005.
9. **"With the Clintons":** Lance Morrow, "Don't Cry for Me, Oneonta," Time.com, July 5, 1999.
10. **"While Mrs. Clinton lost some of her feminist edge":** Ben Smith, "Hillary Hiring Ms. Pac-Man for '06, Beyond," *New York Observer*, November 29, 2004.
11. **"If you think of politics as a sport":** Ann Lewis quoted in ibid.
12. **"If she is our best hope for a woman to be President":** Hilary Rosen quoted in Ben Smith, "Hillary '08: Don't Ask If—It's a Go!" *New York Observer*, December 27, 2004.
13. **Hillary and her kitchen cabinet:** Ben Smith, "Hillary '08: Don't Ask If—It's a Go!" *New York Observer*, December 27, 2004.
14. **"Upstate [New York]—that's [like] the Midwest":** Clinton backer quoted in ibid.
15. **"Hillary is still a polarizer":** Interview with Charles Cook, April 5, 2004.
16. **Team Hillary had one of the best:** Joe Mercurio, "A Modern Campaign Comes to New York and Wins," National Political Services, November 9, 2000.
17. **"The National Committee":** Ibid.

Chapter Forty-four: Nixon's Disciple

1. **"Again and again":** R. W. Apple Jr., "The 37th President, Richard Nixon, 81, Dies; a Master of Politics Undone by Watergate," *New York Times*, April 23, 1994.
2. **"The supreme irony":** Olson, *Hell to Pay*, p. 4.

3. **"President Nixon's 'enemies list' ":** Ibid., pp. 274–75.
4. **Did "the old Hillary" favor:** Stephanopoulos, *All Too Human*, p. 298.
5. **"Some children, however":** Renshon, *The Psychological Assessment of Presidential Candidates*, p. 387.
6. **"My two cents' worth":** www.j-bradford-delong.net

Epilogue

1. **"the best conversation":** Crowley, *Nixon off the Record*, p. 167.
2. **"Your health care":** Hillary Clinton quoted in "Is Teresa Heinz Bottled Up?" *New York Post*, April 7, 2004.
3. **"Had you survived":** Ibid.
4. *Had I survived:* "Is Teresa Heinz Bottled Up?" *New York Post*, April 7, 2004.
5. **"All of this . . . deliberating":** Crowley, *Nixon Off the Record*, p. 181.
6. **"The kid ran right to [Clinton]":** Ibid, p. 172.

INDEX

Acheson, Dean, 61, 107
Acheson, Eleanor "Eldie,"
    61–62, 107
Achtenberg, Roberta, 107
Adams, Ruth, 61
Addington, Ron, 83
Adler, Renata, 81
Afghanistan, 224–25, 241
Ailes, Roger, 98
Allen, Jodie, 227–28
Americans Coming Together,
    239
Ancient Order of Hibernians,
    188–89
Anson, Robert Sam, 212
Apple, R. W., Jr., 249
Arafat, Suha, 188
Arafat, Yasser, 180, 188
Army Signal Corps, 16–17
Arzt, George, 189

Baker, Jerry, 54–55
Baker, Peter, 155–56
Baldwin, Alec, 145
Basinger, Kim, 145
Bay of Pigs, 77
Bayh, Evan, 240
Begala, Paul, 33, 115
Belzberg, Lisa, 212
Bennett, Robert, 29–30, 35,
    104
Bennett, William, 29
Bentsen, Lloyd, 119, 165
Berke, Richard L., 20
Berrigan, Daniel, 58
Binn, Jason, 213
Black Panthers, 71, 126
Bloodworth-Thomason, Linda,
    24, 39, 49n, 118, 159
Blumenthal, Sidney, 125–28,
    133, 139

Bone, Robert L. "Red," 38
Bon Jovi, Jon, 2
Bosnia, 254–55
Bradley, Bill, 203
Branch, Taylor, 104, 121
Branegan, Jay, 146
Brassaloria, Kim, 183
Breaux, John, 218
Brehony, Kathleen A., 63
Brian Lehrer Show, The, 224–30
Broaddrick, Juanita, 88–89, 114
Brock, David, 98
Bronfman, Matthew, 212
Brown-Davis Interiors, 215
Brown, Rita Mae, 58
Brown, Tina, 109, 187
Browning, Dolly Kyle, 84, 91–92
Bruck, Connie, 94, 111
Buddy (Clinton dog), 33, 140, 143
Bullock, Tony, 172, 191–92
Bunch, Charlotte, 58
Burrows, Saffron, 212
Bury, Chris, 120
Bush, Barbara, 20–21, 115
Bush, George H. W., 117
Bush, George W., 210, 218, 237–38, 243
Byrd, Robert C., 207–9

Cadoux, Doris, 183
Calvedt, Sarah, 67
Campbell, Alison "Snowy," 61
Campbell, Naomi, 212
Carey, Ron, 174
Carlson, Margaret, 143
Carroll, Maurice, 218

Carville, James, 33, 116–17, 139, 244
Castro, Fidel, 80
Cattle-futures incident, 37–38
Center for American Progress, 222
Chally, Cliff, 4
Chaney, James, 75
Chesler, Ellen, 181, 184
Children's Defense Fund, 69, 93, 133, 219–23
Clinton, Bill
  as Arkansas attorney general, 87–88
  as Arkansas governor, 22, 93–96
  Arkansas governorship defeat, 95–96
  at Chappaqua residence, 211–13
  Chelsea, relationship with, 92, 94
  childhood of, 127
  DNA testing of, 136, 138–39
  and Hillary Senate campaign, 190–91
  impeachment, 156
  and Jones deposition, 26–31, 33–36
  and Lewinsky, 4–6, 34–36, 103–9, 112–13, 135–37
  Lewinsky affair, denial of, 34, 129–30, 138–39
  meets Hillary, 70–72
  post-presidency, 211–13
  premarital years with Hillary, 31–32, 41, 68–73
  presidential ambitions of, 70
  Radio City birthday party, 1–4

scandals during presidency, 37–40
at Yale Law School, 68–73
Clinton, Chelsea, 25, 91–93, 118, 122, 140–41, 204, 255
Clinton, Hillary
  in Arkansas, compared to locals, 84–86
  body-image of, 24–25
  Brian Lehrer Show call-in, 224–30
  cattle-future windfall, 37–38
  Clinton affairs, handling of, 4–6, 31–33, 38, 70, 72, 83, 87, 89, 94, 98–99, 110–13
  congressional defeat, 86–87
  emotional detachment of, 12–13, 50–51, 64, 92, 111–12
  as enigma, 12–14, 111–12
  family/childhood, 47–52
  FBI files incident, 39
  Foster (Vincent) relationship, 21–23, 236, 250
  and fund-raising, 39, 159, 173–76, 196, 215–17
  and gender feminism, 177–78
  Golden Gavel Award, 214
  and health-care reform, 38, 120, 122, 165
  high school years, 53–55
  kitchen cabinet of, 235–36, 245–47
  left-wing agenda of, 119–20
  left-wing roots of, 57–63, 68–71
  lesbian acquaintances of, 62–65, 107–8
  Lewinsky affair, denial of, 103–4, 124–28, 132–34, 137–39
  Lewinsky, prior knowledge of, 4–7, 42–43, 103–6, 108–9, 112–13
  maiden name, use after marriage, 88, 95–97
  make-overs of, 97–98, 117–19, 122, 190–93, 250–51
  meets Bill, 70–72
  and Nixon impeachment, 17, 37, 74–82
  pardons granted by, 187–88
  pregnancy/birth of Chelsea, 91–92
  premarital year with Clinton, 31–32, 41, 68–73
  presidential ambitions of, 14, 41–42, 73
  privacy needs at White House, 15–17
  public opinion of, 114–16
  at Rose Law Firm, 40, 93
  and Senate 2006 race, 246–47
  Senate campaign, 149–99
  Senate swearing-in, 201–4
  Senate victory, 197
  as senator, 206–10, 214–31
  senators' relationship with, 203, 206–10
  Today interview, 132–34
  travel office firings, 39
  and 2004 presidential election, 217–18, 225, 232–39
  and 2008 presidential race, 225, 236–37, 240–52
  Virginia Kelley (Clinton mother) view of, 85–86, 88
  as Washington intern, 66–67

Clinton, Hillary *(cont.)*
   at Wellesley, 56–67
   White House offices of, 106–7
   White House redecoration, 20–21
   Whitewater, 17, 23, 28, 30, 40, 104
   at Yale Law School, 68–73
   youthful ambitions of, 40–41
Clinton, Roger (brother-in-law), 86
Collins, Gail, 171
Conyers, John, 66, 81–82
Cook, Charles, 247
Cornelius, Catherine, 111
Couric, Katie, 133
Cox, Archibald, 79
Cozy Beach, 72
Cristophe, 19
Cronkite, Betsy, 143
Cronkite, Walter, 143
Cunningham, William, 187
Currie, Betty, 5
Cutler, Lloyd, 30

Dalai Lama, 164, 167
D'Amato, Al, 151–52
Daschle, Thomas, 207, 222
Davis, Lanny, 18
Davis, Sharon, 183
Dawson, Charlotte, 212
Dayton, Mark, 217
Dean, Howard, 225, 229, 239, 251
DeLay, Tom, 209
DeLong, Bradford, 252
Democratic National Committee, 239, 245
Dempster, Nigel, 212

Dickey, Helen, 111
Dickey, Robin, 111
Dinkins, David, 154
DNA testing, of Clinton, 136, 138–39
Doar, John, 75–78, 81
Dowd, Maureen, 191
Doyle, Patti Solis, 235, 246
Drudge, Matt, 35
Duda, Ivan, 98–99
Dunn, Leonard, 22

Edelman, Marian Wright, 69, 78, 219–20
Edelman, Peter, 78
Edwards, Don, 79
Edwards, John, 237–38, 240
Elders, Joycelyn, 107
Emanuel, Rahm, 126
Emery, Christopher, 21
Emery, Noemie, 189
Epstein, Jeffrey, 213
Eskew, Carter, 245

Ferrer, Fernando, 187
Fialkoff, Gabrielle, 174
Fireman, Marilyn, 184
Flowers, Gennifer, 13, 35, 38, 109, 114, 120, 129
Ford, Gerald, 76*n*, 79–80
Foster, Vincent W., Jr., 21–23, 236, 250
Franklin, Aretha, 2
Frank, Barney, 182
Fray, Mary Lee, 85
Fray, Paul, 31, 84, 86
Friedman, Richard, 142
Friends of Hillary, 216

Galster, Michael, 21–22
Galster, Vali, 22
Geffen, David, 39
Georges, Gigi, 245–46, 248
Gergen, David, 112, 120
Gibson, Charles, 232–34
Gingrich, Newt, 105
Gist, Nancy, 66
Giuliani, Rudolph, 160, 180, 183, 188, 194–95, 210
Glenn, John, 40, 203
Glover Park Group, 245–46
Goddell, Charles, 67
Goetz, Isabelle, 19, 25, 214, 219
Goldberg, Whoopie, 2
Golden Gavel Award, 214
Goldwater, Barry, 54, 79
Golson, Blair, 212
Good Morning America, 232
Goodman, Andrew, 75
Gore, Albert, Jr., 106, 111, 119, 122, 129, 138, 201–2
Gore, Albert, Sr., 66
Gore, Tipper, 119, 138
Graham, Katharine, 143
Graham, Lindsey, 209
Greenberg, Stan, 117, 244
Greenfield, Jeff, 172
Greenspan, Alan, 119
Greer, Frank, 117
Griffin, Pat, 207
Grunwald, Henry Anatole, 161
Grunwald, Mandy, 159, 160–61, 170, 182, 191

Hannity, Sean, 242
Harriman, Pamela, 216
Harris, John F., 207
Harrison, Cynthia, 66

Hart, Gary, 126
Hartigan, Laura, 173–75
Hartigan & Associates, 173
Hatch, Orrin, 208
Health-care reform, 38, 120, 122, 164
Health Management Associates (HMA), 22
Helms, Jesse, 150
Helms, Richard, 77
Hentoff, Nat, 58
Herbert, Bob, 152
Herget, Richard, 95
Hillarycare, 38
Hillary's Advocates, 182
HILLPAC, 216
Hockersmith, Katherine "Kaki," 20–21, 23, 203, 215
Hodgson, Godfrey, 164, 170
Hofstadter, Richard, 126
Hope, Judith, 145, 160
Horn, Miriam, 60
Hutchison, Kay Bailey, 193, 208

Ickes, Harold, 27–29, 154–59, 173–76, 180–82, 186, 191–92, 196, 216, 235, 244
Internet fund-raising, 225–26, 239
Irv Kupcinet Show, 57
Isikoff, Michael, 35
Israel Day Parade, 195
Issam M. Fares Lecture, 240
It Takes a Village (Clinton), 123

Jackson, Jesse, 28, 137–38
Jobs, Steve, 39
Johnson, Lyndon, 54, 75, 208
Johnson, Paul, 13, 107

Jones, Don, 41, 53, 57, 193, 201–2, 204, 235
Jones, Paula, 26–27, 30, 34–35, 109, 114
Jordan, Vernon E., Jr., 26, 141–42

Kantor, Mickey, 117
Kastenmeier, Robert, 79
Kaus, Mickey, 69
Kaye, Walter, 105, 204
Kelley, Virginia (mother-in-law), 85–88
Kelly, Michael, 33, 42, 118
Kendall, David, 28–29, 104, 134, 136
Kennedy, Edward M., 77–79, 208, 221
Kennedy, Jacqueline, 156
Kennedy, John F., 77–78, 80–81, 129, 249
Kennedy, Robert, 69, 151, 186
Kerry, John, 226, 233–34, 237–39, 241
Kesey, Ken, 72
King, Martin Luther, Jr., 122
Klein, Joe, 127
Klum, Heidi, 213
Kolbert, Elizabeth, 161
Kramer, Michael, 164–65
Krigbaum, Jan, 66
Kuntzman, Gersh, 186

La Bella, Charles, 28*n*
Lane, Nathan, 2
Lattimore, Neel, 145
Lauer, Matt, 133–34
Lawrence, Jill, 242

Lazio, Rick, 195–97
Legal Services Corporation, 21, 93
Lehrer, Brian, 224–30
Leno, Jay, 25
Letterman, David, 25
Lewinsky, Monica
    Clinton denial of affair, 34, 124–28, 138–39
    at Clinton Radio City party, 1–4
    Hillary denial of affair, 103–4, 124–28, 132–34, 137–39
    Hillary knowledge of, 4–7, 42–43, 103–6, 108–9, 112–13, 138–39
    hiring/White House assignment, 4–6, 105–6, 204
Lewis, Ann, 182, 235, 245
Lewis, Marcia, 105, 113
Lieberman, Evelyn, 4–6, 108, 110, 113
Liebovitz, Annie, 123
Lincoln Bedroom rental, 39
Livingstone, Craig, 23, 39
Lockhart, Joe, 245
Lott, Trent, 203, 209
Luzzatto, Tamera, 209

McAuliffe, Terry, 173–74, 239
McCall, H. Carl, 196
McCarthy, Bob, 157
McCarthy, Eugene, 28, 176
McCormick, Naomi, 63
McCurry, Mike, 18
McGovern, George, 28, 225
McGovern, Nuala, 227
McPhee, Penny, 61

Maine South High School, 53–55
Maraniss, David, 31, 83, 94, 154
Margolis, Jeff, 2
Marshall, Burke, 75, 78, 80–81
Masri, Hani, 195
Mercurio, Joseph, 247–48
Mills, Thomas, 171
Milton, Joyce, 51, 93
Mitchell, Alison, 203
Mitford, Jessica, 32
Molly, Joanna, 212
Morris, Dick, 17, 98, 119, 122–24, 139, 161, 242
Morris, Roger, 50–51
Morrison, Micah, 28
Morrow, Lance, 245
Moskowitz, Eva, 184
Mother Superior. *See* Lieberman, Evelyn
Motive, 57–59
Moynihan, Daniel Patrick, 149–51, 154, 158, 162–72, 194–95, 215
Moynihan, Elizabeth, 150, 163–72, 192
Moynihan, Maura, 161
My Life (Bill Clinton), 212–13

National Education Association, 237
Nayman, Shira, 181
New York Women for Hillary, 183–84
Newlin Carney, Eliza, 217
Newton, Huey, 58
Nickles, Don, 208–9
Nixon, Richard, 249, 251
 Hillary and impeachment investigation, 17, 37, 74–82
 meets Clintons, 253–55
Nussbaum, Bernard, 23, 236

O'Callaghan, Suzy, 48
O'Donnell, Rosie, 2
Ogilvie, Dr. Lloyd, 208
Olson, Barbara, 32, 250
Olson, Kris, 66, 71–72
O'Toole, Tara, 107

Palestinian Liberation Organization (PLO), 180
Panetta, Leon, 110, 230
Pardongate, 187
Patricoff, Alan, 159
Patterson, Robert "Buzz," 230
Penn, Mark, 139
Perot, Ross, 117
Piercy, Jan, 99, 107, 111
Pietrefesa, Nancy "Peach," 94, 97
Podesta, John, 207
Press, Ellen, 54–55
Pressman, Gabe, 149–50, 186
Pullen, Penny, 56–57
Pyke, David, 35

Queen's Bedroom rental, 39

Radkley, Alex, 71
Rangel, Charles, 150–52
Rattner, Steven, 143
Reagan, Nancy, 20, 118
Reno, Janet, 108
Renshon, Stanley, 251–52
Rice, Condoleezza, 193
Ricketts, Rick, 52, 204

Rifkin, Samara, 173
Rockefeller Commission, 76*n*
Rockefeller, Jay, 209
Rockefeller, Nelson, 76*n*
Rodham, Dorothy Howell (mother), 48, 56, 87, 131, 202, 204–5
Rodham, Hugh, Jr. (brother), 50, 84, 187
Rodham, Hugh, Sr. (father), 48, 50–51, 56, 83
Rodham, Tony (brother), 50, 83
Rodino, Peter, 81
Rogers, Jeff, 71–72
Rogers, Kenny, 2
Rogers, William, 71
Roosevelt, Eleanor, 122, 154
Roosevelt, Franklin D., 28, 129
Roosevelt, Theodore, 129
Rose Law Firm, 40, 93
Rosen, Hilary, 246
Rothblum, Esther D., 63
Rupert, David, 63–64
Rush, George, 212
Russell, Richard, 208
Russert, Tim, 154, 196, 226

Safire, William, 222, 226–27
St. Patrick's Day Parade, 188–89
Salon Cristophe, 19, 219
Sanger, Margaret, 181
"Save America's Treasures," 145–46
Schiff, Debra, 111
Schinderman, Donna, 184
Schippers, David, 34, 144
Schmidt, Susan, 127

Schumer, Chuck, 151–52, 192, 201, 246
Schwerner, Michael, 75
Scott, Marsha, 110–11
Senior, Jennifer, 209
Shalala, Donna E., 107–8
Shalit, Ruth, 29*n*
Sheehy, Gail, 154, 208
Sheldon, Timothy, 53–54
Shepard, Alan, 40
Shepard, Geoffrey, 77
Shriver, Maria, 145
Shrum, Robert, 137
Shulsky, Rena, 183
Sills, Beverly, 143
Simon, Carly, 143
Simon & Schuster, 202
Six, Dr. Claudia, 64
60 Minutes, 38, 129
Skadden, Arps, Slate, Meagher & Flom, 29
Skenazy, Lenore, 189
Smith, Ben, 245
Solidarity for Israel rally, 195
Sommers, Christina Hoff, 177
Soros, George, 239
Spielberg, Steven, 39
Starr, Kenneth, 17, 26, 104, 127, 130, 135–37
Stephanopoulos, George, 33, 36, 115–16, 123–24, 220
Stock, Ann, 106
Stone-Davis Hall, 59
Strategic Frameworking, 181
Stronach, Belinda, 212
Styler, Trudie, 183–84
Styron, Rose, 143
Styron, William, 143
Sullivan, Andrew, 108

Talk, 187
Thomases, Susan, 108, 159, 176–82, 191, 235, 244
Thomason, Harry, 24, 29, 39, 130–31, 159
Thomasson, Patsy, 23
Thurmond, Strom, 150, 203, 209
Today, 132–34, 145
Tomasky, Michael, 6–7, 145
Toobin, Jeffrey, 29*n*, 126
Torre, Joe, 187
Torricelli, Robert, 154
Travel Office firings, 39
Treuhaft, Robert, 32
Truman, Margaret, 19
Tucker, Jim Guy, 87
Tunney, Gene, 50

Vallone, Peter, 174
Verveer, Melanie, 133
Viacom, 202

Wallace, Doug, 84
Wanderer, Nancy, 62, 65
Watergate, 17, 37, 74–82
Watkins, David, 39
Weiner, Anthony, 206
Weinstein, Harvey, 143
Wellesley College, 56–67

West Wingers, 207
White Boys, 207
White, Frank, 95–96
White, Gay, 95
White, Maureen, 143
Whitehaven, 215–16
Whitewater, 17, 23, 28, 30, 40, 104
Wiggins, Charles, 81
Wilhelm, David, 117
Willey, Kathleen, 34, 106
Williams, Maggie, 23, 159
Williams and Connolly, 28
Wolfe, Tom, 72
Wolfson, Howard, 246
Women's Leadership Forum, 184
Woodward, C. Vann, 77–78, 81, 153*n*
Wright, Betsey, 32, 98
Wright, Susan Webber, 27

Yale Law School, 68–73
Yale Review of Law and Social Action, The, 71
Yeltsin, Boris, 254
Yrigoyen, Jim, 47–49, 52

Zeifman, Jerry, 79
Zucker, Jeff, 133